ECHOES OF THE DEAD

Recent Titles by Sally Spencer from Severn House

THE BUTCHER BEYOND
DANGEROUS GAMES
THE DARK LADY
DEAD ON CUE
DEATH OF A CAVE DWELLER
DEATH OF AN INNOCENT
A DEATH LEFT HANGING
DEATH WATCH
DYING IN THE DARK
A DYING FALL
THE ENEMY WITHIN
FATAL QUEST
GOLDEN MILE TO MURDER
A LONG TIME DEAD
MURDER AT SWANN'S LAKE
THE PARADISE JOB
THE RED HERRING
THE SALTON KILLINGS
SINS OF THE FATHERS
STONE KILLER
THE WITCH MAKER

The Monika Paniatowski Mysteries

THE DEAD HAND OF HISTORY
THE RING OF DEATH
ECHOES OF THE DEAD

ECHOES OF THE DEAD

A DCI Monika Paniatowski Mystery

Sally Spencer

severn
House

This first world edition published 2010
in Great Britain and in 2011 in the USA by
SEVERN HOUSE PUBLISHERS LTD of
9–15 High Street, Sutton, Surrey, England, SM1 1DF.
Trade paperback edition first published
in Great Britain and the USA 2011 by
SEVERN HOUSE PUBLISHERS LTD.

British Library Cataloguing in Publication Data

Spencer, Sally.
  Echoes of the dead.
  1. Paniatowski, Monika (Fictitious character) – Fiction.
  2. Woodend, Charlie (Fictitious character) – Fiction.
  3. Police – England – Fiction. 4. Detective and mystery
  stories.
  I. Title
  823.9'14-dc22

ISBN-13: 978-0-7278-6980-7   (cased)
ISBN-13: 978-1-84751-307-6   (trade paper)

All Severn House titles are printed on acid-free paper.

Severn House Publishers support The Forest Stewardship Council [FSC],
the leading international forest certification organisation. All our titles that
are printed on Greenpeace-approved FSC-certified paper carry the FSC logo.

Typeset by Palimpsest Book Production Ltd.,
Falkirk, Stirlingshire, Scotland.
Printed and bound in Great Britain by the
MPG Books Group, Bodmin, Cornwall.

PART ONE
Whitebridge, October 1973

PROLOGUE

George Street was right at the heart of old, industrial Whitebridge. It was narrow and cobbled, and it climbed the steep hill with complete disregard for the old and frail who lived along its route. The street was lined with terraced houses which had front doors opening directly on to the pavement, and the large sash windows of all the front parlours were strung with lace curtains, in order to give those who lived there a little privacy from those who merely passed by.

It was the lace curtains that the priest noticed as he toiled his way up the street – noticed them because each and every one twitched angrily as he passed it by.

The women lurking behind the netting – their eyes following every step of his reluctant progress – knew exactly where he was going, and exactly why he was going there, he thought. And though many of them were his own parishioners – and believed, as he did, in a merciful God – they did not approve of what he was doing.

The priest looked up at the autumnal sky. Black clouds hung there – as they had all morning – like the heavy drapes in an undertaker's parlour.

It was not a day that any man would *choose* to die on, Father O'Brien thought.

But he had no doubt that – for the curtain twitchers of George Street – the imminent death of the man he was about to visit was nothing less than a sign that the Almighty shared their own feelings of righteous revulsion.

The priest felt the need to stop and catch his breath, and came to a halt in front of a house with a chocolate-brown door. His mouth was dry, and he was just wondering if he dared to lift the polished brass knocker and ask for a glass of water when the door itself opened – barely a chink – and he found himself staring into the blazing eyes of a tiny, bent woman.

'Ah, good morning, Mrs Gilligan,' he said, in a voice which he was hoping would appear friendly and at ease, but came out as cracked and uncertain. 'I wonder if I might trouble you for—'

'So you're off to see *him*, then, are you, Father?' the old woman interrupted.

'I am, Mrs Gilligan,' the priest replied.

'Don't do it, Father,' the woman implored him.

'I have to,' O'Brien told her.

And even as the words left his mouth, he knew that they were the *wrong* words, knew that a priest should never sound so *defensive* – so *ashamed* – of what he was doing.

'You weren't in this parish when Lilly Dawson was killed, were you?' Mrs Gilligan demanded.

'No, I wasn't,' O'Brien admitted.

Of course he hadn't been there! The girl had been dead for *twenty-two* years! Generations had been born – and died – in the time since Lilly Dawson left this life. But for Mrs Gilligan – and no doubt for all the other women who lived on this street – it seemed as if no time had passed at all.

'She was a lovely little kid. Very quiet – maybe a bit sad – but lovely,' the old woman said.

'I'm sure she was,' O'Brien agreed

'And she never even got to see her fourteenth birthday, did she?' the old woman asked.

'When you think of her, you should not dwell so much on how she died,' the priest said uncomfortably. 'Instead, you should rejoice that she is now reaping her reward in heaven.'

'You do realize what he did to her *before* he killed her, don't you?' the old woman asked, as if he had never spoken.

'I . . . I know that he interfered with her.'

'He *defiled* her,' the old woman said. 'That's what he did to her – he *defiled* her.' Mrs Gilligan paused to draw breath. 'Don't go and see him, Father. Let him die alone. It's all he deserves.'

'I have to go and see him,' O'Brien said. 'It's my duty.'

'But you'd rather not – if you had the choice?' the woman asked.

She was offering him an escape route, he realized – giving him the chance to admit that he felt just like she did, to express a loathing as deep as her own. And, for a moment, he was tempted to take that route, because, as a man, he wanted to be well thought of. Then he reminded himself that he was a priest – that when he put on his cassock that morning he had ceased to be a man at all, and had become one of God's representatives on earth.

'I'll see you in church, Mrs Gilligan,' he said.

'Maybe you will – and maybe you won't,' the woman replied ominously.

And then she closed the door – like a voice of conscience which had given up on him.

As Father O'Brien pressed on up the hill, he found his mind wandering back to another time – to his childhood in rural Ireland.

Back then, things had seemed so much simpler, he thought. No, he corrected himself, not just *seemed* simpler – had *been* simpler. The life of the village and the life of the church had been at one with each other. And, even more importantly, there had been a certainty to everything which was never questioned – because how *could you* question certainty?

He wished he had never been posted to this parish, where the people were as alien to his own experience as beings from outer space would have been – where, once the familiar ritual within the church was completed, he felt he had nothing in common with his parishioners.

'You're a very bad priest,' he mumbled to himself.

And there was no mock-humility in the statement, he decided.

No, on that charge, at least, he was not guilty – for a *good* priest would never have questioned God's wisdom in sending him to Whitebridge.

He had reached his destination, and – with a heavy heart – knocked on the door.

The woman who opened the door was in her late thirties. He saw her nearly every day in church, and when he studied her thin, pinched face as she knelt in prayer, he had never been quite sure whether she was expressing her devotion *to* God or her anger *at* Him. Perhaps, he had finally decided, it was both.

'You came,' she said – as if she had suspected that he might not.

'It was my duty, Elizabeth,' O'Brien said, rather woodenly. 'Where is he? Upstairs?'

'Of course he's upstairs,' Elizabeth Eccles said, with a harshness entering her voice which could almost have been contempt. 'Where else *would* he be? The poor man can hardly move.'

'Of course,' the priest agreed, and tried to sound understanding.

Elizabeth looked over his shoulder, out on to the street.

'Have you seen enough?' she screamed, her hands defiantly on her hips. 'Have you all had your fill?'

'Please, Elizabeth, show a little decorum in this house of sickness,' the priest said.

'There's sickness, all right, but it's out there!' the woman retorted, now angry with the priest as well as with her neighbours. 'Do you know how hard it's been for me, since my father came to live with me?'

'I'm sure it must have been very—' the priest began.

'You wouldn't believe the things they've done,' the woman interrupted him. 'You wouldn't believe the kinds of things they've posted through my letterbox.'

'It must have been almost as hard on them as it has been on you,' the priest said. 'You must learn to understand them, and forgive them.'

'And will they forgive him?' Elizabeth asked, jerking her finger towards the upstairs bedroom.

'They must,' O'Brien said solemnly.

'Well, they needn't bother!' Elizabeth told him. 'My father doesn't *need* their forgiveness.'

They were still standing on the doorstep, and the priest shivered as a chill breeze suddenly blew down the street.

'You'd better come in,' Elizabeth said. 'He's been waiting for you.'

'I'm sure he has,' the priest agreed.

'He's been *hanging on* for you,' Elizabeth said, in case he had missed the point.

And O'Brien was sure of that, too – for no man wanted to face his maker with the weight that must be pressing down on Fred Howerd's soul.

The priest followed the woman up the stairs which led off the hallway, and, even halfway up them, his nostrils were already filled with stink of death and desperation.

From the narrow landing, they looked in on the bedroom. The dying man was lying on an old-fashioned oak bed. A large crucifix had been nailed above the bed, and on the wall opposite it was a painting of the Sacred Heart.

O'Brien stepped into the room, and the woman followed him.

'You must leave us now, Elizabeth,' the priest said.

'I want to stay,' the woman told him.

'You can't.'

'He needs me by his side,' Elizabeth protested. 'What little strength he has left, he draws from me.'

'It's not possible,' Father O'Brien said – and for once, it seemed to him, God had deemed him worthy of that tone of authority which appeared to come naturally to most other priests. 'You cannot be here during the Sacrament of Penance and Reconciliation.'

For a moment, it seemed as if the woman would defy him, then she stepped back on to the landing and closed the door behind her.

Father O'Brien looked down at the sick man. Howerd had once been a powerful figure, he'd been told, but his illness had eaten away at him, and now he was little more than a husk.

And he looked in pain – he looked in *so much* pain.

'It was good of you to come, Father,' the dying man said with the merest rasp of a voice.

And O'Brien, who wanted to say more – he knew he *should* say more – could only manage to repeat, 'It's my duty.'

Fred Howerd nodded – though it was hardly a nod at all – as if that was all he had expected.

'I was in prison for twenty-two years, Father,' he said, with effort.

'I know.'

'I'd still have been there now, if I hadn't been dying.'

'Yes.'

'You can't imagine what hell I've been through for the last twenty-two years, Father. You can't imagine what the other prisoners did to me.'

And didn't you deserve it? an unwelcome voice at the back of O'Brien's mind screamed. After what you did, could *any* punishment be enough?

But that was the *man* in him talking.

The *priest* in him said, 'Do you wish to confess your sins, my son?'

'I do, Father,' the dying man said.

The priest knelt down beside the bed. 'Let us begin.'

'Forgive me, Father, for I have sinned,' Fred Howerd said. 'It has been twenty-two years since my last confession.'

And now, in his final moments, he wants to get it all off his chest, the priest thought. Wants to confess to the terrible things he did to that poor, innocent girl and obtain absolution for his monstrous acts. And I – God help me – will guide him along that path.

'You start with your worst sin, don't you?' the dying man asked.

'You do.'

'Then I confess to having committed a mortal sin.'

'Go on,' the priest said encouragingly.

'I lied,' the dying man said. 'I took an oath before God to tell the truth – and I lied.'

'Your worst sin first,' the priest said firmly.

'That's it,' the dying man told him.

'But Lilly Dawson . . .' the priest gasped.

'*That's* who I lied about,' Howerd said. 'I swore under oath that I killed her – but I didn't.'

Am I going mad? the priest wondered. Am I *dreaming* this?

'You . . . you didn't kill her?' he asked, almost choking.

'No, Father.'

'Then why did you . . . ?'

'They sent two policemen up from London to investigate her murder,' Howerd said. 'They had to arrest *somebody* – and they chose me.'

'But if you were innocent, as you claim, then why did you . . . ?'

'Have you ever been interrogated by the police, Father?' the dying man asked, and there was contempt in his tone, as there had been contempt in his daughter's – and in Mrs Gilligan's.

'No,' the priest admitted weakly. 'No, I haven't.'

He saw the harsh realities of life every day, he thought, but his cloth protected him from actually touching them, so that it was as if he were viewing them through a steamed-up window.

I'm a very bad priest, he told himself, for perhaps the fifth or sixth time that morning.

'If you've never been put through an interrogation, then you've no idea what it's like,' the dying man croaked. 'After a few hours of it, you'll say anything they want you to – just to make them stop. So when they handed me the confession, I signed it.'

'But couldn't you have recanted later?' the priest asked.

'They said that would only make matters worse for me,' Fred Howerd told him. 'They said I'd be convicted of the murder whatever happened, and if I fought them, they'd see to it that I suffered more once I was inside.'

He coughed, and a drop of blood spattered on to the edge of the clean, white sheet he was gripping.

'As if it *could have* been any worse,' he added. 'As if I *could have* suffered more.'

'Is there anything you wish to add?' the priest asked, still shaken by what he'd heard.

'No.'

O'Brien made an effort to compose himself. 'God the Father of mercies,' he intoned, 'through the death and resurrection of his Son, has reconciled the world to Himself and . . .'

He heard the door click open behind him, and, turning round, saw Elizabeth Eccles standing there with a tray in her hands.

'Not yet!' he said.

'I didn't notice the time, God forgive me,' the woman said, clearly on the verge of hysterics. 'Father has to have his medicine. He has to have it *now*.'

'Two minutes!' the priest pleaded. 'Just give me two minutes.'

'My medicine,' the dying man moaned. 'I want my medicine.'

He could cut the Absolution short, O'Brien told himself. At times like these, he was *allowed* to cut it short.

'I absolve you from your sins in the name of the Father and of the Son and of the Holy Spirit,' he said, trying, even now, not to rush the sacred words.

The daughter, licking her lips with concentration, was beginning to fill the syringe with morphine. The father, wracked with pain, was watching her with an intensity that was almost frightening.

'They don't even know I'm still here,' the priest thought, as an all-too-familiar feeling of inadequacy swept over him.

The sick man and his ministering angel – locked together in a world of pain and dying – did not even look up when O'Brien turned and left room. As the priest walked heavily down the stairs, he was aware of the fact that though Howerd had craved spiritual relief, it did not hold a candle to the relief that his daughter was about to deliver to him.

The dark clouds had finally opened, and the rain was lashing down as O'Brien stepped out on to the pavement.

The priest watched as the rainwater rushed down the hill, carrying the filth from the street with it – and found himself wishing all filth was so easy to wash away.

He had not wanted to come to this house of death, he told himself. There had part of him, at least, which had hoped he would arrive too late to give absolution – because there was a part of him which had hoped that Fred Howerd would burn in hell for all eternity.

But Fred Howerd's fate had not been his to decide, and in

merely holding on to that hope he had failed – not for the first time – to carry out the task that God had entrusted him with.

'But I will not fail again,' he promised, as he felt the rain trickling down his neck. 'I will see that justice is done – here on earth – for Fred Howerd.'

ONE

Monika Paniatowski had only ever had one bad experience with a priest, but that had been more than enough to make her wary of them as a breed, and the moment she saw Father O'Brien sitting in the 'cosy' corner of George Baxter's office, her stomach lurched.

Priests had no business visiting chief constables, she told herself, in an attempt to rationalize what was beyond rationalization.

Priests and chief constables inhabited different worlds – worlds which rarely touched.

But they must be touching now, mustn't they, Monika? asked a mocking voice somewhere in the back of her mind. The very fact that this priest is here at all must mean they're bloody near colliding!

Baxter stood up – he was always a gentleman, even in the presence of his minions – and said, 'Ah, Chief Inspector Paniatowski! Would you care to join us?'

No, Paniatowski thought, I wouldn't.

But she crossed the room, and sat down in the armchair opposite her boss, anyway.

Baxter ran his hand through his shock of sandy hair – something he always did when he was nervous.

'This is Father O'Brien,' he said. He turned his attention back to the priest. 'Tell the chief inspector what you told me, Father.'

'May I smoke?' O'Brien asked.

Baxter glanced involuntarily down at the almost over-spilling ashtray in front of the priest, smiled, and said, 'Of course, Father.'

As the priest lit up, Paniatowski took the opportunity to study him. He was around forty-five, she guessed. His black clerical shirt was stained grey with the ash of innumerable cigarettes, and though he had shaved that morning, he had done so either hurriedly or distractedly.

He was a man who would always try to do the right thing in every situation, she decided, but he was not a strong man – a confident man – and if other priests were available, she suspected his parishioners would much prefer to take their problems to them.

The priest cleared his throat. 'Yesterday, I administered the last rites to a man called Frederick Howerd,' he said.

He paused, as if expecting Paniatowski to react in some way.

'The case was before our time, Monika,' George Baxter explained. 'Howerd served twenty-two years for the rape and murder of a young girl. He was only finally released because he was dying.'

Paniatowski nodded, as if she understood – though she didn't.

'Just before he died, he told me that he was not guilty of the crime,' O'Brien said portentously.

Paniatowski shrugged uneasily. 'That's not at all unusual,' she said. 'I've known men who killed their victims in front of half a dozen witnesses, but who still refused – right to the end – to admit that they did it.'

'When you say "right to the end", you mean right to the end of their *trials*, don't you?' the priest asked.

'Yes,' Paniatowski agreed.

'But not to the end of their *lives*,' the priest said, with emphasis. 'Are you a member of the Faith, Chief Inspector?'

'I don't see what that has to do with *anything*,' Paniatowski replied, suddenly defensive.

'Frederick Howerd knew he was dying,' the priest said slowly. 'There can be absolutely no doubt about it.'

Paniatowski shrugged again. 'I'll accept that,' she conceded.

'And he knew more,' the priest continued. 'He knew that if he died in a state of mortal sin, he would burn in the everlasting pit forever. That is why you can be certain that what he told me was the truth.'

Paniatowski felt a tingling which Charlie Woodend – her mentor, the man she most admired in the whole world – would have called a 'gut feeling'. She was treading on dangerous ground, she warned herself, and though she had no idea why that ground *should* be dangerous, it would be best to get clear of it as soon as possible.

'Surely, whatever he told you under the seal of confession should be absolutely confidential,' she said.

'So you *are* a believer,' the priest countered.

Paniatowski shook her head.

But sometimes she was! Sometimes, despite herself, she *was*.

'I have struggled long and hard with the knowledge I have been entrusted with,' the priest told her. 'And I have finally decided that since what Fred Howerd confessed to me was that he had *not* committed a sin, I am not bound by the seal.'

Paniatowski's already queasy stomach did another somersault. This was going to be bad – she just knew it was.

'Even if he was innocent, there'll be no proof of that – not after twenty-two years,' she said, realizing how desperate she sounded – and wondering *why* she sounded so desperate. 'And if mistakes were made, there's nothing you can do about it now.'

'No *mistake* was made,' the priest said heavily. 'It was all very deliberate. Fred Howerd was "fitted up".'

The last two words fell uncomfortably from his lips.

As if they were not natural to him.

As if he had made a conscious effort to speak to the police in their own language.

'It's *twenty-two years*,' Paniatowski repeated. 'The officers responsible are probably dead by now. And the same will be true of the real murderer, for God's sake! That is, if it really *wasn't* Howerd who did it.'

'Do not take the name of the Lord your God in vain,' the priest said sternly.

'I'm sorry, I didn't mean to offend you,' Paniatowski said contritely.

'It is not I you have offended,' O'Brien told her.

Paniatowski turned to Baxter – looking for support, waiting for him to tell the troublesome priest that he was on a hiding to nothing.

The chief constable gazed back at her, with eyes that were filled with pain.

And the pain was for *her*, she suddenly realized – for his ex-lover who he'd never quite been able to bring himself to stop caring for just a little.

'What . . . what do you want?' she asked the priest, stuttering over her words. 'Are you asking for compensation for Howerd's family?'

'I want justice for a man who has been sorely wronged,' the priest intoned. 'I want the officers who framed him to be punished for their crime.'

'You're asking for the impossible,' Paniatowski said harshly. 'Good God . . .' and this time she used the phrase with baiting deliberation, 'do you even know their names or where they are now?'

'Yes,' the priest said. 'I do. The sergeant involved still works at Scotland Yard. His name is Bannerman.' He paused for a moment. 'And the chief inspector – the one who was in charge of the investigation and who must therefore shoulder most of the blame – is retired and lives in Spain.'

Now, finally, Paniatowski understood why her gut had been playing her up from the second she walked into the room. Now, finally, she could read the look of pain in George Baxter's eyes. Now, finally, it was all brutally – horrifically – clear.

'You're . . . you're talking about Charlie Woodend,' she gasped.

'Yes,' the priest agreed. 'That is the man's name.'

From time to time – and this was one of those times – DI Colin Beresford caught himself wondering if he was in love with DCI Monika Paniatowski. It was not a comfortable thought to have bouncing around in his head, because not only was Monika his boss, she was also several years older than him, and – if *that* was not enough – she was still in love with a dead man. And, besides, he usually concluded angrily at end of this train of thought, what did he – a thirty-two year old virgin – actually *know* about love anyway?

'Are you still with me, Colin?' he heard Paniatowski's voice say to him across the table in the public bar of the Drum and Monkey.

'Yes, boss. Sorry, boss,' Beresford replied.

But he was thinking that the problem was that when Monika looked as vulnerable as she did at that moment, it was hard *not* to love her.

'The whole idea that Charlie Woodend would ever even think of fitting anybody up is insane, isn't it?' Paniatowski asked passionately.

'It doesn't seem likely,' Beresford said.

Paniatowski gave him a hard stare. 'Well, that's scarcely what I'd call a ringing endorsement,' she said. 'For God's sake, Colin, you *worked* with the man. You knew him as well as anybody.'

'The Charlie Woodend I knew was a giant,' Beresford admitted. 'A legend! He was the kind of detective I aspired to be – even though I always accepted that I'd never quite make it.'

'Well, there you are, then!' Paniatowski said.

'But that wasn't the same Charlie Woodend who arrested Fred Howerd in 1951,' Beresford cautioned.

'I don't know what you're talking about,' Paniatowski told him.

'*That* Charlie Woodend had only just been made up to chief inspector. *That* Charlie Woodend still had to prove himself.'

'Are you saying that he *could have* doctored the evidence?' Paniatowski demanded angrily.

'Not deliberately, no,' Beresford replied. 'But in his eagerness to get a result, he might have unconsciously decided to overlook any evidence which didn't help his case.'

'He'd *never* have done that,' Paniatowski said stubbornly. 'And the investigation will *prove* that he didn't.'

'The investigation?' Beresford repeated, alarmed. 'You never said anything about an investigation.'

'George Baxter says there has to be one,' Paniatowski stated flatly. 'He thinks that if we don't have an investigation, Father O'Brien will take his story to the newspapers – and they'll have a field day with it.'

'Criminal Complaints will never agree to reopen the case,' Beresford said. 'There's simply not enough evidence to justify a fresh inquiry.'

'You're right,' Paniatowski agreed. 'There's not enough evidence for an official inquiry – that's why it will have to be an *unofficial* one.'

'And who'll be leading it?'

'Who do you think?'

'You?' Beresford exploded. 'He wants *you* to lead it?'

'As our dear chief constable was at pains to point out, I've got a lot of leave due to me, and it's about time I took some of it.'

'Is he *ordering* you to lead it?'

'No, he's merely offered it to me if I want it.'

'Turn it down, Monika,' Beresford pleaded.

'Now why should I do that?' Paniatowski asked, with deceptive mildness.

'Because you're too close to it – too close to Charlie Woodend.'

'It's because I'm close to Charlie that George Baxter wants me involved,' Paniatowski explained. 'He says I know how Charlie would have thought and how he would have acted.'

'And what happens if you uncover evidence that shows Woodend in a bad light?' Beresford asked. 'What will you do then?'

'I won't find any – because there'll be none to find.'

'But suppose you do?' Beresford persisted. 'How do you handle
it? Do you put it in your report, and bring down the man who's
been a guiding light to you? Or do you go against everything
you've ever believed in and bury it?'

'There's one very compelling reason I have to be involved,'
said Paniatowski, sidestepping the question, 'and that's that it
won't be a purely local inquiry.'

'What do you mean?'

'Scotland Yard will be sending its own man – a DCI – to be
in joint command.'

'Then that's your let-out, isn't it?' said Beresford, sounding
relieved. 'You can step aside and let him do all the dirty work.'

'It's dirty work that I'm worried about,' Paniatowski told
him.

'What do you mean?'

'The officer who worked with Charlie on the case – Sergeant
Bannerman – is now *Assistant Commissioner* Bannerman.'

'So what?'

'So that means he's got the power and the influence to see to
it that if this inquiry drags *anybody* down, it won't be him.'

'If that *is* Bannerman's aim, and you get in the way of it, he'll
crush you,' Beresford said worriedly.

'That's a possibility,' Paniatowski admitted.

'So you'll be ruined and you still won't save Charlie Woodend,'
Beresford said hotly. 'Bloody hell, Monika, that's no more than
pointless heroics!'

'My father was in the Polish Cavalry at the start of World
War Two,' Paniatowski said.

'I know that, but . . .'

'His regiment charged German tanks – *on horseback*. It must
have known it would be cut to pieces.'

'Doesn't that prove my point?'

'My father knew he was going to die, but he went through
with it anyway – because he wouldn't have been able to live
with himself if he hadn't.'

'That was war,' Beresford said.

'And so is this,' Paniatowski countered. 'If I'm right, then the
whole of Scotland Yard is behind Bannerman. And who's behind
Charlie? Me! I can't let him down, Colin.'

Beresford sighed. 'No,' he admitted, 'I don't suppose you
can.'

TWO

Whitebridge Central railway station – like the rest of the town – had seen better days, and the mirror in the ladies' lavatory was a perfect reflection of this fact. Much of the silvering at its centre had been worn away with time, leaving dull brown patches in its place, and any traveller who wished to examine her whole face could only do so by first looking at one half and then moving sideways so that other half became visible.

Monika Paniatowski, standing in front of the mirror, performed the crablike manoeuvre necessary to reveal the left side of her features.

Her hair was as blond as it had always been, she decided. Her Polish nose – unfashionably large for some Lancastrians' tastes, but appealing enough to others for her not to worry about it – had lost none of its firmness over the years. There were perhaps more lines around her blue eyes than there had been a few years earlier, but that only served to give her more character.

'You're not here to admire yourself, Monika,' she reminded herself angrily.

What she *was* there for was to prepare the face that would greet DCI Hall, the hotshot from London, who would be arriving on the next train – and as far as *that* face went, it was more important to look competent than pretty.

She had to set the right tone from the start, she thought – had to establish that though he came from almighty Scotland Yard, this was *her* patch, and they would work according to *her* rules. Because if she didn't establish that, she suspected, Charlie Woodend's precious reputation – and perhaps his pension – would be doomed.

She was starting at a disadvantage, she accepted, because, unlike Hall, she had yet to see the Scotland Yard file on the case. But she had done all that she could locally, and – by trawling through the newspapers and talking to colleagues who had been around at the time – she now had a pretty fair idea of how the investigation into Lilly Dawson's murder had gone.

* * *

It is on a mild Saturday afternoon in the early spring of 1951 that Lilly Dawson goes missing. She has spent the morning working at her aunt's fish stall on Whitebridge covered market, and, when the market closes at one o'clock, she sets off for home, where she has been told that her favourite meal – Lancashire hotpot – will be warming on the stove for her.

At two o'clock, when Lilly still hasn't arrived, her mother starts to be vaguely concerned. At two thirty, as her apprehension grows, Mrs Dawson puts on her coat and goes down to the Market Tavern, where she knows she will find her sister – Big Gertie Hardy, fore-arms of a man and a drinking capacity to match – already imbibing her third or fourth pint of Thwaites' Best Bitter.

'It's not like our Lilly to be late, especially on a hotpot day,' Mrs Dawson tells her sister.

'Why don't you cut the lass a bit of slack, our Elsie?' Gertie Hardy asks indulgently. 'She's been workin' her arse off for me all mornin'. Why shouldn't she spend a bit of time with her mates?'

'She doesn't really have any mates,' Elsie Dawson says dubiously.

Gertie chuckles. 'None that you *know about, any road,' she replies, 'but it wouldn't surprise me if she was steppin' out with some lad on the sly.'*

'She's thirteen*!' Elsie protests.*

'Aye, she is,' Gertie agrees. 'An' do you remember when you were thirteen, lass?' She takes off the flat cap she is wearing and scratches her head for comical effect. 'Now what was the name of the lad that you *were knockin' about with?'*

'Jackie Taylor,' Elsie confesses, flushing slightly. 'But that were innocent enough.'

'It may well have been – but you still didn't have the nerve to tell our dad about him,' Gertie points out.

'Lilly was late home from school yesterday, as well,' Elsie frets.

'Well, there you are then, it's almost bound to be some lad,' Gertie counters, as if she had just won her argument for her.

By six o'clock, Elsie Dawson has grown frantic, because even if Lilly has been out with a lad – and Elsie still doesn't believe she has – she would have been home by now.

The duty sergeant at the local police station is kindly and understanding – but not very helpful.

'It's just the sort of thing that kids do, Mrs Dawson,' he says.

'An' I should know, because I've got three young buggers of me own.'

'But . . .'

'You just get yourself off back home, an' I'll guarantee you that within a couple of hours she'll turn up at the front door with an excuse that has such big holes in it, you could drive a double-decker bus through it.'

But Lilly does not turn up that evening – and by the following morning, even the bobbies are starting to show concern.

By Sunday afternoon, it has gone beyond mere concern. Local volunteers – many of whom know Lilly personally – join forces with the Whitebridge policemen and other officers drafted in from neighbouring divisions, and together they start searching all the likely places.

They begin with the old abandoned mills – and even though Whitebridge's industrial decline is still a whisper of what it will become, there are enough of them. Next, they criss-cross the wild, savage moors – redolent with early spring flowers – which surround the town. And, when neither of these searches produces any results, they finally admit things might have turned really nasty, and begin dragging the canal.

We'd never treat it so casually nowadays, Monika Paniatowski had thought, as she'd read the old newspaper reports and remembered a similar case which she'd had to deal with when she was only a sergeant. We'd have given the matter top priority, right from the start.

It is early on Thursday morning that a man called John Smith – out walking his equally prosaically named Labrador, Blackie – makes a discovery which will remain burned on to his brain until the day he dies.

Their route takes the man and his dog across a stretch of wasteland that, until recently, has been full of thriving allotments which have produced more than their fair share of prize-winning marrows and amusingly shaped carrots.

As he walks, Smith looks down at the ground – at the previously carefully cultivated patches of land where, even now, a few neglected vegetables are still struggling for survival.

'It's a bloody disgrace, what's been allowed to happen here,' he tells the dog. 'And for why?'

The dog, earnestly sniffing the ground, seems completely oblivious to his owner's outrage.

'I'll tell you for why,' Smith says. 'For that!'

He is pointing beyond the allotments, at a cutting in the ground – perhaps twenty feet wide and three feet deep – and at the heavy machinery which has been responsible for gouging it.

'It's been allowed to happen so they could build a bloody bypass,' the man amplifies, in case the dog has missed the point. 'A bloody ring road.'

There is a roar in the distance, as one of the bulldozers fires up at the start of another day's destruction.

'An' if you think that it's noisy now, just wait until the bypass is opened,' the man warns the dog. 'There'll be big lorries trundlin' along it at all hours of the day an' night.'

But the dog continues to show little interest in urban planning, and instead saunters over to one of the huts where, in happier days, the allotment owners had potted their plants and brewed their tea on small spirit stoves.

'Have you found somethin' interestin', Blackie?' the man asks, as the dog paws at the door of the shed. 'What is it, lad? A rabbit?'

But even as he speaks, he thinks the prospect unlikely, because there has been little sign of any wildlife since the road builders embarked on their act of desecration.

The dog continues to paw at the door, and the man – willing to indulge his pet – lifts the latch.

And that is when he sees her – lying there.

He looks down at her in horror. The glance lasts only for a second or two before he turns away, but that is enough to register the fact that her arms and face are badly bruised, and that her thick blue knickers are around her ankles.

He turns and rushes from the hut, the dog at his heel. He has only one desire – which is to get away from the dreadful sight as quickly as he can – but he has not gone more than a few yards when he doubles up and is violently sick.

The Chief Constable of Mid Lancs, Eliot Sanderson, has never had to handle a case of rape and murder before, but, with a stunning mixture of ignorance and arrogance, he assumes it will not present him with too much of a problem.

'There's no need to call in Scotland Yard,' he says, with an airy gravity, to the assembled local reporters at his first press *conference after the body has been discovered. 'My lads are perfectly capable of sorting it out.'*

Then he sits back and waits for the quick result which can not but reflect well on him.

Thursday slides into Friday, and Saturday, and Sunday follows with almost breathless speed – and still the killer has not been found. Sanderson, bowing to pressure from the papers, gives more press conferences, and – despite his brave words – seems shakier each time.

'What he's really burstin' *to do,' the veteran bobbies inform each other, in whispered conversations in the corridors of their headquarters and over steaming mugs of tea in the police canteen, 'is to call in Scotland Yard – as he should have done in the first place. But he* can't *do that straight away, not after all the braggin' he's done about how good he is. So what he's waitin' for* now *is some kind of excuse which will allow him to call the Yard in without losin' face.'*

On the following Monday morning – a full nine days after Lilly Dawson went missing – the excuse that Sanderson has been praying for finally presents itself.

There is another murder. This time, it is a man called Bazza Mottershead, who has done a stretch for robbery with violence and is well known for his association with what – in provincial Whitebridge – passes for the criminal underworld. His body is discovered behind a garage which the police have long suspected of dealing in stolen cars. His throat has been cut and he has bled profusely – but not so profusely as to mask the fact that someone else who has been at the scene has also bled.

It is clearly a matter of 'thieves falling out', and the general opinion at Whitebridge HQ is that even the greenest bobby on the beat could solve the case – as long, that is, as he is prepared to use his boots as part of his interrogation technique when questioning the known felons likely to be involved.

The chief constable quickly calls another press conference.

'The death of little Lilly Dawson is a tragedy which has affected each and every one of us,' he tells the hacks, with a sincerity he has been practising in the mirror. 'But it is nonetheless an aberration – a once-in-a-generation crime. The murder of Barry Mottershead, on the other hand, is part of a worrying trend towards criminal violence which is sweeping the whole country, and which must be nipped in the bud, here in Whitebridge, before it is allowed to spread any further. With that

*in mind, I have reluctantly decided to concentrate the resources
available to me on bringing Mottershead's killer to justice, and
have asked Scotland Yard to take over the investigation into poor
Lilly's murder.'*

One of the reporters raises his hand in the air. *'Can I just
ask you, Chief Constable—'* he begins.

*'I'm afraid, with all I have to do this morning, there will be
no time for questions,'* Sanderson interrupts.

And having – in his opinion – managed to successfully dodge
the bullet, he steps hurriedly down from the podium and goes
straight to his office, where he dials Whitehall 1212, and asks
to be connected to the Murder Squad.

'He wasted six days,' Paniatowski muttered, as she finished
inspecting herself in the mottled loo mirror. 'The first forty-eight
hours of any investigation are the crucial ones – everybody knows
that – and he wasted *six whole days.'*

She walked out on to the platform to await the arrival of the
train from London. It would be an electric train – they were all
electric on this line now – and she smiled as she remembered
Charlie Woodend's comments on the demise of the old steam
engines.

'Electric trains are all right for kids to play with,' Woodend
had said, 'but they'll never be suitable for transportin' grown
men around.'

Well, suitable or not, they're what we're stuck with, Charlie,
she thought.

She closed her eyes, and could almost see him – a big man
with a face that looked only half-finished, clad in a hairy sports
jacket which was quite unsuitable for an officer of his rank.

She wondered how he'd looked that morning, twenty-two years
earlier, when he climbed down from the steam train – suitable
transportation! – on to this very platform.

And, more importantly, she thought, she wondered how he'd
felt as he embarked on his first major case as a chief inspector.

PART TWO
Whitebridge, April 1951

THREE

Charlie Woodend had never travelled First Class before, and though he'd long ago accepted – on an intellectual level – that such luxury was one of the perks of his new rank, he was finding the practice rather more uncomfortable than the theory had been. It bothered him, for example, that just by paying more for the ticket, he had acquired the services of attendants who were more . . . well, attentive. And while it was grand to have so much space to yourself, it didn't seem quite right when, further down the train, women with small babies on their knees sat sandwiched between building workers puffing on their hand-rolled cigarettes and commercial travellers clutching their sample cases.

'You'll probably get used to it, Charlie,' he told himself.

But he was not entirely sure that he *wanted* to get used to it. In fact, he found the idea that there might come a time when he *didn't* notice the women with their babies really quite worrying.

The railway track was following a gentle curve. Looking through the carriage window, Woodend saw the Black Moss railway viaduct ahead. The journey was almost over, and – for the first time in over a year – he would soon be in the town which he had once called home.

His gaze shifted from the window to the man sitting opposite him. Sergeant Bannerman had had his head buried in a copy of *The Times* since they left London, and even if he was an inordinately slow reader – and his academic record said otherwise – he must have virtually memorized every article in it by now.

So perhaps he just doesn't want to talk to me, Woodend thought. Perhaps he simply doesn't know what to say.

'See that viaduct, Sergeant?' he asked.

Bannerman lowered his newspaper and glanced briefly out of the window.

'Yes, sir, I see it,' he said, in a bored, uninterested way.

'There's folk round here who will tell you – straight-faced – that it was built by the Romans,' Woodend chuckled, 'and when you say that you didn't know the Romans *had* trains, they look at you as if you're a *nutter*.'

'Indeed?' Sergeant Bannerman replied.

Woodend felt a sudden – unexpected – wave of shame wash over him.

Now why was that, he wondered.

It could have been the other man's tone which brought it on, he thought – or it could have been the fact that he himself had chuckled while telling his story.

He had been trying to make the people of Whitebridge seem quaint and funny, he realized.

And perhaps they were. Perhaps their narrow view of the world – their firm belief that Whitebridge, for all its industrial ugliness, was the centre of the universe – *was* humorous. But it was a belief that he had largely shared before he had gone away to fight in the war. And even if the people of Whitebridge *were* slightly ridiculous, they were still *his* people – and he had no right to make fun of them for the amusement of an outsider.

Not that, despite his efforts, Bannerman *had* appeared amused, he admitted. Instead, the detective sergeant had seemed rather superior – as if he found Woodend's attempt to convey quaintness to be quaint *in and of itself*!

Perhaps takin' that promotion was a mistake, he thought, as he felt the rat of doubt gnawing away at his self-confidence. Perhaps I should have waited for a couple of years.

He hadn't felt like that when the Assistant Commissioner – who hated his guts – had offered him a double promotion because that was quickest way of getting him out of London and *keeping* him out of London. No, back then, he'd been delighted. But now he was beginning to see the advantages of spending some time as a detective inspector – of growing slowly towards the role of DCI, rather than of suddenly being dropped into it from a great height.

But even if he *had* served his time as a DI, working with Bannerman would still have been a problem, he thought, though – in all fairness – that was due less to Bannerman himself than it was to the fact that they were a classic mismatch.

A classic mismatch, he repeated silently, rolling the words around in his brain. Yes, that was exactly the way to phrase it.

He found himself imagining sitting in the opposite corner from Bannerman in a boxing ring, and the master of ceremonies – always an impartial outsider – introducing them to their eager, bloodthirsty audience.

'My lords, ladies and gentlemen,' said the imaginary MC,

'may I present to you, in the red corner, Slugger Charlie Woodend – an elementary-school-educated ex-mill worker from Whitebridge; a private soldier in North Africa who managed to claw his way to the rank of sergeant by the time of the D-Day Landings in France; a "big bugger" as they say in Lancashire; a man you might mistake for a bricklayer's labourer or a digger of ditches, but who is, in fact, no less than a chief inspector from Scotland Yard.'

And what would he say about the man in the blue corner? Woodend asked himself.

'And in the blue corner, my lords, ladies and gentlemen, Ralph St John Bannerman, educated at one of England's finest and most ancient schools; a man who missed the war only by virtue of his youth, but nevertheless served with distinction as a second lieutenant in the peace which followed it; a gentleman, in every sense of the word, who carries his slim yet muscular frame with an elegance quite beyond the ability of the bruiser opposite him; a man who could have become a diplomat or a merchant banker, but instead chose to become a humble policeman.'

'Have you ever done any boxin', lad?' asked Woodend, carried along by the whimsy.

Bannerman crinkled his nose in disdain.

'No, sir, can't say that I have,' he answered in a lazy drawl which was already starting to drive Woodend crazy. 'Rugger's more my sport.'

'Rugger', Woodend noted.

Not *rugby*, which was what they called the game in down-to-earth Whitebridge, but *rugger*, as played by the gentlemen of England.

As the train began to slow, Woodend looked out of the window again, and saw the whole of the town spread out before him.

Every town or city had something distinctive about it – something which set the tone of the place – he thought.

Paris had its Eiffel Tower, a symbol of both its past glory and its hopes for the future. New York had the Empire State Building, a colossus which proclaimed the city's energy and confidence.

And Whitebridge?

Whitebridge had its forest of factory chimneys – built from finest Accrington Iron Brick – which were still belching out poisonous black fumes, twenty-four hours a day, just as they had always done.

*   *   *

The uniformed constable, who was waiting for them on the platform, saluted smartly, then said, 'Hello, Charlie, it's right good
to see you!'

A look of haughty irritation crossed Bannerman's face. 'What
you mean, constable, is, "Hello, *Chief Inspector Woodend*, it's
right good to see you, *sir*",' he growled.

Prick! Woodend thought.

Although he supposed that, in a way, his new sergeant was
right. He was no longer the *old* Charlie Woodend – the lad in
short trousers who'd gone bird nesting with this constable in
Sparrows' Copse, long ago. Now he was the *new* Woodend – a
Scotland Yard man who was only in Whitebridge to solve a
crime that the locals seemed unable to solve themselves.

But even taking the change in circumstances into account,
you could still push things *too* far.

'It's good to see you, an' all, Sid,' he said, patting the other
man on the shoulder. He grinned. 'So, is this a chance meetin'
– or are you here to make us feel like VIPs?'

'I'm here to take you to police headquarters, sir,' PC Sid Smart
said, looking, as he spoke, at Bannerman, to see if he'd got the
tone right. 'Mr Sanderson said he wanted to see you the moment
you arrived.'

Aye, Woodend thought, he probably had.

'They tell me you're a local chap, Mr Woodend,' the chief
constable said, gesturing to the two men from London to take a
seat in front of his desk. 'If that's the case, it's surprising we've
never run into each other before.'

No, it isn't – not really, Woodend thought. Not when you
remember that my dad *worked* in a mill, and your dad was the
part-owner of one.

'Yes, that is strange,' he said aloud.

'You, on the other hand, definitely remind me of someone,
Sergeant Bannerman,' the chief constable continued. 'You're not
related to Samuel Bannerman, the polo player, by any chance?'

'Yes, sir, he's my father,' Bannerman said.

'Is he, by God! He has a damn fine seat, your father. We
played against his team at Hurlingham once, and they gave us
a real thrashing.'

Bannerman smiled. 'My father *does* like to win,' he admitted.

'Indeed he does,' Sanderson agreed. 'And I should imagine
that you take after him.'

The whole conversation was getting far too cosy – far too tea-and-cucumber-sandwiches – for Woodend's liking.

'Do you think we could talk about the Lilly Dawson murder now, sir?' he suggested.

'Yes, I suppose it *is* time we got down to discussing the more unsavoury aspects of life,' the chief constable conceded – though he did still manage to look slightly offended at being pushed into it quite so quickly. 'Let me start by laying down what I consider to be the ground rules.'

'All right,' Woodend agreed cautiously.

'While I'm more than willing to assist with your investigation in any way I can, I hope you'll be able to appreciate that, with a second major murder case on my hands, my resources are somewhat stretched,' Sanderson said.

He sounded as if he was addressing a press conference, rather than talking to colleagues, Woodend thought.

And Bannerman obviously felt that too, because he leant forward, rested his hands on the chief constable's desk, and – with a cold edge to his voice that Woodend had never heard before – said, 'With respect, sir, we're not here by our own choice – we came because you requested us to,'

'I . . . err . . . beg your pardon, Sergeant?' the chief constable said, clearly taken aback.

'We're here to do the job *you* asked us to do, and in return *we* have every right to expect you to provide us with everything we need to see that job through to the end,' Bannerman amplified.

The lad certainly wasn't lacking in confidence, Woodend thought, and – in a way – it was a pleasure to watch him cutting this stuffed-shirt down to size. But however ineffective it might turn out to be, they did still *need* the chief constable's cooperation.

'I don't expect we'll require a great deal of help from your officers, sir,' he interjected quickly, before the chief constable had time to express the outrage which was probably building up inside him. 'Havin' said that, of course, I am assumin' that they'll already have done the basic spadework for us.'

The chief constable nodded, and switched back into press conference mode. 'They have indeed done the basic spadework – if not a great deal more than that,' he said. 'In fact, I think I can say without fear of contradiction that, under my guidance, they've done everything that can be expected from a modern police force.'

He should have let his pit bull of a sergeant rag at the chief constable's pomposity a little longer, Woodend decided.

'Yes, I'm sure you *have* done everything that can be expected from a modern police force,' he said, then paused for a second, before continuing, 'except, of course, make an arrest.'

'Yes, apart from that,' the chief constable admitted.

'What can you tell us about the progress of your investigation so far?' Woodend asked.

The chief constable laughed, awkwardly. 'I naturally don't have all the details at my fingertips.'

Well, he bloody well should have, Woodend thought.

'A broad outline will do,' he said, aloud.

'As I understand it, Lilly Dawson left the market at the usual time, and never arrived home,' the chief constable told him.

'When was she last sighted?'

The chief constable waved his hands in the air. 'I couldn't say, offhand, but I expect it will be in the reports.'

He expected it would be in the reports! If the rest of the Mid Lancs Constabulary was as useless as the man who was supposed to be running the whole show, then they were in deep shit, Woodend thought.

He stood up, and held out his hand. 'Thank you for sparing us so much of your valuable time, sir. You've been a great help,' he said, hoping that he'd managed to squeeze at least a semblance of sincerity into the words.

FOUR

If there'd been just his mam and dad at home, when Woodend snatched half an hour to go pay a visit, the three of them would have sat around the kitchen table and drunk tea out of thick blue-and-white striped mugs. But, as chance would have it, his parents already had visitors – in the shape of an ageing couple who clearly still expected him to address them as 'Auntie' May and 'Uncle' George, even though they were not relations – and so the whole event had to be transferred to the front parlour, which was normally only used for christenings, weddings, funerals and birthday parties.

It soon became obvious to Woodend that it wasn't chance *at all* that these non-relatives were there, but rather as a result of their hearing, through the grapevine, that Mr and Mrs Woodend's only child was back in town, and in charge of the most sensational murder case to hit Whitebridge in living memory. 'Auntie' May, especially, was eager to hear all the gory details, and seemed most put out when Woodend explained that, at the moment, he knew little more than they would have read in the papers.

Mam let the pretend aunt and uncle continue their fruitless interrogation for the best part of fifteen minutes, then stood up and said, 'Well, we mustn't detain you any longer, May an' George. I expect there's lots of things you'll need to have got done before the day's over.'

'Well . . .' 'Auntie' May began to protest disappointedly.

'I'll show you to the door,' Mam said firmly. 'Drop around any time. You're always welcome.'

As Woodend watched his mother relentlessly shepherding her visitors to the front door, he found it hard to restrain a chuckle. This was vintage Mam, he thought – as polite as could be, but as immovable as the Rock of Gibraltar.

While Mam shooed the visitors out into the street, Woodend took the opportunity to glance around the parlour.

Had it always seemed so pokey? he wondered.

Had there always been this danger that, even by making the slightest move, you ran the risk of knocking over one of the occasional tables on which Mam displayed her precious knick-knacks?

Mam closed the front door firmly behind the visitors.

'That May!' she said, in a voice which was half-disapproval and half-amusement. 'She's got a bigger appetite for tragedy than I have for pickled gherkins. Still,' she continued, 'I don't suppose I can blame her – especially when she used to hold the man in charge of the case on her lap.' She smiled. 'Imagine it, Charlie, you a *chief inspector.*'

'Aye, just imagine it,' Woodend agreed, balancing the delicate china tea cup – which he knew had been brought out of the display cabinet especially for the occasion – on one of his sturdy knees.

'Where's this sergeant of yours?' his father asked.

'He's settlin' into the hotel at the moment,' Woodend said, more gruffly than he'd intended.

'An' what hotel might that be?' his mother wondered.

'The Royal Victoria.'

'The Royal Victoria! Will you be stayin' there, an' all?'

Well, of course he would be! What did they think? That his
sergeant would have a room in the best hotel in town, while he
made do with a modest bed and breakfast?

Yes, that probably was what they *would* think, he decided,
because while they accepted the fact that he *was* a chief inspector,
they still hadn't quite got used to the idea.

And, to tell the truth, neither had he.

'We're so glad you're here, Charlie,' his mother said.

'I'm pleased to see you, an' all,' Woodend replied.

'That's not what I meant,' his mother told him.

And suddenly the rosy glow of approval in which he'd been
basking – albeit uncomfortably – was gone, and in its place was
the practical level-headedness of a mam who, despite the trauma
of her hysterectomy, had held the family together through the
lean times in the thirties.

'So what *did* you mean?' he asked.

'In some ways, this is a big town, Charlie,' his mother said.
'There's a dozen cinemas and three dance halls now, you
know.'

'No, I didn't know that,' Woodend admitted, realizing just
how *little* he actually knew of Whitebridge any more.

'But in other ways, it's little more than a village,' his mother
continued.

He nodded, well aware that what she was saying was true.

'Lilly Dawson's death is tearin' the place apart,' his mother
continued. 'It's not just that she died so young – though that's
bad enough – it's *how* she died.'

'I know, Mam,' Woodend said.

'An' she looked such a sweet little thing, didn't she? So
completely trustin' and innocent?'

'I don't think that I've actually seen any pictures of her yet,'
Woodend confessed.

His mother looked shocked. 'Not seen any pictures of her?
But you're the one who's in charge of the case.'

Woodend sighed. He wanted to explain to his mother that
however sweet Lilly had been, it had nothing to do with the
case – that his task was simply to track down her murderer.
He wanted to make her see that it was a job like any other
job, and that becoming personally involved with the victim –
as he *had* become in the Pearl Jones case – was a mistake,
and one he was unwilling to repeat. But he knew he would

be wasting his time, because he would never be able to make her understand.

'I thought she was just bein' naive, you see,' he would explain to Monika Paniatowski, many years later, 'but what she was actually doin' was pointin' me in the direction I've been travellin' in ever since.'

Mam disappeared into the kitchen for a second, and returned with a copy of the *Whitebridge Evening Telegraph* in her hand.

'Here's a picture of the little lass,' she said, holding out the paper in front of her son. 'Look at it!'

The tone in her voice made him grin. It was almost, he thought, as if he were five years old again – back in a time when Mam's words carried as much force as those of any benevolent dictator who had ever lived.

The grin disappeared from his face the moment he looked at the picture. Mam was right – as she invariably was. Lilly Dawson *had* looked like a 'sweet little thing'. There *was* a trust and innocence in her eyes. But there was something else about the picture – something which made Woodend's stomach lurch.

'I saw it, too,' his mother said sombrely.

'Saw what?' Woodend asked.

But he knew. He already *knew*.

'She looks just like our Annie might look, in a few years' time,' his mother said.

Annie! His golden girl! His only child! And there would be no more – the doctors had been quite clear about that.

'I don't see it,' he said, his eyes still on the photograph.

But what he really meant was that he *didn't want* to see it!

'The man who killed her has to be caught, Charlie – an' caught *quickly*,' Mam said. 'Not just to bring a little peace an' consolation to Lilly's mother – although, God knows, the poor woman must be sorely in need of it – but for the good of the whole town.'

'I'll do everything I can,' Woodend said – aware of just how inadequate the response seemed, even to him.

'You should go down to the market, like I have, Charlie,' the mother continued. 'There's so much fear an' suspicion in the air that you could cut through it with a bread knife. Everybody's wonderin' if it was one of their neighbours who did them terrible things to Lilly. An' everybody's wonderin' if he'll do it *again*. So when I said earlier that I was glad you were here, *that's* what I meant.'

'Of course, we're also pleased to see you here for yourself,' his father added, hastily.

But his mother was not to be deflected from her point.

'You understand Whitebridge in a way an outsider never ever could, Charlie,' she said. 'Besides, you're my lad, an' I know you like only a mother can. Once you've set your mind to somethin', you won't rest until you've seen it through to the end. That's the way you've always been – and the way you always will be.'

Woodend carefully laid the delicate cup on the fragile table, and – even more carefully – stood up.

'I have to go,' he said. 'My sergeant will probably be expectin' me back at the hotel.'

'Well, we'd better not detain you any longer, had we?' his father said, and smiled to show that he was well aware he was using the same words as his wife had used to get rid of Auntie May and Uncle George.

Woodend kissed his mother and shook hands with his father – had the old man *always* been so small? – then walked across to the door which led out directly on to the street.

'Remember, Charlie, we're all relyin' on you,' he heard his mother say behind him.

Woodend stepped out on to the pavement and closed the front door behind him. He looked first up the street of narrow terraced houses and then down it. It somehow didn't feel real any more, he thought. It was as if it were a place he had only read about, and which now – examining it for the first time – seemed to be nothing like he had pictured it in his mind.

He lit up a cigarette, and set off towards the 'better' part of town, where the Royal Victoria was located.

His mam expected a great deal from him, he thought, as he walked down the cobbled street.

And it wasn't just his mam who expected it – it was the whole bloody town of Whitebridge.

Because he was not so much the local hero returning home to his justly earned acclaim as he was one of their own who they had allowed to get on in life – and who they now expected to fix things for them.

And that was a lot of pressure to put on a newly-promoted chief inspector, he told himself.

FIVE

The Drum and Monkey public house was just fifteen minutes' walk from the Royal Victoria Hotel, and had a historical importance in the life and development of Charlie Woodend.

It was here, as a youth inexpertly puffing on a Park Drive cigarette, that Charlie had first tried to pass himself off as old enough to drink. He had been nervous when he entered the public bar, but he need not have been. Even at sixteen, he was half a head taller than most of the other customers, and the landlord had pulled him a frothy pint of best bitter without a second thought.

Looking around him as he drank, he had savoured the moment. This was the adult world, he'd told himself – this was the world of *men* – and a lifelong love affair between Charlie Woodend and old-fashioned pubs had begun to blossom.

Now, approaching the pub for the first time in perhaps a dozen years, Woodend felt butterflies in his stomach, just as he had done that first time.

Well, not quite like the first time, he admitted. *This* time, there was no danger at all that the landlord would refuse to serve him because of his age.

But perhaps other things would be different, too.

Perhaps this shrine to his coming-of-age would have changed beyond all recognition – the oak counter replaced by something modern and plastic, the brass foot-rail removed, the wall between the public bar and the snug knocked down in order to create one vast soulless room . . . the possibilities were horrifically endless.

He opened the door, and breathed a sigh of relief. It was, he saw, exactly how he remembered it – exactly how it *should* be.

'What do you want to drink?' he asked Sergeant Bannerman, as they strode over to the bar.

He was half-expecting that the sergeant would ask for something exotic – something that not only did the pub not stock, but had never even heard of.

But what Bannerman actually said was, 'Is the best bitter any good in here, sir?'

'It's champion.' Woodend replied with enthusiasm. 'But you'll have to treat it with caution, because after that thin London ale you're used to, it'll probably knock your socks off.'

Bannerman gave him a smile – the first sign of genuine amusement Woodend had seen from his new sergeant – and said, 'I'll risk it.'

They took the pints to the nearest table.

'Well, you certainly made your disdain for the chief constable evident enough,' Woodend said.

'The man's an idiot,' Bannerman replied simply. 'He's a third-rate polo player and a fourth-rate policeman.'

'I agree with you – on the second part, at least,' Woodend said. 'But he is *still* the chief constable, an' he could seriously damage your career if you're not careful.'

Bannerman smiled sardonically. 'As I see it, there are two main skills to getting on in life,' he said. 'The first is to achieve the results you're expected to achieve, and the second is to know *who* you can step on and *who* you can't.'

'An' you think you can step on Sanderson, do you?' Woodend asked, interestedly.

'Definitely,' Bannerman said. 'If we manage to get a result on this case, then the people who matter back at the Yard won't give a damn about what Sanderson thinks of me. And if we *don't* get a result, well,' he waved his hands carelessly through the air, 'I can at least point out, in my own defence, that when I told the chief constable we needed more resources, he ignored me.'

An' you can also point out that I said we *didn't* need them, Woodend thought.

'I've got two questions for you,' he said. 'Firstly, do you see solvin' the case as anythin' more than a step up the promotions ladder for you?'

'Of course I do,' Bannerman replied. 'Life is about justice and order, and I wish to see justice prevailing and order maintained. That's why I joined the police.'

Woodend did no more than nod non-committally.

'What's the second question, sir?' Bannerman asked, when some time had elapsed.

'Oh aye,' Woodend said, as if he'd completely forgotten there *was* a second question. 'What sort of feller am I?'

'I'm sorry, sir?

'Am I the sort you can step on – or the sort you can't?'

'Definitely the latter,' Bannerman said, just a little too quickly. 'You're my boss, and I intend to learn all I can from you.'

An' then kick me up the arse when you've learned it, Woodend thought.

He opened the file that the Whitebridge Police had given to him, and spread it out on the table.

'Accordin' to this report,' he said, 'Lilly Dawson left the covered market at one o'clock. Now it's a twenty-five minute walk from the market to the Dawson's home . . .'

'How do you know that?' Bannerman interrupted.

'Because I've clogged it,' Woodend told him.

'I beg your pardon, sir.'

'While you were settlin' yourself in at the hotel, I went to see me mam an' dad.'

'I know that, sir.'

'An' *after* I'd seen them, I walked from the market to Lilly's house. Now, I can't say I did it at exactly the same speed the little lass would have done, but I tried my best, an' I don't think I can have been more than five minutes out, one way or the other.'

'I'd never have thought of that,' Bannerman said, with what just might have been a hint of admiration.

'It's what's called "old-fashioned police work",' Woodend replied. 'You can learn a fair bit from reports – especially if they've been written by a bobby who really knows his job – but there's no substitute, to my mind, for cloggin' it around the scene of the crime.'

'I'll remember that,' Bannerman said.

'Anyway, things are quiet at that time of a Saturday,' Woodend continued. 'By one o'clock, most people are either busy still shuttin' up shop or sittin' down to their dinner, so it's hardly surprisin' that the last reported sightin' of Lilly was at ten past one. Now it's possible that she went wanderin' off on her own somewhere, but what's most likely is that she was snatched off the street by her killer some time between ten past one and twenty-five past, which was when she should have arrived home. So what we're lookin' for, Sergeant, is somebody who can't account for his movements between those two times.'

'But we could be talking about *hundreds* of people!' Bannerman said.

'Do you think so, Sergeant?' Woodend asked.

'Yes, sir. Don't you?'

'No, I think it's more like *thousands* – but at least it's a start.'

Bannerman pondered on the enormity of the task for a moment, then said, 'So what do we do next?'

'Next, though I'm not lookin' forward to it at all, we go an' see Lilly's mother,' Woodend replied heavily.

He took a last look around the bar before they departed. He was glad it hadn't changed since the last time he'd been there, but he accepted, fatalistically, that the *next* time he was in Whitebridge and visited it again, it would probably be a completely different pub entirely.

He had no way of knowing, back then, that when he had his *last* drink in the Drum and Monkey – twenty-two years later, on the very day of his retirement – he would be sitting in exactly the same chair as he was sitting in at that moment.

Like Rome, Whitebridge was built on hills, but there the comparison with the eternal city ended.

The terraced houses which made up most of the housing stock in the town had been hastily constructed, a hundred years earlier, to accommodate the workers in the booming textile industry. They were two-up two-down dwellings, with no front garden and a back yard (containing the wash-house and the outside lavatory) which opened on to a narrow alley and a view of *someone else's* backyard. The houses clung precariously to the hills, each one with a front door at an angle to the pavement, each with a roof which was a little lower than the neighbour's on the right, and a little higher than the neighbour's on the left.

'Must be a bit of a change to what you're used to,' Woodend said to Bannerman, as they laboured up the steep slope.

'Oh, I wouldn't exactly say that,' Bannerman replied. 'There are slums in the south, as well, you know, sir.'

'Aye, maybe there are,' Woodend agreed. 'But, you see, lad, the people round here don't regard *these* houses as slums – to them, they're little palaces.'

They came to a halt in front of a door which had been inexpertly painted in royal blue, and Woodend lifted the knocker and tapped it against the door.

The woman who answered his knock was in her middle thirties. Her hair was lank, her eyes were red, and there could be no doubt that she was Lilly Dawson's mother.

'We're from Scotland Yard, Mrs Dawson,' Woodend said softly.

'I know who you are,' the woman replied, in a flat, dead voice. 'Would you like to come in?'

'If you wouldn't mind.'

She stepped back to admit them, then gestured towards the front room.

'If it's all the same to you, love, we'd prefer to go into the kitchen,' Woodend said.

Bannerman gave him a questioning look, as well he might.

What the sergeant didn't understand, Woodend thought, was that if they wanted Mrs Dawson to relax – or, at least, be as relaxed as she *could be*, under the circumstances – then the kitchen, her natural environment, was where the interview should be conducted.

Mrs Dawson nodded, and led them through.

'It's a bit of a mess,' she said apologetically. 'I've not had time to tidy up, what with . . .' She waved her hands helplessly.

What with your daughter havin' been murdered, Woodend supplied mentally. What with havin' to live through every parent's worst nightmare.

'It's fine, love,' he assured her.

'Well, sit yourselves down,' Mrs Dawson said, doing her best to sound the brisk and efficient housewife that she probably normally was.

They sat at a solid old table which would serve as both the surface on which the food was prepared and the place at which it was eaten.

'Cup of tea?' Mrs Dawson asked.

Bannerman looked at Woodend for guidance, and Woodend said, 'That would be most welcome. After walkin' up that hill, I feel as if I'm spittin' feathers.'

Mrs Dawson rewarded him with a thin laugh. 'You get used to the climb,' she said, then added sadly. 'You can get used to everythin' in time.'

I doubt that, Woodend thought. The ache may dull over the years, but it isn't goin' to go away, love.

Mrs Dawson brewed the tea in a dark-brown teapot which, in Bannerman's 'social circles' would have been considered almost an antique, but in hers was just an old teapot.

'Lilly's dad died when she was nine,' Mrs Dawson said, when she joined them at the table.

'That must have been difficult for her,' Woodend said, sympathetically. 'For you, as well,' he added.

'If he'd got hit by a bus, it wouldn't have been so bad,' Mrs Dawson continued. A look of horror came to her face. 'I . . . I didn't mean that the way it sounded. Ted's death would have been terrible, however it had happened, but if it had have been quick, it might at least have been easier to take.'

'I understand,' Woodend said.

He took a sip from his cup. The taste of tannin filled his mouth. This was how he liked his tea – strong enough to build bricks out of.

'It was cancer that Lilly's dad had,' Mrs Dawson said – and her voice dipped when she used the dreaded word, as it did with all women in Whitebridge when they referred to the killer disease.

'It's a terrible way to go,' Woodend said.

'Yes, it is,' Mrs Dawson agreed. 'A terrible way. It took him over a year to die, an' he was here at home for most of it. Our Lilly was marvellous with him. When she wasn't at school or asleep, she hardly ever left his bedside. She was just a little kid, but he couldn't have asked for a better nurse.' A tear came to the woman's eye. 'She really loved her dad. She never got over losin' him.' Mrs Dawson gulped. 'An' now she never will.'

'Tell me about her friends,' Woodend said softly.

'She didn't really have any – not after her dad died. It was like . . . it was like, lookin' after him robbed her of somethin'.'

'It forced her to grow up quickly,' Sergeant Bannerman said.

And he sounded as if he thought that that was a *good* thing, Woodend told himself – as though Bannerman believed that childhood innocence was a thing to be discarded as rapidly as possible.

'That's the thing, it *didn't* make her grow up,' Mrs Dawson said. She shook her head in frustration, desperate to express herself and yet unable to find quite the right words. 'It . . . it froze her,' she concluded, finally.

'I'm afraid I really have no idea what you're talking about, Mrs Dawson,' Bannerman said.

Then you should bloody well take a few lessons in sensitivity! Woodend thought angrily.

'What you mean is, she stayed the little girl that she'd been when her dad took ill,' he said to Mrs Dawson.

'That's right,' the woman agreed, gratefully. 'She clung on to her dolls, long after all the other girls had got bored with them. An' then there were the animals.'

'What animals?' Bannerman asked.

Mrs Dawson stood up. 'Come an' see,' she said.

She led them into the backyard. Next to the hand-turned mangle stood a rabbit hutch, in which three plump complacent rabbits twitched their pink noses and scratched at the straw.

'It wasn't just rabbits she kept,' Mrs Dawson said. 'There were her guinea pigs and hamsters as well. An' just before she . . . just before she died, she was mitherin' me to get a budgerigar. She'd have turned the whole house into a zoo, if I'd let her.' She paused for a moment. 'I . . . I don't know what to do with the rabbits now she's gone.'

'I'm sure there's some little kid down the street who'll be glad of them,' Woodend said.

They all went back into the house.

'Would it be all right if we had a quick look at Lilly's bedroom?' Woodend asked.

'Why would you want to go in there?' Mrs Dawson wondered, with something close to panic in her voice.

'It might assist us in gettin' a clearer picture of Lilly,' Woodend told her.

'But I don't see how that would help,' the grieving mother protested.

No, she wouldn't, Woodend thought.

Because, to her, her daughter's death had nothing to do with Lilly herself. The girl had been killed by an evil man – a monster – and there wasn't anything that Lilly had done – or had failed to do – which could have prevented it.

She had to think that way, of course, because the idea that Lilly had contributed to the tragedy would have been unbearable to her.

But the sad fact was that while some victims were selected randomly, others were chosen because of a weakness that the killer detected in them – and while he thought that he already knew what Lilly's weakness was, he needed to go the girl's room to confirm it.

'I don't know . . . I'm not sure that I want you to . . .' Mrs Dawson said hesitantly.

He was within his rights to insist, of course, but he didn't want to do that unless he absolutely had to.

'What about if I left Sergeant Bannerman here – to keep you company – an' just went for quick look myself?' he suggested.

'Well . . .' Mrs Dawson said, weakening.

'I promise you, I won't disturb anything,' Woodend pressed her.

Mrs Dawson shrugged, as if she wanted to continue resisting but didn't have the strength.

'It's the second door on the left, at the top of the stairs,' she said.

'I'll not be more than five minutes,' Woodend promised her.

And then he shot a look in his sergeant's direction which he hoped would convey the message that, while he *was* upstairs, he didn't want Bannerman saying anything that would make Mrs Dawson feel any worse than she already did.

SIX

'How the hell can Lilly's room be the second on the left?' Woodend wondered, as he climbed the steep stairs which led to the first floor of Elsie Dawson's home. 'There is no second on the left.'

At least, he amended, there'd been no second on the left in *any other* terraced cottage he'd ever visited. Two-up two-down was what this type of house was called, and two-up two-down was exactly what you got – one bedroom over the front parlour, and another over the kitchen.

And yet, when he reached the top of the stairs, he saw that there was not just the small landing he had been expecting, but a narrow corridor to his left, with two doors opening on to it.

He opened the first door, and looked inside.

'Well, bugger me!' he said softly to himself.

The house had a *bathroom*! The Dawson family didn't need to go *outside* to the toilet on cold, wet winter nights. They didn't need to bathe in a large tin bath in front of the kitchen fire. They – unlike most of the other working-class families in Whitebridge, including Woodend's own parents – had an *indoor* bathroom!

Up until that moment, he had been picturing Mr Dawson as the helpless invalid he must have been towards the end of his life. What he was looking at now changed all that. It showed him a man who had so wanted to make a comfortable home for his wife and daughter that he had done what few men from his background would ever dream of doing – he had scrimped and saved and built them a bathroom.

The man was a hero, Woodend thought – not the towering

hero of legend, but a hero nevertheless. And his death, which already seemed tragic enough, took on a new poignancy.

The journey from the dead man's monument to the dead girl's bedroom was just two short steps along the cramped corridor.

Lilly's room looked out on to the back yard, where she had kept her rabbits. It was small, and furnished with only a single bed and a cheap dressing table. There was a shelf above the bed, where most kids would have kept their books, but Lilly seemed to have no interest in reading, and instead the shelf was filled, from end to end, with stuffed toys – most of them cuddled threadbare.

Woodend sighed. What he was seeing was pretty much what he had *expected* to see – but, even forewarned, it was still sad.

What did come as a surprise were the drawings. They were pinned to the walls, and there were so many of them that very little of the purple-flowered wallpaper underneath managed to show through.

Some of the pictures were of animals – rabbits, hamsters and donkeys, inexpertly but loving drawn – but the majority of them were of a girl and a man.

'So why are there no pictures of her mother?' Woodend said softly.

Then, as he studied the pictures in more detail, the answer to his question slowly came to him – and, as it came, he started to feel nauseous.

The girls in the pictures never varied. They were all excessively small – totally out of proportion to the men – and had a desperate fragility about them. None of the men, in contrast, looked like any of the others. Some had dark hair, some were fair. Some smoked a pipe, others a cigarette. The only thing that they had in common was that they were holding the little girl's hand.

There are no pictures of her mother because her mother's not bloody well *dead*, Woodend thought, angry with himself that he'd taken so long to grasp this simple point.

What he was looking at, he now realized, were not pictures of her *real* dad – she had seen him slowly waste away, and knew he was not coming back.

No, they were an attempt to create a *new* dad for herself – someone who would fill the aching void she felt deep inside her.

She had tried, and she had failed. None of the men had seemed quite right, and so she had kept on drawing, hoping against hope that she could eventually produce a figure who she could believe in.

Her coloured pencils lay on the dressing table. They were Lakeland brand, Woodend noted, some of the most expensive available. Lilly's mother, living on a meagre widow's pension, must have thought long and hard before buying them. So perhaps the fact that she *had* bought them meant she understood her daughter's need, and had seen to it that she had best tools available to her as she embarked on her hopeless quest.

He picked up one the pencils, and saw that the end had been bitten into so deeply that the coloured lead was exposed.

'It didn't really help, did it, Lilly?' he asked, as he felt a great wave of sadness wash over him. 'However hard you tried to draw yourself a new dad, it didn't really help.'

He found himself thinking of his daughter, Annie – who, as his mother had pointed out, resembled the dead girl in so many ways.

The two girls' faces merged together in his mind, and he pictured Annie in this room, drawing frantically as tears slowly slid down her cheeks.

'Don't do it, Charlie,' he told himself urgently. 'For Christ's sake, don't bloody do it!'

But the idea was in his head – the connection was made – and the thought would simply not go away.

He imagined Annie being dragged into a car against her will . . . taken to a shed on an abandoned allotment . . . having her legs roughly forced apart as she screamed out for a little kindness . . . gasping desperately as her killer's hands closed around her throat . . .

He felt the sudden urge to vomit.

'Easy, Charlie!' he ordered himself, as he tried to regulate his breathing. 'Remember who you are. You're a hardbitten copper – a professional – an' you should be able to keep all this under control.'

But he was fighting a losing battle – and he knew it.

He turned and rushed from Lilly's bedroom to the bathroom. He only just had time to lean over the toilet bowl before his stomach heaved and all the sadness – and all the anger and all the fear – came spewing out.

It was a full ten minutes before Woodend felt he could face the world again, and even then his legs were still shaking as he re-entered the kitchen.

Bannerman was sitting at the table, a copy of the *Evening*

Telegraph spread out in front of him, and his lips set in a super-cilious twist. There was no sign of the woman.

'Where's Mrs Dawson?' Woodend demanded.

Bannerman looked up. 'She said she needed to go outside for a breath of fresh air,' he replied, with marked unconcern.

'Why was that?' Woodend asked, suspiciously. 'You've not said anythin' to upset her, have you?'

'Me?' Bannerman said, with a look of comic surprise on his face.

'Well, I don't see anybody else in the room, so, yes, I do mean *you*,' Woodend countered.

'Now what could *I* possibly have said to upset her?' Bannerman wondered innocently.

'Do you want me to give you a list?' Woodend demanded. 'Because, if you do, it'll be a bloody long one!' He sighed. 'Sorry, lad, I didn't mean it. I needed to lash out at somethin' – an' you just happened to be in the way.'

'That's all right, sir,' Bannerman said, with easy grace. 'What's that you've got in your hand?'

Woodend looked down, and – though he didn't even remember picking them up – saw that he was holding some of Lilly's pictures.

'Look at these,' he said, laying them out on the table.

Bannerman studied the drawings for a few moments, then said, 'Well, if we're to believe her mother, she may indeed have been immature in some ways – but she certainly seemed to have a very grown-up attitude to men.'

An' to think, it's barely a minute since I apologized to this bastard! Woodend thought angrily.

'Are we lookin' at the same pictures, do you think, Sergeant?' he asked, in a tone which was much leveller than the rage he was feeling inside.

'I'm sorry, sir?'

'Aye, an' so you bloody well should be! From what you've just said, it sounds as if you think she was the kind of girl who was so hot for men that she had no elastic in her knickers.'

'Well, you must admit, she did seem to have had something of an obsession for the opposite sex,' Bannerman replied.

For the briefest of instants, Woodend seriously contemplated showing his sergeant the error of his ways by the simple expe-dient of smashing his fist in Bannerman's face and breaking his upper-middle-class nose. But the moment passed, and before he

had time to substitute a verbal beating for the – much more satis-
fying – physical one, the back door opened, and Mrs Dawson
walked into the kitchen.

'I . . . err . . . I needed to get out for a bit,' she said to Woodend.

'Aye, love, my sergeant said,' Woodend replied, as he noted
that she had obviously been crying again. 'We've got a few more
questions,' he continued. 'Do you feel strong enough to answer
them?'

'I . . . I think so.'

'Then sit yourself down, an' it'll be all over before you
know it.'

Mrs Dawson sat, deliberately positioning herself so that, while
she could look directly at Woodend, Bannerman was just out of
her line of vision.

'Did anythin' unusual happen in the week before your Lilly
disappeared?' Woodend asked softly.

'Unusual?' Mrs Dawson repeated.

'Did you, for example, see any strangers hangin' around in
the street?'

Mrs Dawson shook her head. 'That sort of thing doesn't
happen round here, Chief Inspector. People would notice
strangers. They'd ask them what they thought they were doin'.'

Of course they would, Woodend agreed silently. This wasn't
a leafy southern suburb, in which every house had a substantial
garden and the residents lived completely separate lives. This
was the shoulder-to-shoulder terraced-housed north – where
people not only knew their neighbours' business, but thought
they had a *right* to know it.

'There was one thing,' Mrs Dawson said tentatively.

'Go on.'

'Lilly was very late home on the Friday night before . . . before
it happened. I had words with her about it.'

'Why was that? Was it because she was normally a very
punctual girl?'

'Well, exactly. You could have set your watch by our Lilly.'

'Did she give you a satisfactory explanation for her tardi-
ness?' Bannerman asked.

Mrs Dawson looked completely mystified.

'Pardon?' she said.

Bloody idiot, Woodend thought.

'Did she give you any reason for why she was late?' he asked.

'Not really. She said she'd just been for a walk. But I could tell she was lyin' – I could *always* tell when she was lyin' to me! I nearly stopped her goin' to her Saturday job on the market because of it.' Mrs Dawson suppressed a sob. 'I wish to God I *had* stopped her.'

'It wouldn't have made any difference if you had,' Bannerman told her, bluntly. 'Once one of these animals has a girl in his sights, he's not likely to put off by the fact that she doesn't follow her normal routine.'

'My sergeant's got a talent for sayin' just the right thing in just the wrong way,' Woodend told Mrs Dawson. 'But what he says *is* true, you know. None of what happened is any of your fault – an' nothin' you could have done would have prevented it.'

'Thank you, Chief Inspector,' Mrs Dawson said, looking Woodend straight in the eye and ignoring Bannerman's gaze completely. 'I really needed to hear that.'

They were sitting in the Balmoral Bar of the Royal Victoria. The best bitter that the bar served was passable – maybe even better than passable – but the tartan wallpaper was starting to give Woodend a headache.

'What line of investigation do you think we should pursue in the morning, sir?' Sergeant Bannerman asked.

'What line do *you* think we should follow?' Woodend countered.

'Well, there *is* a long list of possible suspects who should be investigated,' Bannerman said.

Woodend took a sip of his pint. 'Is there? I didn't know that.'

'It's all in the reports, sir.'

'Oh, you mean the fellers that the local bobbies have already pulled in for questionin'?'

'That's right, sir.'

'But – an' correct me if I'm wrong, Sergeant – haven't they already been ruled out?'

'Yes, sir – but you shouldn't forget *who* ruled them out.'

'I'm not followin' you,' Woodend said.

But he was – he was following every twist and turn of Bannerman's blinkered thought process.

'It's the *local coppers* who have ruled them out, sir.'

'Yes?'

'And whilst they *are* our colleagues – and thus entitled to our professional respect – I have to say that I don't think they'd recognize a lead if you slapped them in the face with it.'

Arrogant young sod, Woodend thought.

'So it's your opinion that we could do worse than re-interview all the usual suspects, is it?' he asked.

'That's right,' Bannerman agreed.

He hadn't solved the Pearl Jones murder case by sitting on his arse and glaring at some poor twisted sod on the other side of the table, Woodend reminded himself – he'd done it by clogging his way around Canning Town, breathing in the air that Pearl had breathed herself, and talking to the people who Pearl had known. And that was how he intended to crack this case – by planting himself firmly in the middle of Lilly's world.

On the other hand, even though he was personally convinced that nothing would come from re-interviewing people whose alibis had already been checked out – and *however* incompetent the Whitebridge police were, they would surely have checked the alibis – Bannerman might just have presented him with the perfect way of getting his sergeant off his back.

And the fact was, he admitted, there were a number of good reasons why he really *wanted* Bannerman off his back.

The sergeant was an outsider, whose very presence would be likely to make the people in Whitebridge clam up.

Besides, from the way he'd spoken to Elsie Dawson, it was clear that Bannerman didn't regard sensitivity to other people's grief as the quality that he most needed to cultivate.

And then there was the clincher – that he neither liked Bannerman as a person nor entirely trusted him as a policeman.

'But hang on, Charlie,' cautioned a slightly uneasy voice from somewhere at the back of his head. 'Isn't it your job to train up your sergeant – to lead by example, and make him into a policeman just like you?'

'No!' a stronger voice – one which he clearly recognized as his own – immediately countered. 'It's my job to catch the animal who killed poor little Lilly Dawson – an' catch him before he has the chance to strike again! It's my job to help the town I grew up in to heal itself. An' if that involves cuttin' this bumptious little prick out of the loop, it's a price well worth payin'.'

'Sir?' Bannerman said questioningly.

And Woodend realized that it must be quite some time since he had last spoken.

'I've been thinkin' about what you said,' he told the sergeant, 'an' I've decided you've probably got a point. It might well be very useful to re-interview all the possible suspects.'

Bannerman nodded seriously. 'If that's your considered opinion, sir, then I'm sure that you're right.'

He thinks he's manipulated me! Woodend told himself. The bugger really thinks he's got me wrapped around his little finger!

'And not only do I think it's a good idea, but I've decided I'll leave that particular job in your very capable hands,' he said aloud.

Bannerman beamed, as if he'd just been told he'd won first prize in a school debating competition.

'Really, sir?' he asked.

'Really,' Woodend confirmed.

He checked his watch, and was surprised to see that though it felt like it had been a very long day, it was still only a quarter to nine.

'Do you fancy another pint?' he asked.

Bannerman shook his head. 'If it's all the same to you, sir, I think I'll turn in for the night.'

He really *didn't* know the ropes, did he, Woodend thought – still didn't appreciate one of the most important unwritten rules of being part of a team, which was that the boozing stopped when the boss decided it should stop.

Even so, he was far from displeased by his sergeant's ignorance – because he had had quite enough of the bloody man for one day.

Left alone, with only the garish wallpaper for company, Woodend wondered what he should do next.

He wasn't ready to go to bed, but he didn't want to remain in the Balmoral Bar, either. The obvious solution would be to pay a visit to one of the dozen or so pubs within easy reach of the hotel – pubs where he would not have to drink alone because he was almost bound to run into someone who he had known in his childhood or his youth.

But he was starting to realize that to do that would be a mistake, because his life had moved on, and things could never again be as they once were.

The old mates who he talked to in one of these pubs wouldn't see him as the lad who had scored the goal which put his club at the top of the local amateur football league (and only later realized he had done it with a broken leg).

They wouldn't connect him with the youth who, when the

lead singer of a visiting jazz band collapsed due to a surfeit of alcohol, had had the brass balls to climb on stage and take over the vocals.

They wouldn't even conjure up an image of him as the callow young man, in a new suit bought on the never-never, who'd been so nervous when he took Joan out on their first date that he'd spilled his pint all over her – and then torn her dress in his desperate urge to clean up the mess.

No, they wouldn't see any of that at all.

What they *would* see would be Chief Inspector Woodend – up from London to solve a horrendous crime which had sent the town into a state of shock and baffled the finest minds in the local constabulary.

And he didn't want that – he *really* didn't want that.

He lit a cigarette and signalled to the waiter to bring him another pint. When it arrived, he sat looking at it without his customary enthusiasm, and then sighed softly to himself.

That's what it's going to be like from now on, Charlie, he told himself, so you'd better bloody well get used to it.

SEVEN

There had been a market on the spot where Whitebridge now stood since early medieval times, which – as local historians were fond of pointing out – was long before there'd even been a white bridge to name the town after. Back then, the town had been no more than a hamlet – a few dozen mud-and-wattle huts, clustered together around a ford in the river – but on market day, when peddlers came to sell their wares and tinkers to carry out their trade, it had been the busiest and most exciting place in whole of central Lancashire.

The modern market had been built towards the end of the Victorian era. It was a solidly reassuring cast-iron structure with an arched roof. And under that roof, over three hundred traders conducted their business from tubular-steel stalls which had been specifically designed for easy erection and disassembly – but had stood rooted to the same spot for as long as anyone could remember.

When Charlie Woodend entered the covered market at

half past eight that morning – a half-smoked cigarette in one hand and a half-eaten bacon sandwich in the other – he saw that although a few of the stalls were already open for business, most were still in the process of setting up shop.

It was a grand place, he thought, as he watched the traders at work.

If it was fruit and veg you were after, there were at least forty stalls offering everything from the mundane potato to the still-slightly-exotic banana. If you fancied a piece of fish, the stalls displayed salmon, trout and North Sea cod in abundance. There were new clothes and second-hand clothes; cotton, thread and wool; suitcases and duffel bags; screwdrivers and spanners; old radios and new 'antiques'.

Anything and everything was available, just for the asking, in this wonderful market.

His gaze fell on one of the stalls which still had its green canvas cover tightly held down by cords and clearly would not be opening that day. He ambled over to it and saw that a hand-written note had been taped to the canvas.

'HARDYS FISHMONGERS,' the note read. 'CLOSED UNTIL FURTHER NOTICE DUE TO A FAMILY BEREAVEMENT.'

The pleasant sense of nostalgia that he been experiencing since entering this time machine of a market drained away in an instant, and was replaced with an anger which had never been entirely absent since the moment his mother had shown him Lilly Dawson's photograph in the newspaper.

'Family bereavement' was such a neutral, antiseptic term, almost as bland as 'Closed for renovations' or 'Gone on holi-day'. It gave no idea of the hell that Lilly's family was going through, but he had talked to her mother – and *he* knew.

The market was starting to fill up, and as Woodend scanned the newly arriving faces, he wondered what had been on the mind of Lilly's murderer on the fateful Saturday morning.

When the killer wakes up, he knows – from the pressure which has been building up in his brain – that he must fulfil his fantasies soon, but he has no idea it will come about on that particular day. Then, driving around on quite some other mission, he sees Lilly leave the market and the urge becomes just too strong to fight any longer.

Possible?

Yes!

But it wasn't the *only* possibility.

When the killer wakes up, it feels as if his loins are on fire. He knows that if he does not get relief soon he will either throw himself under a bus or go completely insane. He sets out with the deliberate intention of finding a girl – any girl – and it is Lilly who is unlucky enough to be in the wrong place at the wrong time.

It hadn't happened in either of those ways, Woodend's instinct and experience told him. In all probability, Lilly had been targeted for days – or possibly even weeks – before she was actually taken.

And that was why it was such a bugger, in terms of the investigation, that she'd had her bloody Saturday job!

The Saturday job complicated everything, because it vastly widened the circle of suspects. If it hadn't been for the job, there would only have been limited opportunities for the killer to study her – on her way to and from school, or when she was out shopping with her mother, for instance. But working on the market, she would have been under the constant observation of thousands of pairs of eyes – and any one of those thousands of pairs could have belonged to her killer.

His thoughts still on the murder, Woodend absent-mindedly slipped the remains of his sandwich into his mouth. The bacon had been deliciously crisp and warm only minutes earlier, but now it was cold and congealed, and tasted like a piece of old carpet straight out of the dog's basket. He forced himself to swallow, then headed for the cafe stall at the edge of the market, intent on disinfecting his throat with a mug of hot, strong tea.

There were several stallholders already standing around the cafe, and when Woodend ordered his tea, one of them slid four pennies across the counter and said, 'Have this one on me, Charlie.'

Woodend looked at his unexpected benefactor – a late-middle-aged man in a flat cap.

'I'm sorry, but do I know you?' he asked.

The expression which came to the man's face was a mixture of mild surprise and mild hurt.

He certainly *thinks* that I ought to know him, the chief inspector realized.

But then, people *did* think that, didn't they? And it was understandable in a way, for while he had moved on, into a world in which he was surrounded by a sea of so many ever-changing faces that even his dustbin of a mind couldn't store them all, this man's world had remained as fixed and immutable as it had always been.

'I'm Len Bowyer,' the man said awkwardly, as if he still could not quite believe such an introduction was necessary.

Woodend grinned. 'Of course you are,' he said. 'Len Bowyer of Bowyer's Bakery – purveyor of the tastiest meat pies in Central Lancs.'

Bowyer returned his grin. 'That's right,' he agreed. 'An' I trust you'll be eatin' a few of them pies while you're up here.'

'You can put money on it – I'd be a fool to miss the opportunity,' Woodend told him.

The smile drained from Bowyer's face, and he said, 'It's terrible what happened to that little lass, Charlie.'

'Yes, it is,' Woodend agreed. 'Did you know her?'

'Well, *of course* I knew her. I know pretty much everybody who works on this market.'

'I assume the local bobbies have already asked you if you've noticed anybody in particular hangin' around her auntie's stall recently,' Woodend said.

'Then you assume wrong,' Bowyer replied. 'I've seen neither hide nor hair of them.'

Woodend sighed. Ever since he'd first started working at Scotland Yard, he'd heard other officers talking about the yokels who inhabited the provincial police forces, and had forced himself to bite back a scornful response. Now, out in the provinces himself – back on his old stamping ground – he was learning that all the sneers and lip-curling were not entirely without foundation.

And it was a bitter pill to swallow.

'Well, if they didn't ask you about it, I certainly will,' he said. '*Did* you notice anybody?'

The expression on Bowyer's face showed he was giving the matter serious consideration. 'She was a pretty girl, so naturally she attracted her fair share of attention from the lads,' he said finally. 'You know what that's like, don't you?'

Oh yes, Woodend thought, he knew all right, because, in his time, he had been one of those lads himself.

He remembered hanging around the market on a Saturday, directing cheeky and flirtatious comments at the girls behind the stalls in an effort to make them blush. But it had all been good-natured, and though the girls pretended to be annoyed, they would probably have been disappointed if the lads had *not* bothered them.

'How did Lilly *feel* about all the attention she was gettin'?' he asked Len Bowyer.

'The whole business seemed to make her a bit uncomfortable,' Bowyer replied. 'To tell you the truth, she didn't really get on with people of her own age. She was more drawn to—'

He stopped, abruptly.

'Go on,' Woodend encouraged.

'I'm not one to talk ill of the dead,' Bowyer said awkwardly. 'I mean, strictly speakin', what she did was all very innocent, but put it into cold, hard words an' you might end up getting' the wrong impression.'

'I won't,' Woodend promised.

'Well, you know, it's easy enough for you to say that now, but once I've told you . . .' Bowyer fretted.

'Do you want her killer caught, or not?' Woodend asked bluntly.

'She . . . she used to get very friendly with some of the stall-holders,' Bowyer said uncertainly, then added in a rush, 'and I'm not referrin' to the young ones now – I'm talkin' about them that are close to my age.'

'What exactly do you mean by "get very friendly"?'

'Well, she'd go all giggly when they were around, an' sometimes she'd brush up against them. But there wasn't nothin' sexual in it. I mean to say, if one of them had tried to touch her where he shouldn't, I'm sure she'd have—'

'All she wanted was a bit of affection,' Woodend interrupted.

'That's right,' Bowyer agreed, with some relief. 'All she wanted was a bit of affection.'

The rabbits, the guinea pigs, the hamsters and the older men – they were all a desperate attempt, on Lilly's part, to fill the gaping hole which her dad's death had left in her life.

It was more than likely her killer had understood that, Woodend thought, and had used it to lure her to the potting shed on the abandoned allotment – which meant, in turn, that he had been no stranger, but had spent some time studying her before making his move.

And where would have been better to study her than in the market, where her loneliness had been so apparent that even a casual observer like Len Bowyer had noticed it?

Woodend pictured the girl walking towards the shed where she would meet her end. He saw the smile on her face, and the sparkle in her eyes. Perhaps she even held her killer's hand, and pretended it was her father's.

As they reached the shed, the image in Woodend's mind's eye changed, and though the girl still had the body of a gawky thirteen-year-old called Lilly, it was his own daughter's head on top of the thin shoulders.

'Are you all right, Charlie?' Len Bowyer asked worriedly.

'I'll have that bastard,' Woodend growled. 'If it's the last thing I do, I'll have him.'

The police surgeon, Dr Stuart Heap, was in his mid-forties, and had an air of self-importance and self-congratulation which clung to him like an ostentatiously heavy fur coat.

'I can spare you five minutes – but no more,' he told Woodend.

'That should be more than enough, sir,' Woodend said. 'Five minutes of *your* time must be worth – oh, I don't know – at least seven and half minutes of almost anybody else's.'

'*Much* more than that,' the doctor said, slightly huffily. 'Well, I expect you'd like to see the stiff.'

'Aye, I thought I might as well, now that I'm here,' Woodend replied, with the deceptive mildness which would serve as a warning signal to later police surgeons, but went right over the head of this one.

The doctor took hold of the handle of the refrigerated drawer, and slid it smoothly open.

'There you go,' he said, with all the flourish of a music hall magician.

Woodend gazed down at the girl's body, and felt a sudden stabbing pain in his chest.

She was so young, he thought.

So *very* young – and so *very* vulnerable.

'Thank you, you can close it up again now,' he told the doctor.

Heap slid the drawer closed. 'Well, if that's all . . .'

'It isn't actually,' Woodend said firmly. 'I'd like you to tell me about the post-mortem, if you don't mind.'

Heap glanced pointedly at his watch. 'There's no need to – it's all in my report,' he said.

'Ah, but you see, I don't like wearin' out my eyes readin' reports,' Woodend replied. 'I'd rather hear directly from the fellers who wrote them.'

'As I think I've already explained, my time is very valuable . . .' the doctor began.

Woodend put his massive hand on the other man's shoulder. 'Just tell me in your own words, Doc,' he said. 'An' do try to steer clear of all the jargon, because I'm really not very bright.'

'Well . . . err . . . she was raped and then she was strangled,' the doctor said.

'There's no chance that she was a willing participant, is there?' Woodend asked.

The doctor grinned. 'In the strangulation?' he asked.

'That'd be a joke, would it?' Woodend said stonily.

'Yes, I suppose you might call it a little "mortuary humour",' Heap admitted.

'The thing is, I've got a little lass of my own,' Woodend said softly, as he increased – ever so slightly – the pressure on the doctor's shoulder. 'An' when I see *this* little lass lyin' there, I think of my Annie, an' I start getting' angry.'

'You really shouldn't . . .'

'Which means, in turn, that while your little stand-up comedy act might go down a storm with your fellow quacks after they've had a few pints, it doesn't actually do a lot for me. Do you see what I'm gettin' at?'

'Err . . . yes, I suppose I do,' Heap said reluctantly.

'So let's start again, shall we?' Woodend suggested, removing his hand from the doctor's shoulder. 'Is there any chance at all that Lilly Dawson was a willin' participant?'

'None,' the doctor said, doing his very best to sound both serious *and* unintimidated. 'The bruising on her thighs indicates that she was being held down, and the further bruising around the vaginal area shows that entry was forced. And then, of course, there's the skin under her nails.'

'*What* skin under her nails?' Woodend demanded. 'There was no mention of that in your report.'

'I thought you told me you didn't read reports,' Heap said accusingly.

'I lied,' Woodend countered. 'It's one of my worst habits.' He paused for a moment. 'So there *was* skin under her nails?'

Heap frowned. 'Yes, and, do you know, I could have sworn that, when I was writing the report, I—'

'Was it her *attacker's* skin?'

'Almost definitely.'

'So what have you learned from the skin? Can you give me any idea of the rapist's age or what he did for a livin'?'

The doctor laughed. 'Good heavens, no – not with the kind

of sample we had. I'm a forensic scientist, not a miracle worker.'

'What about the girl's personal effects?' Woodend asked, finally giving up on the man. 'Are they still at the police lab?'

'No, they sent them back here, so that they could be released to the mother at the same time as the body.'

'I'd like to see them.'

'Certainly. No problem at all. I'll get one of my girls to show them to you.'

'What's it like, bein' one of the doctor's "girls"?' Woodend asked the smartly dressed young clerical officer, Mrs Walton, as she laid out Lilly's clothes on the table.

'It's like a dream come true,' the woman replied.

And they both knew what she meant by that.

Lilly had been wearing a navy blue skirt, a white blouse, blue serge bloomers, a scarlet cardigan and grey knee socks. There was no brassiere – the poor little kid hadn't needed one.

'That'd be her school uniform,' Mrs Walton said.

'Yes, it would,' the chief inspector thought.

And the fact she'd been wearing her uniform on a Saturday came as no surprise to him, because uniforms were expensive and swallowed up most of the money that working-class mums had budgeted for clothing.

'Where are the envelopes?' Woodend asked.

'What envelopes?'

'The evidence envelopes.'

'There aren't any.'

There weren't any?

'Yokels!' Woodend's colleagues at Scotland Yard jeered at him from inside his head.

And he had nothing to come back at them with.

Had the Whitebridge police lab done anything with the clothes, other than give them a cursory examination and straighten them out?

On the face of things, it didn't seem likely.

'I'd like some surgical gloves, please,' Woodend said.

Though that was probably a waste of time, he added mentally. Because it wouldn't come as a total surprise to him if – having given the clothes the once-over – the lab team hadn't sent them out to be bloody dry-cleaned!

The collar and cuffs of the blouse had been skilfully darned to disguise the fact that they were fraying. The socks had been darned too, in a lovingly careful way that almost reduced Woodend to tears.

And it was while he was examining the socks that he came across something that the technicians appeared to have overlooked – and he himself had never expected to find.

EIGHT

The moment Woodend walked in though the main entrance of Whitebridge police headquarters, he could sense a feeling of anticipation in the air. No, it was more than just anticipation, he decided, as he walked up towards the desk sergeant's counter – the air was positively crackling with excitement.

The desk sergeant himself was leaning back in his chair and chatting into the phone.

'Well, it's what I've always said,' he was telling the person at the other end of the line. 'These bobbies from London might *think* they're the bee's knees, but when you're talkin' about doin' a bit of real police work, you're far better off leavin' it up to the—' He looked up, and saw Woodend standing there. 'I'll have to call you back,' he said into the phone, before hanging up.

Woodend held out his warrant card. 'I'd like to speak to DCI Paine, if he's available,' he said.

'Oh, I'm sure he's available *now*, sir,' the sergeant said, cockily.

'Meanin' what, exactly?' Woodend wondered.

'Meanin' that seein' as he's just wrapped up the job he was assigned, I imagine he'll have bags of time on his hands for talkin' to Scotland Yard.'

'I take it you've caught your murderer,' Woodend said.

'That's right, we have,' the sergeant agreed. 'You'll find the DCI's office through them double doors an' down the end of the corridor. Is there anythin' else I can do for you, sir?'

'Aye,' Woodend said. 'You can stop bein' so bloody insufferable.'

The first thing Woodend saw when he pushed open the double doors and stepped into the corridor was the four men approaching him from the other end of it. Three of the men were uniformed officers, and the fourth, dressed in a shabby blue suit, was in handcuffs.

The prisoner was as big as he was, Woodend guessed – and maybe even harder. His nose had been badly broken at some point in the past, and there were numerous scars on his chin, cheeks and forehead. He didn't exactly seem enthusiastic about taking this walk along the corridor, and it was only by considerable effort on their part that the three officers were managing to make any progress at all.

Just looking at the scene made Woodend's hands start to twitch, but before he could take it any further, a warning voice in his head said, Don't get involved, Charlie. It isn't any of your business, an' they probably wouldn't thank you for stickin' your oar in.

Good advice, he told himself, stepping into an open doorway, in order to give the local bobbies more room to manoeuvre.

Mind you, he added, as he watched the officers continue to struggle against their prisoner, they do look as if they could *use* a little help.

The party had almost drawn level with him when the prisoner finally noticed him.

'You're that bobby up here from London, aren't you?' the man demanded.

'Come on now, Walter, don't make this any more difficult than it has to be,' urged PC Sid Smart, Woodend's old bird-nesting mate.

But Walter had come to halt, and refused to be budged.

'Aren't you?' he insisted. 'Aren't you that bobby from London?'

'Yes, he is,' Sid Smart agreed wearily. 'But he's here on another case entirely, an' the last thing he wants is to talk to you.'

'They say I killed Bazza Mottershead,' the prisoner told Woodend. 'But I didn't. I swear to you, I never touched him.'

'Like I said, what you did or didn't do is nothing to do with Scotland Yard,' Sid Smart countered, giving his prisoner a shove in the right direction.

A warning that something was about to go seriously wrong flashed across Walter's eyes. Woodend saw it, but knew – even as he was registering the fact – that it was already too late to prevent it.

Walter moved with the speed of a veteran street fighter.

He raised one leg no more than eighteen inches off the ground,

then brought it down again, scraping the heel of his shoe along
the calf of the man on his right. The officer screamed, tried to
keep his balance for no more than a split second, and then crumpled to the floor.

Walter turned quickly to his left and headbutted the man on
the other side of him. A loud cracking sound – suggesting breaking
bone – echoed down the corridor, and the officer joined his
colleague on the ground.

The only constable left standing was Sid Smart, and he was
still reaching for his truncheon when the prisoner swung his
arms in a wide arc and struck him under the chin with the edge
of the handcuffs.

If they'd handcuffed his wrists *behind* his back, like they did
in America, that could never have happened, Woodend thought,
as he tensed himself for the attack he was sure was coming.

But Walter seemed to have no interest at all in attacking him.
Instead, he held his hands out in front of him in a pleading way,
and said, 'You've got to help me. I'm innocent.'

Woodend glanced quickly down at the three fallen policemen.
The first one down was rubbing his leg, the second holding his
nose, and the third – Sid Smart – gingerly fingering his jaw.
None of them would be feeling too happy for a while, he thought,
but it could have been much worse.

He switched his attention back to the man responsible for all
the mayhem. 'What you've just done isn't goin' to help your
case at all, you know, Walter?' he said, matter-of-factly. 'If I
was in your shoes, I'd try to calm down an' wait until my lawyer
arrived.'

The look of supplication which had filled the prisoner's face
was replaced by one of blind fury.

'You're a bloody bastard!' he screamed. 'You're just as bad
as the rest of them.'

'Take it easy now, Walter,' Woodend said soothingly. 'I
really don't want to hit a feller in handcuffs – so please don't
make me.'

But Walter was now in such a rage that it was doubtful he
even heard the warning. He leapt at Woodend, then went flying
backwards – almost doubled over – as his stomach came into
contact with the chief inspector's fist.

The three uniformed officers were, slowly and painfully,
climbing to their feet.

'Thanks, Charlie,' Sid Smart gasped.

'My pleasure,' Woodend told him.

The three bobbies surrounded Walter, and half-carried, half-dragged him along the corridor, while Woodend watched them and massaged the knuckles of his right hand with the fingers of his left.

'My men could easily have handled the situation, you know,' said an angry voice behind him.

Woodend turned around, and saw the chief constable glowering at him from one of the office doorways.

'I said, my men could have easily have handled the situation,' Eliot Sanderson repeated.

'Aye, they seemed to be makin' a right good job of it,' Woodend replied. 'I don't know why I even bothered to put my two penn'orth in.'

'If you hadn't been there, they wouldn't have been distracted,' Sanderson said.

'Yes, I knew it must be *my* fault,' Woodend agreed.

'And at least *we've* caught *our* murderer,' Sanderson told him.

Woodend grinned. 'Not if you listen to what Walter has to say on the subject, you haven't.'

'It was just as I thought from the very start – a case of thieves falling out,' the chief constable said, ignoring both the comment and the grin. 'Walter Brown is a well-known burglar, and – before their fateful disagreement – Bazza Mottershead was his fence.'

'Well, there you are,' Woodend said easily. 'A nice simple murder – all neatly tied up an' filed away.'

'I'm beginning to regret the fact that I ever called in Scotland Yard,' the chief constable said.

Me an' all, Woodend thought, as another heartbreaking image of Lilly Dawson flashed across his brain.

DCI Paine had a shiny bald head, and his rounded cheeks were almost entirely occupied by a wide smirk of self-congratulation.

'We've caught *our* murderer, you know,' he said.

'Aye, I ran into him earlier,' Woodend said, rubbing his knuckles again.

'We could probably have caught Lilly Dawson's killer by now, too, if the chief constable hadn't panicked and called in you so-called "experts",' Paine continued.

'Is that a fact?' Woodend asked. 'So tell me, Chief Inspector, how far did you actually *get* with that investigation?'

'It's all in my report,' Paine said.

First the police doctor and then the chief inspector – they were buggers for writin' reports, this lot, Woodend thought. It was just a pity that they all seemed to confuse neat typing with useful information.

'Have you actually gone to the trouble of *reading* my report?' Paine asked.

'Yes, I thought I might as well – since it was obviously goin' to be such a *quick* read,' Woodend said. 'As far as I could see, you didn't make much use of your boffins, did you?'

'I'm afraid I have no idea what you mean by that,' Paine said, sucking in his cheeks to show his displeasure. 'The forensic team carried out a thorough examination of all the evidence available, and produced an excellent report.'

'I'm sure it was – I'll bet there wasn't a single spellin' mistake in the whole document,' Woodend said softly.

'What did you say?' Paine demanded.

'If they did as thorough a job as that, I'm surprised they didn't find any evidence on Lilly's clothes.'

'And I don't suppose it occurred to you, did it, that perhaps the *reason* they didn't find any evidence was because there *was* no evidence to find?'

'No, as a matter of fact, that *hadn't* occurred to me,' Woodend said, running his thumbnail along the edge of the plastic envelope in his pocket.

DCI Paine smiled like a man who thought he had just scored a point.

'However good they are – and, as I've just told you, they're *very* good – the lab men still can't spin gold out of sand,' he said.

'True,' Woodend agreed. 'Nobody would expect them to – but they didn't find anythin' in the pottin' shed where Lilly's body was discovered, either.'

'And, again, that's because there *was* nothing to find.'

'I think I just might go an' have a quick look at that shed myself,' Woodend mused.

'Well, if that's what you want to do, by all means be my guest,' Paine said magnanimously. 'But I warn you, you'll only be wasting your time.'

Woodend had no need to ask anyone for directions to the allotments where Lilly Dawson's body had been found. As a kid, he had walked past them regularly on his way to Fuller's Pond, which

was generally acknowledged to be the best place in Whitebridge
to catch tadpoles and sticklebacks.

In those days, he recalled, these allotments had been the last
outpost of the man-made world – separated from the wild and
majestic moors by no more than a country lane and a thick copse
of elm trees – and the whole area around them had been a haven
for all kinds of wildlife.

Rooks and pied wagtails had nested high in the trees. Hares
had made their homes in the tall grass. Shrews and voles had
scampered back and forth as they pursued their furry business.
Hedgehogs had trotted across the open spaces, secure in the
belief – proved erroneous by the gypsies, who caught them and
baked them in mud – that their spiky quills made them invin-
cible.

All that had now changed. The gentle elms had gone, and in
their place were diggers which roared as they ripped up the earth,
and bulldozers which rumbled ominously as they forced the helpless soil from one spot to another. There were lorries which
screamed out their protests as their drivers fought a never-ending
battle with the gears, and pneumatic drills which pounded relentlessly. And all the birds and beasts, tired of the disruption – and
perhaps even terrified of it – had left in search of a quieter place
in which to live out their simple lives.

It was like being robbed of part of your childhood, Woodend
thought sadly, as he watched the heavy plant move on relentlessly.

'But at least *you* were allowed to *finish* your childhood,' he
reminded himself, 'which is more than can be said for Lilly
Dawson.'

As he approached the potting shed in which Lilly had spent
the last few terrifying moments of her life, he realized that
something was very wrong – from a procedural point of view –
with the scene as it was laid out before him.

He had never imagined that there would be a policeman permanently on duty outside the shed – no police force had the
manpower for that kind of luxury – but he *had* thought that there
would at least be a strong police padlock newly fitted to the
door, and official notices which warned the general public to
keep away.

Instead, the shed just looked like any other shed, with no indi-
cation at all of the horror that had been committed within it.

He lifted the latch, and the door to the shed simply swung
open.

If this had happened in London, he'd have had the balls of whoever was responsible, he thought.

But this wasn't London. It was Whitebridge, where the technicians had come up with nothing during their 'thorough' examination of Lilly's clothes, and, having made what had probably been – at best – a cursory examination of the murder scene, had left it open to all kinds of contamination.

He looked around the shed. This had once been one man's little kingdom – the citadel from which he tended his own tiny garden of Eden – yet apart from a few broken plant pots in one corner, and a tattered seed catalogue in another, there was no longer any evidence of it.

But there was evidence aplenty of the tragic struggle which had occurred here less than two weeks earlier, Woodend thought, looking at the scuff marks in the packed earth floor which had been gouged out by Lilly's heels, as she battled desperately – and hopelessly – for her life.

He felt his anger rising again, and though the hardened professional he was trying to be fought against it, that anger would not go away.

He got down on his hands and knees and, slowly and methodically, began to search the ground.

It was behind one of the broken plant pots that he found the feather.

It was the second one he had discovered in less than two hours – and it had to mean something!

Most of the drinkers in the Clog and Billycock that lunchtime were either chatting to their mates or else playing darts, though there were a few who sat silent, blankly gazing into space as they grappled with the problems that life had thrown into their paths.

The weedy middle-aged man at the end of the bar was doing none of these things. He was *reading*. And not *just* reading, Woodend thought – the book, positively bursting with colour plates, seemed to have totally absorbed him, to have whisked him away from the public bar and into some entirely different world.

The chief inspector walked over to the man, and tapped him lightly on the shoulder.

'How you doin', Stan?' he asked.

Stan Watson tore his eyes from his book with reluctance, but his look soon changed when he saw who was addressing him.

'Charlie!' he said delightedly. 'I *heard* you were back.'

Woodend grinned inwardly.

Typical Whitebridge understatement, he thought.

I heard you were back.

As if Watson had gained that knowledge from some hurriedly whispered rumour, rather than from seeing it splashed across the front page of the *Whitebridge Evening Telegraph*.

'I see you're still as big a fan of our feathered friends as you ever were,' Woodend said, glancing down at the still-open book.

'That's right,' Watson agreed. 'Only, I don't get bullied for it any more.'

He had certainly been bullied at Sudbury Street Elementary School, Woodend remembered. The playground thugs back then had looked for any excuse to pick on their weaker brethren – and a lad who showed more interest in birds than in football was a natural target.

'I wasn't bullied for that long, though, was I?' Watson asked. 'The moment you saw it happenin', you put a stop to it. You became my protector.'

Woodend's neck prickled with embarrassment. 'Aye, well, that's what the big lads did for the little lads back in them days,' he said awkwardly.

Watson grinned at his obvious discomfort. 'There were other big lads at Sudbury Street – not as big as you, but big enough – an' *they* didn't see it as their duty to protect the weak,' he pointed out.

Woodend shrugged. 'You might be right about that, Stan, but the thing is, I'm not here to talk about what a paragon of virtue I used to be. I've come because I need your help.'

Watson's grin widened. 'You need *my* help?' he asked. 'The big-shot detective from London needs the help of a nutty local birdwatcher?'

'That's right,' Woodend agreed.

Watson shook his head in wonderment. 'Funny old world, isn't it? So what can I do for you, Charlie?'

Woodend reached into his pocket, and took out two transparent plastic envelopes. In one was the feather he had found snagged in Lilly Dawson's knee sock at the morgue. In the other was the one he had discovered in the potting shed where she had been raped and murdered.

'Are these both from the same bird?' he asked.

Watson studied the two envelopes. 'They're from the same *breed* of bird, certainly,' he said finally.

'An' what breed might that be?'

'They're pigeon feathers.'

Woodend did his best not to feel too dispirited. It had always been a long shot – at best – he told himself, and though he'd been hoping his old friend would identify the feathers as belonging to a rare breed of guinea fowl or some other such exotic bird, he'd never really believed that would be the case.

But, even at his least optimistic, he'd still been expecting something a bit better than feathers from the common *pigeon*!

'Domesticated birds aren't my speciality, as you know,' Stan Watson continued, 'but from the red tinge on these feathers, I'd say they almost definitely come from a Sheffield tippler.'

Woodend felt the spark of hope reignite.

'Domesticated birds?' he repeated. 'Are you sayin' that these feathers are from a *homin'* pigeon?'

Watson shook his head, as if he almost despaired at the extent of Woodend's ignorance.

'Nay, lad, they're not homin' pigeons' feathers at all,' he said. 'Have I not just told you they come from a tippler?'

'What's the difference?' Woodend wondered.

'If you've got homin' pigeons, then you have them sent a long way away from home an' time how long it takes them to fly back to their loft – hence the name,' Watson said, explaining slowly, now he realized he was talking to a real idiot.

'An' how does that differ from tipplers?'

'It's not about speed an' distance with tipplers at all – it's about endurance. They never go far from home. They just fly round an' round in big circles, an' it's how long they stay in the air that counts. That's what makes them the natural choice of the workin' man.'

'Come again?' Woodend said.

Watson sighed. 'It costs money to transport your pigeons some-where else, just so that they can fly back, doesn't it?' he asked.

'I suppose so,' Woodend agreed.

'But it doesn't cost you owt to have them fly round and round your own house. Are you startin' to get the picture now?'

'I think so,' Woodend said cautiously.

'So if you've got tipplers, you can compete with breeders of other tipplers from places as far away as Australia an' America without ever having to leave home – because if their birds stay in

the air for twenty hours, an' your birds are up there for twenty
hours an' one minute, you've won.'

'How many tippler lofts would you say there are in
Whitebridge?' Woodend asked.

'Certainly a lot less than there were before the War,' Watson
replied. 'Folk have got very lazy, you see. They sit in front of the
television, watching somethin' that somebody else has done, rather
than get off their fat arses an' do somethin' for themselves.'

'How many?' Woodend repeated, with a patience that he was
a long way from actually feeling.

'That's hard to say.'

'Then just take a guess.'

Stan Watson scratched his head. 'I'd say there can't be more
than twenty or thirty. Why the interest? Is it important?'

'Important!' Woodend repeated. 'It could be bloody *vital*.'

NINE

The pigeon loft was located on a patchwork quilt of allotments which – so far – the enthusiasts for redevelopment in the town council planning department had not been able to get their hands on. It was an oblong wooden building, and was painted white, except for the cross slats which were picked out in black. Ordinary (common or garden) pigeons were perched on its roof, as if they were waiting – without much hope – for the opportunity to be admitted to the exclusive club which lay below their clawed feet. And, in the long grass, a large ginger cat watched patiently for one of the feathered creatures to make a mistake.

A man was sitting on a garden chair in front of the loft, reading the newspaper. He was around seventy, Woodend guessed as he got closer, and the glasses that were perched on his nose had lenses as thick as jam-jar bottoms

Hearing Woodend's approach, the man folded the newspaper, laid it neatly on his lap, and looked up expectantly.

'If you don't mind, lad, I won't get up,' he said. 'That might sound a bit rude, I know, but me rheumatism's been givin' me jip all mornin', an' I'd rather not do anythin' to encourage it.'

'No problem,' Woodend assured him. 'Are you Mr Ramsbotham?'

'Aye, an' from the pictures I've seen in the paper, you must be young Charlie Woodend. I used to know your dad quite well. How's he gettin' on?'

'He's fine.'

'Well, that's the pleasantries neatly out of the way,' Ramsbotham said. 'Now why don't you tell me what it is that you want?'

He had missed the direct Northern approach while he'd been living down south, Woodend thought, grinning.

'I hear that you're the president of the Whitebridge Tippler Association,' he said.

'President, secretary, treasurer an' chief cook an' bottle washer,' Ramsbotham replied.

'I also hear that you know the complete history of every tippler that's ever flown in Whitebridge.'

'And so I do,' Ramsbotham agreed. 'But you're not here for a history lesson, are you? You're here because you're a bobby – an' you're investigatin' one of my members who you think might be involved in this murder of yours.'

'An' does that bother you?'

Ramsbotham shrugged. 'Not if he's done wrong. My loyalty's always been to the birds, not to the fellers what happen to fly them. Who is it that you want to know about?'

'I'm not sure,' Woodend admitted. 'But the chances are he owns some Sheffield tipplers.'

'Well, that narrows it down a bit, because Sheffields are nowhere near as popular as they used to be. Let me see, for a start, there's old Harry Knox . . .'

'How old *is* he?'

'He'll be eighty, if he's a day.'

'Then I'm not interested in him. The man I'm lookin' for will be much younger than that. Say – forty-five at tops.'

'Then you really *are* narrowin' it down,' Ramsbotham said. He counted off the names on his fingers. 'Thad Robinson keeps tipplers, but he's had his leg in plaster ever since he came off his motorbike, so he won't be of much interest to you. Then there's Mike Thomas – but he's been away for the last three months, buildin' a railway in Canada.'

'An' who's been lookin' after his pigeons while he's been gone?' Woodend asked. 'One of his mates?'

The old man chuckled. 'One of his mates?' he repeated. 'Nay, lad, Mike'd no more think of lettin' another man get his hands on his birds than he'd think of lettin' him get his hands on his missus. An' if he had to choose between the two, I'd bet on it bein' his missus he'd let go.'

'So who *is* lookin' after them?'

'The selfsame missus of which I spoke.' Ramsbotham's eyes twinkled behind the thick lenses. 'Well, that's killin' two birds with one stone, in a manner of speakin', isn't it?' He suddenly grew more serious, and paused for a moment, before speaking again. 'I've got one more name, for you – Fred Howerd.'

'What does he—?' Woodend began.

Ramsbotham raised a hand in the air to cut him off.

'Nay, lad, I've said all I'm sayin'.'

Perhaps there would come a time when he wouldn't attach quite *so* much importance to the best lead that an investigation had thrown up, Woodend thought, as he tried to enjoy the pint of bitter he was holding in his hand. Perhaps – when he'd had more experience as a DCI – he would learn to be philosophical if a promising line of inquiry failed to lead anywhere.

It was possible.

But, for the moment, he was desperate that the one lead that he actually had *would* work out – that Fred Howerd would indeed be revealed as the killer. Because if he didn't have Fred Howerd, he had *nothing* – and the prospect of starting again from scratch was truly daunting.

The bar door swung open, and PC Sid Smart walked in. There was a very noticeable bruise on his jaw. It was still a light purple shade – a little like watered-down blackcurrant juice – but by morning would almost definitely have turned black.

'Hairline fracture,' Smart said, noticing Woodend looking at the bruise as he sat down. 'Still, it could have been worse, I suppose. With just a bit more force behind the blow, the bastard would have broken my bloody jawbone.'

'Will you be pressin' charges?' Woodend asked.

'I thought about it, but that'd be a bit like scorin' a goal when the match is already over,' Smart said. He grinned, then winced as his bruised muscles registered their protest. 'Walter Brown's got a lot more to worry about than hurtin' a bobby,' he continued. 'When he's convicted of killin' Mottershead – an' he *will* be convicted – he'll have a life sentence to look forward to.'

Well, that's the pleasantries neatly out of the way, Woodend thought, echoing Mr Ramsbotham. Now let's get down to what really matters.

'What have you got on Fred Howerd?' he asked.

'Quite a lot,' Smart replied. 'As you must have already suspected, our Fred's a bit of a villain.'

Yes! Woodend thought triumphantly. Bloody *yes*!

'Were any of the offences that he was charged with of a sexual or violent nature?' he asked aloud.

Smart shook his head. 'I said he was *a bit* of a villain,' he reminded Woodend.

'So what's he done?'

'Mostly small-time stuff – drunk an' disorderly or causing an affray – that kind of thing.'

It was disappointing – but Woodend was still not prepared to give up on his best lead quite yet.

'Has Howerd ever been inside?' he asked.

'No, but he came damn close to it once, when he borrowed a car from somebody he didn't know, an' ended up smashin' it into a tree. They do say it was only his father's influence that stopped him from bein' locked up.'

But it was a big leap from stealing a car to kidnap, rape and murder, Woodend thought downheartedly.

'So Howerd's father has influence, does he?' he asked, more out of politeness than interest.

'He does,' Sid Smart confirmed. 'Arthur Howerd's a very big wheel in this town. He has a chain of electrical goods stores that stretches from here to the Yorkshire border. If you own anything that runs on electricity in Whitebridge, the chances are you bought it from Arthur.'

'Is there anything else you can tell me about Fred?' Woodend asked.

And he was thinking, Please give me one thing – just one little thing – that will help to put him back in the frame.

Sid Smart gently fingered his bruised jaw. 'Well, let me see. He got married sometime in the early thirties, an' has one daughter, Elizabeth her name is, who must be sixteen or seventeen now. He was called up by the army early in the war – but he didn't serve long. Got invalided out with a stomach complaint – an' we both know how easy *that* is to fake – so while you an' me were gettin' shot at by the Jerries, he was havin' a cushy time as a fire warden back in Whitebridge.'

It was no good, Woodend thought – none of it was *any good*.

'What else?' Smart continued. 'Oh yes – he lives with his wife an' daughter on Mafeking Street, and, as far as I know—

'Hang about,' Woodend said, experiencing a sudden flicker of curiosity. 'Did you say he lived on *Mafeking Street*?'

'That's right.'

'But that's just a terraced row, like the one my mam an' dad live in, isn't it?'

'It is.'

'That doesn't seem the sort of place I'd expect a man whose father runs a chain of shops to live in.'

'Ah, but you see, Fred's sort of workin' his passage back,' Sid Smart explained.

'What do you mean?'

'Arthur Howerd's not only a big man in the business community, he's a big man in the local Catholic church as well. He takes his religion very seriously – an' he's not the sort of feller who likes havin' a black sheep in the family.'

'So?

'So, for a number of years he wouldn't have anythin' at all to do with his youngest son, an' Fred had to get by as best he could. But then the old man had a heart attack, an' decided it was time to accept the lost sheep back into the fold, while he still had the chance.'

'Accept him – but not exactly welcome him with open arms,' Woodend guessed.

'You've got it,' Sid Smart agreed. 'Before he could reclaim his birthright, he had to prove he was worthy of it. An' the *way* he had to prove it was by startin' at the bottom of the business an' workin' his way back up.'

Pointless, Woodend thought miserably. All this is *pointless*.

'So while Arthur bought his elder brother Robert a nice detached house on the edge of town, Fred had to continue living in Mafeking Street,' Sid Smart said. 'An' while Robert swanned around as assistant general manager—'

'Fred was stuck behind the counter, as a humble assistant,' Woodend interrupted, just to show he was still listening.

'Well, it wasn't quite as bad as that,' Sid Smart told him. 'Fred was allowed to have his own little business, but, you must admit, runnin' a stall doesn't really compare to runnin' a shop, does it?'

'Runnin' a what?' Woodend exploded.

'Runnin' a stall,' Sid Smart repeated. 'Didn't I say? I thought I'd already mentioned that he was given a stall on Whitebridge covered market.'

*   *   *

The house on Mafeking Street was three doors down from Fred Howerd's home. Woodend had had no real reason for selecting it over any of the others on the street, except that while the rest had their front doors and window frames painted in chocolate brown or sombre black, the owner of this one had – intriguingly – plumped for a pale lilac.

His knock was answered by a slim man in his early thirties, who was wearing a shirt which almost matched the colour of his paintwork, and a pair of trousers which seemed – to Woodend, at least – to be uncomfortably tight.

'Yes?' he said.

Woodend produced his warrant card. 'Police, sir,' he announced. 'DCI Woodend.'

The man in the doorway blanched, and then made a visible effort to recover himself.

'But I haven't done anything wrong!' he said.

'It never occurred to me, even for a moment, that you had, sir,' Woodend replied. 'By the way, I don't think I quite caught your name.'

'It's Harper,' the man said, in what might almost have been called a guilty mumble. 'Ronald Harper.'

'I'd like to ask you a few questions, Mr Harper,' Woodend said. 'Would it be all right if I came inside?'

Harper shrugged. 'I suppose so,' he said, reluctantly.

There was no hallway, because the downstairs of the house had been converted into a single large room. There was a kitchenette in the left-hand corner at the back, and a dining table in the right-hand corner. The remaining space was dominated by the largest sofa that Woodend had ever seen, and sitting on the sofa was a second man, wearing trousers that were almost identical to Harper's, and a yellow shirt.

The man jumped to his feet when he saw Woodend.

'I . . . er . . .' he began.

'This is Mr Bell, my tenant,' Harper said hastily. 'He lives upstairs, and,' he added with emphasis, '*I* live down here.'

So where did Harper sleep? Woodend wondered.

'The sofa converts into a bed at night,' Harper told him, reading his mind. He turned to the other man. 'I have made a note of your complaint, Mr Bell, and will instruct my builder to call on you and make the necessary repairs,' he said, woodenly. 'And now, perhaps, you'd like to return to your own apartment.'

'I think I'd prefer Mr Bell to stay,' Woodend said.

'We're not doing any harm. Why can't you just leave us alone?' Bell asked – and looked as if he were about to burst into tears.

It would have been comical if they hadn't both been so worried, Woodend thought.

'The best mate I had in the army was called Tommy Jenkins,' he said. 'He was a homosexual, though not many people knew that, an' he was one of the bravest men I ever met. The night he was killed, I cried, an' sometimes just the thought of him is enough to set me off again.'

'What is this?' Harper demanded. 'Some kind of trick?'

'No trick,' Woodend replied. 'What people do behind their own closed doors is no business of mine. I'm only here because I'm investigatin' a murder, an' I thought you might be able to help.'

The two men looked at each other questioningly, and then Harper, taking the lead, nodded and said, 'What do you want to know?'

'You can start by tellin' if you have a view of the pigeon loft that's on the field behind this house,' Woodend said.

'Not from down here,' Harper told him, 'but you get a pretty good view of it from our bed— from the back bedroom upstairs.' He giggled. 'Tinker spends half his time gazing out of that window.'

'I like to watch the rabbits playing in the grass,' Bell said defensively. 'Nothing wrong with that, is there?'

'Nothin' at all,' Woodend agreed. 'So you'll often see Mr Howerd, when he's comin' and goin' from the loft, will you, Mr Bell?'

'If he happens to be coming and going when I happen to be looking out of the window,' Bell said cautiously.

'Is he usually alone?'

'Yes,' Bell replied, and this time he spoke far too quickly.

'But you've seen him take someone else there?'

'Once in a while.'

'What about a week last Friday?' Woodend pressed. 'Did you see anybody then?'

The look on Bell's face told Woodend that he was trying to make up his mind between telling a complete lie and a half-truth.

'He . . . went there with his daughter,' Bell said, opting for the latter course.

Harper giggled again. 'Oh, really, you're such a scatterbrain, Tinker,' he said.

'Please, Ronnie, don't say any more,' Bell begged.

'The lovely Elizabeth wasn't even here a week last Friday,' Harper said, ignoring him. 'She was away! On her honeymoon! Don't you remember?'

'Then . . . then it must have been some other day,' Bell mumbled.

'Or some other *female!*' Woodend said.

'No, I . . .' Bell whined.

'Or some other female,' Woodend persisted.

A tear appeared in the corner of Bell's right eye. 'I don't want to go to prison,' he said.

'Who mentioned anythin' about prison?' Woodend wondered.

'If there's a trial, and I have to give evidence, it will come out that I've been . . . that Ronnie and I have been . . . And then they'll lock me away – because that's what they do to homos.'

'Hang on a minute!' Harper said. 'Do you think Fred Howerd killed that poor little girl, Chief Inspector?'

It was not a question he was supposed to answer, Woodend thought – but bugger that.

'Yes, Mr Harper,' he said. 'I think it's very likely that he did.'

Harper crossed the room and placed his hands on his friend's shoulders. 'You can't shield a murderer, Tinker,' he said softly. 'Whatever it costs us, you have to tell the chief inspector what you know.'

'I . . . I did see him go the loft that Friday night,' Bell said, almost in a sob. 'It was just as it was going dark. He had a girl with him, and once they were inside, he lit the lantern.'

'Was it the girl who was killed?' Woodend asked. 'Was it Lilly Dawson?'

'I couldn't say,' Bell told him. He looked at his partner. 'Honestly, Ronnie, I really couldn't say.'

'But it was definitely a girl – rather than a woman?' Woodend asked.

'Oh yes,' Bell admitted. 'It was a girl, all right.'

TEN

I t was the middle of the afternoon. Much had already happened that day, and much more might happen yet, Woodend thought, as he and Bannerman walked across the field to Fred Howerd's pigeon loft.

'Did you *know* I'd be wasting my time re-interviewing all the usual suspects, sir?' Bannerman asked, with a hint of resentment in his voice.

'It was what you wanted to do,' Woodend replied.

'You haven't answered my question, sir,' Bannerman persisted.

'I *suspected* it was probably a waste of time,' Woodend said frankly, 'but I didn't actually *know*. In this kind of investigation you *never* know until all the pieces finally slot together.'

And they *did* all slot together, he told himself. Lilly had been desperate to make friends with older men, and, working on the market, Howerd would have had ample opportunity to learn that. Lilly loved all kinds of dumb creatures, and Howerd had a pigeon loft, which was the perfect bait. There had been a Sheffield tippler feather snagged in Lilly's stocking, and another in the shed where she had been murdered. And – to cap it all – 'Tinker' Bell had seen Howerd take a girl to his pigeon loft the night before she was abducted.

It all added up. It really *did*. Each bit of evidence dovetailed so neatly into all the other bits that he just *had to be* right.

Why then, Woodend wondered, did he still – even at this stage – have qualms?

It's because this is your first major case, lad, he told himself. You're *bound* to be a *little* worried that, somewhere along the line, you've made a mistake.

They had reached the loft. There was a heavy padlock on the door, but they had come well prepared, with a search warrant in Woodend's pocket and a set of bolt cutters in Bannerman's hand.

'Shall I break the lock, sir?' Bannerman asked.

'That's what we're here for,' Woodend told him.

Bannerman cut through the shackle, and the lock fell to the ground, hitting the soft earth with a slight thud.

Woodend pulled on the hasp, and the door swung open.

They were in!

It was gloomy in the loft, but once Woodend had drawn back the bolts and opened the shutters, the light from the outside flooded in.

The caged pigeons, surprised by this unexpected visitation, ruffled their feathers and cooed worriedly.

'You're all right, lads,' Woodend said softly. 'I've never been a big fan of pigeon pie, myself, so you've really nothin' to worry about.'

Apart from the pigeon cages, there was not much to see. Two battered armchairs stood at the opposite end of the loft from the door, and a small rickety table had been placed next to them. There was an oil lamp on the table – the lamp which, presumably, 'Tinker' Bell had seen Howerd light the night he had taken the girl to the loft. And on the floor next to the chairs were several empty brown ale bottles and a half-full bottle of lemonade.

Woodend crouched down, so that he could take a closer look at the bottles. They were all covered with a thin layer of dust, which suggested to him that they had been standing there for some time.

He straightened up again.

'It's significant that there's no sign of any glasses, don't you think, Sergeant?' he asked.

'Is it, sir?' Bannerman replied, puzzled. 'Why?'

'Because that means that nobody's been drinkin' *shandy* in here,' Woodend said.

'I'm still not following you,' Bannerman admitted.

'Most men, when they're drinkin' beer, will do it straight from the bottle,' Woodend explained. 'Well, it saves washin' up, doesn't it?'

'Yes, I suppose so,' Bannerman said dubiously.

'But if they're goin' to drink shandy, which is a *mixture* of beer an' lemonade, they need a glass to do the mixin' in. An' like I said, there are no glasses here.'

'Howerd didn't buy the lemonade for himself – he bought it for a visitor!' Bannerman said, finally getting the picture.

'That's right – an' it was a visitor who he knew, in advance, wouldn't want to drink beer.'

'Lilly Dawson!'

'It's more than likely. An' since Howerd couldn't be bothered to remove the bottles once Lilly had left, it's also more than likely he couldn't be bothered to wipe the fingerprints off them, either.'

'We've got him!' Bannerman said.

'Not yet, we haven't,' Woodend cautioned him. 'Not by a very long chalk.'

'What's that on the floor, sir?' Bannerman asked suddenly.

'Where?'

'There. By your feet.'

Woodend looked down, and saw the coloured pencil. He bent over, picked it up, and took the pencil over to the window, where the light was stronger.

It was a *red* pencil – a *Lakeland* red pencil – and there were bite marks around the top of it.

'*Now* we've got him,' Woodend said, with a sigh of relief.

It was almost closing time at the Whitebridge covered market. Only a few customers still lingered, and many of the stallholders had already started the process of closing up their stalls for the day.

Woodend and Bannerman stood next to Hardy's Fishmongers' – which still had the sign announcing it was closed for a family bereavement taped to its canvas cover – and watched the man three stalls up from them, packing his electrical goods away.

What kind of man was it who could rape and murder a girl, and then go about his normal business so close to the place where she had worked that he could almost touch it? Woodend asked himself.

But the answer was simple – a man like Fred Howerd!

Howerd had a thin, sharp-featured face – the sort of face, Woodend thought, which clearly announces to the world that it has treated him unfairly, and then offers that as an excuse for granting himself the right to snatch back, from that same unfair world, anything he has a fancy for.

The chief inspector wondered if Howerd knew that he was being watched – and, more to the point, if he *did* know, whether he had been expecting it.

Probably not! As Howerd's police record clearly showed, he was an impulsive criminal, rather than a reflective one. He did things – got blind drunk or stole a car – because he wanted to at that particular moment, and he worried about the consequences (if he did, actually, worry about them that all) once he had slaked his yearning.

'Do you want us to make the arrest now, sir?' Bannerman asked, with an edge of impatience to his voice.

'No, I don't,' Woodend replied. 'In fact, I don't think I want *us* to make it at all. Let's just leave it to the local lads, shall we?'

'Are you *sure* you want them to do it?' Bannerman asked, disappointedly.

'Yes, I'm sure,' Woodend replied.

He understood his sergeant's disappointment – and even sympathized with it. This was their chance to be like the men in the white hats, who they had watched admiringly on the cinema screens of their childhoods. This should be the moment when – in one dramatic swoop – they restored order and brought the guilty to justice.

Yet he wanted no part of it, because he couldn't trust himself – because he couldn't be certain that, instead of cautioning Fred Howerd, he wouldn't simply put his big hands around the evil bastard's throat, and break his neck.

'You're absolutely certain that you want to do it that way, sir?' Bannerman persisted.

'For Christ's sake, yes!' Woodend snapped angrily.

Bannerman made a discreet signalling gesture with his hand, and two uniformed constables approached the suspect, one from his left side and the other from his right.

The constable on the right started to speak, and though Woodend was too far away to hear the words, he knew exactly what the officer would be saying.

'*Frederick Anthony Howerd, I am arresting you for the murder of Lilly Dawson. You do not have to say anything, but anything you do say may be taken down and used in evidence against you.*'

Fred Howerd tensed, and then began to wave his hands frantically about in the air.

He was probably saying that this whole thing was a stupid mistake, and it would be much better if the policemen just left him alone, Woodend thought.

Because men like him – however careless they'd been while committing their crimes – often simply refused to believe it when they were finally tracked down.

The constable shook his head, and said something else, probably to the effect that it would be better for Howerd if he agreed to come quietly.

And the message seemed to have finally got through, because now Howerd held his wrists out, and allowed the constable to slip the handcuffs on them.

A small crowd of stallholders, noticing that something unusual was happening, had started to gather, but they kept their distance from Howerd's stall, and watched in complete silence as the whole drama was played.

Were *they* surprised about the turn of events? Woodend asked himself.

Or had they perhaps *always* thought there was something a little *strange* about Fred Howerd?

The two policemen each put one of his hands firmly on Howerd's shoulders, and led him away. Without any bidding from the officers, the small crowd parted to let them pass.

He had solved his first major crime as a chief inspector in less than *two days*, Woodend reminded himself. He would return to Scotland Yard – where there were many who still had their doubts about him – as a conquering hero.

He should, by rights, have been elated.

But he wasn't!

Because there was a large part of him which wished that this triumph of his had never been possible.

That he had *won* no victory because there had been no victory to win.

That instead of being raped and murdered in a derelict potting shed, Lilly Dawson had been allowed to go home, with the prospect of a full and happy life ahead of her.

This feeling – this near-despair that life could be so brutish – was one that would revisit him many times over the years, but this *particular* experience of it, he knew even then, would never leave him – because it had been branded onto his soul.

Solving this case was bit like desperately looking forward to losing your virginity – and then realizing, once it was over, that it wasn't at all it was cracked up to be, he thought.

He turned to Bannerman and said, 'Well, I suppose we'd better go back to the station and tie up all the loose ends.'

'And then we can crack open the champagne,' replied the sergeant, sounding as though *he*, at least, felt as if he was riding the crest of a wave.

PART THREE
Whitebridge—Costa Blanca, October 1973

ELEVEN

The London train was right on time, and Paniatowski – who was not usually superstitious – caught herself wondering whether that was a good sign or a bad one.

She had thought of waiting on the platform to greet DCI Hall, but instead had decided to stand just beyond the ticket barrier.

'That way,' she told herself, 'I'll have a chance to study him before he even knows I'm here.'

It wasn't much of an advantage, she realized, but at that moment she was prepared to grab any advantage – however small – that was going.

The train doors opened, and as the passengers began to spill out on to the platform, she ran her gaze quickly from one end of it to the other.

She had a very clear idea of what she should be on the lookout for. The man from the Yard would be young, and he would be tall – high-fliers were always both. He would be the kind of police officer who can find always time to play a punishing game of squash, even in the middle of the most demanding investigation, and his slim, athletic body would reflect that. He would be smartly, though not flashily, dressed. He'd have the sharp features of the typical hatchet man, and the cunning eyes of a consummate politician.

Yes, that was how he'd look – and she was sure she'd dislike him from the second she set eyes on him.

Most of the people who'd got off the train were already rushing towards the barrier, but the last man to disembark was still standing there, as if he was quite content to wait until the rush was over.

He was of no more than average height, Paniatowski noted. He was chunky, rather than athletic, and was wearing a sports jacket which had seen better days and a pair of grey flannel trousers.

'That can't be him,' she said to herself. 'That simply *can't* be him.'

Yet all the other passengers continued to sweep past her, and when the man in the jacket and grey trousers finally reached the barrier, he looked her and said, 'DCI Paniatowski?'

Paniatowski nodded.

The man smiled. 'And I'm Tom Hall,' he said. 'I must admit, you're not at all what I expected.'

He was a few years older than she was – which probably made him no more than a couple of years younger than Assistant Commissioner Bannerman. He had a face which – though even the kindest of observers would have been pushed to call it attractive – was pleasant enough. And while his eyes were as intelligent as she'd pictured them, they seemed to be quite lacking in guile.

'You're not what I expected, either,' she admitted.

'No, I shouldn't think I am,' Hall said, 'but the difference between us is that people are usually disappointed when they see how *I* look.' The smile, which had never quite left his face, now turned into a grin. 'You're not one of those coppers who insist on driving their visitors straight to their hotel and ignore all the pubs on the way, are you?'

'No,' Paniatowski agreed. 'I'm not.'

'Excellent!' Hall said.

The hill on which Charlie and Joan Woodend's villa stood had once been shared – in almost equal parts – by a few herds of scavenging goats and a handful of determined peasants who had cultivated their almonds on its steep terraces. Now the goats had gone, and most of the almond groves were in terminal decline. Building work had begun almost a decade earlier, but it was a slow, leisurely process, and though Woodend knew several people who lived close enough to him to be called neighbours, most of the building plots still stood empty.

It would all change, he accepted, with just a touch of regret. More and more houses would spring up, and the hillside would eventually become a full-blown village. But it hadn't happened yet, and – in the meantime – he still had his virtually uninterr-upted view.

And what a bloody marvellous view it was, he told himself, as he stood on his sunny terrace that afternoon, a glass of Mahou beer in one hand and a Ducados cigarette in the other.

Straight ahead of him lay the Mediterranean Sea, a carpet of deep, rippling blue which stretched from the shoreline to the far horizon. To his right, the Peñon Ifach – a vast, breathtaking, outcrop of rock which the ancient Phoenicians had regarded as the younger sister of the Rock of Gibraltar – reared out of the water like a fierce primeval monster. And to his left – less dramatic, but equally enchanting – there was the sleepy fishing village of Moraira, dancing lazily in the heat haze.

'Looking back on it, are you happy with the way your life has gone, Charlie?' asked a voice from somewhere to his left.

Woodend turned to face the man who had posed the question – a wiry, seventy-three-year-old Spaniard whose full name was Francisco Ibañez Ruiz, but who was better known simply as Paco.

'That's a strange question to ask on a warm afternoon, after half a dozen bottles of beer, Inspector Ruiz,' he said.

'It is the *perfect* question to ask on a warm afternoon, after half a dozen bottles of beer,' Paco replied, with a smile.

Yes, Woodend agreed, it probably was.

Though he liked *most* people, there were few he actually *admired*, and Paco was one of that select band. He was in awe of the way that Ruiz had put the horrors he had seen during the Civil War behind him, and grateful for the fact that, since they had solved a murder together, several years earlier, they had become firm friends.

'Am I happy about the way my life has gone?' he said. 'Yes, I think so. I've had a very good marriage an' I've got a wonderful daughter. An' as far as my work went—'

'You were an honourable policeman,' Paco interrupted.

Woodend grinned. 'Honourable!' he repeated. 'You're very fond of that word in Spain, aren't you?'

'It's at the root of our being,' Paco told him. 'If you cannot understand what honour means to a Spaniard, then you will never understand Spain.'

'It's probably not that different in Lancashire,' Woodend admitted. 'But we'd never call it "honour" – that's far too poncey a word for a mill town like Whitebridge.'

'So what *would* you call it?' Paco asked.

'Decency, I suppose,' Woodend said. 'I was a very *decent* policeman. In all the time I was on the Force, I never once did anything that I was ashamed of.'

'I wonder how many men could honestly say that?' Paco mused.

'I wouldn't know,' Woodend replied. 'But it's important to me that *I* can – because everything I am now is based on everything I was then.'

*   *   *

DCI Hall looked around the public bar of the Drum and Monkey and said, 'Now this is what I *call* a pub. Where shall we sit?'

'Over there, at the table in the corner,' Paniatowski told him.

'But there's already somebody sitting there,' Hall pointed out.

'I know there is,' Paniatowski agreed. 'He's my inspector.'

'Is he, now!' Hall asked. 'Well, isn't that a pleasant surprise?'

They walked across to the table. Beresford and Hall shook hands, and Paniatowski signalled the ever-vigilant waiter.

Once the drinks had arrived, Hall immediately launched into a series of amusing stories about life at Scotland Yard, as if he were that one guest at a dinner party who is expected to pay for his supper by keeping the other guests entertained.

Paniatowski let him talk for ten minutes, and then said, 'I think we'd better get down to business.'

'Yes, we had,' Hall agreed, his face growing more serious. He turned to Beresford. 'I don't want you to take this the wrong way, son, but I think it's time you left.'

'Time he left? But he's my inspector,' Paniatowski protested.

'And that's exactly the problem,' Hall said. 'The deal that's been worked out between your bosses and mine is that we're the only two involved in this investigation. If my bosses read in my report that your inspector was also involved, they'll want to know why I didn't have back-up as well – and then they could create a real stink.'

'So leave it out of your report,' Paniatowski suggested.

Hall shook his head. 'I can't do that. I've always played things by the book, and I'm too long in the tooth to change my ways now.' He turned to Beresford again. 'I expect Monika will tell you everything in the morning, anyway – I know I would if you were my inspector.'

Beresford looked questioningly at Paniatowski. 'Boss?'

'You go, Colin,' Paniatowski said. 'Tom's right – I can tell you everything you need to know in the morning.'

Beresford stood up – but reluctantly, as if he worried about leaving Paniatowski alone with the man from the Yard – and said, 'I'll see you again, then, Chief Inspector.'

'Undoubtedly,' Hall agreed. 'And next time you do, please call me Tom.'

They watched Beresford walk to the door, then Paniatowski said angrily, 'So exactly what is it that you don't want my inspector – who I'd trust with my life – to know?'

'There's *nothing at all* I don't want him to know,' Hall said, apologetically, 'but – given the snakepit in which I'm forced to work – there's plenty that I don't want him to be able to say he got *directly from me*.'

'Like what?'

'Well, for a start, the way the people who really matter at the Yard view this investigation.'

'And how *do* they view it?'

'Their main concern, above all else – and that "all else" includes seeing justice done – is to protect Assistant Commissioner Bannerman's reputation.'

'And what about Charlie Woodend's reputation?' Paniatowski demanded. 'He used to work at the Yard, as well.'

'So he did,' Hall agreed. 'But that was a long time ago, and if the Blessed Charlie comes crashing down off his pedestal – so the thinking goes – the vibrations from his fall will hardly be felt in London at all. But Bannerman's an entirely different case. He's still at the Yard. He still has a future. And, most important of all, he's owed a lot of favours – which he can call in any time he chooses to.'

'Or, to put it another way, he know where all the bodies are buried,' Paniatowski said.

'Exactly,' Hall agreed. 'But the truth is, for all they're in a sweat over this situation, they've really got nothing to worry about – because if Fred Howerd *was* fitted up for the murder, Bannerman had nothing to do with it.'

'How can you be so sure of that?' Paniatowski asked, sceptically.

'Because the very fact that *I'm* here in Whitebridge is the living proof of it.'

'How is *that* proof?'

'I know for a fact that Bannerman played no part in assigning this investigation to me – but he didn't block it, either, and he could have easily done that, if he'd wanted to.'

'So?'

'We've never worked together, but he knows me by my reputation – just as I know him by his. And that means he also knows that if you want something sweeping under the carpet, Tom Hall is the last man you should think of sending.'

'You're saying that if Bannerman *did* have something to hide, he'd have made certain that it was one his cronies who came to Whitebridge?'

'Spot on.'

'Which means you're also saying that you think Fred Howerd's conviction was sound – that there *is* no dirt to sweep under the carpet?'

Hall frowned. 'No, I don't think I'd go *that* far, Monika,' he replied, cautiously. 'At the moment, you see, I'm not really in a position to.'

'Then what you're *actually* saying is that if *anyone* twisted the evidence, that person was Charlie Woodend?' Paniatowski demanded.

Hall looked embarrassed. 'Look, Monika,' he said uncomfortably, 'I've never even met Charlie Woodend, so you can't expect me to . . .'

'That *is* what you're saying, isn't it?' Paniatowski persisted.

'Yes,' Hall agreed reluctantly, 'If you're going to pin me down, then I suppose it is.'

'Charlie would never have sent an innocent man to jail,' Paniatowski said fiercely.

Yet Fred Howerd had claimed – with what was almost his dying breath, and under the seal of the sacrament of confession – that he had not killed Lilly Dawson.

'At least, he would never *knowingly* have sent an innocent man to jail,' she amended, realizing how weak that sounded.

'I think we've been getting a bit ahead of ourselves – and that's probably entirely my fault,' Hall said apologetically. 'At this stage of the investigation it was wrong of me to assume we could rule Bannerman out. I see that now. I should *never* have done it – however good my reasons were.'

'No,' Paniatowski said firmly. 'You shouldn't.'

And she was thinking to herself, If only I'd sounded half so firm – half so decisive – just a minute ago, when I was supposed to be defending Charlie.

Hall smiled in an ugly-charming way. 'I promise you that I'm not a habitual assumption-maker, so do you think you could let me off with a caution this time?' he asked.

'No, I don't think I could,' Paniatowski told him. Then she smiled back – because it was hard not to – and added, 'but I'm prepared to give you a suspended sentence.'

'That'll do,' Hall said cheerfully. His face grew serious again. 'I'd like to make a suggestion, if that's all right with you.'

'It's all right with me.'

'I think that instead of just sitting here and debating who should get blamed for what, we should get off our arses and go and see if there's any need to blame *anybody* for *anything*.'

'A good idea,' Paniatowski agreed. 'Where do you want to start?'

'A little chat with Fred Howerd's daughter, Elizabeth, might be as good a place as any,' Hall said.

TWELVE

'If I'd known you had streets like this in your lovely city, I'd have gone into training from the moment I knew I was being sent here,' DCI Tom Hall puffed good-naturedly, as he and Paniatowski walked up the steep street, towards the house where Fred Howerd had taken his last breath.

Paniatowski grinned. 'You get used to it, Tom,' she said.

She found herself wondering if Sergeant Bannerman had said something similar to Charlie Woodend, twenty-two years earlier, when the pair of them were clogging it around the hilly streets of Whitebridge.

Probably not.

Back then, Bannerman would have been young and fit, and driven by a burning ambition which would eventually land him in the post of Assistant Commissioner. He would have seen any hill – whatever the gradient – as no more than a minor obstacle in what he must already have known was going to be a long, hard climb.

The real question was whether, at some point, he had decided to look for a short-cut – because despite Hall's protestations that he *had to* be clean, she was still convinced that if anybody had fitted Fred Howerd up, that somebody could not be Charlie Woodend.

As they drew closer to Elizabeth Eccles's house, they saw that a car was just pulling away from it. And not just any old car, but a Bentley with a personalized number plate which read 'RJH 1'.

'Mrs Eccles would appear to have some rich and powerful friends,' Hall commented wryly. 'Let's hope, for all our sakes, that *they're* not taking too personal an interest in the case.'

A woman answered their knock on the door. Her black hair was drawn tightly in a bun, and she had the pale complexion of someone who rarely left the house. Her eyes were hostile, her mouth seemed permanently fixed in a downward turn, and her chin jutted out aggressively.

She must have been quite a pretty woman once, Paniatowski thought, but years of giving in to resentment and bitterness had indelibly marked her face, and though she was probably no more than forty, it was not a *good* forty.

'Mrs Eccles?' Hall asked politely.

'Who are you?' the woman demanded rudely.

Paniatowski produced her warrant card. 'I'm DCI Paniatowski, and this my colleague, DCI Hall, from Scotland Yard.'

'Are you here about my father?' Elizabeth Eccles asked.

'Yes, we are,' Paniatowski replied.

'Then you should have let me know exactly when you were coming – so I could have had some witnesses here.'

'Now why would you need witnesses?' Hall asked mildly.

'Because I don't trust you as far as I could throw you,' Elizabeth Eccles said. 'Because I think the only reason that you're here is to protect your own – and anything else will just be for show.'

'It's not like that at all, Mrs Eccles,' Paniatowski assured her. 'We're both here with completely open minds, and if your father was innocent of the crime for which he was convicted . . .'

'He was!'

'. . . then we're more than willing to uncover any evidence which could prove that.'

For a moment it really looked as if Elizabeth Eccles was about to slam the door in their faces. Then she seemed to change her mind and said gracelessly, 'Well, I suppose you'd better come in.'

She led them the short distance down the hallway to the front parlour.

It was a neat, tidy room, Paniatowski noted. A three-piece suite – in almost-neutral blue mock velvet – faced the fireplace, and both armchairs had been carefully placed at precisely the same angle to the sofa. The dark-brown hearth rug which lay stretched in front of the grate did not have a single wrinkle in it. The wallpaper had a floral pattern – which could have been cheerful, but wasn't – and if there had ever been pictures hanging on the walls, there was no evidence of it now. The only thing that gave the place a personal touch was the line of photographs arranged along the mantelpiece.

It was a cold room, Paniatowski thought – a room in which
it was almost impossible to imagine there had ever been fun and
laughter.

'Sit down, if you want to,' Elizabeth Eccles said, indicating
the two armchairs. 'I won't be offering you tea because—'

'Quite right, Mrs Eccles,' Hall interrupted her. 'You shouldn't
even have bothered to mention it. The last thing that either of
us would want to do is to put you to the trouble.'

And he sounded as if he meant it, Paniatowski thought –
sounded as if even the idea of Mrs Eccles making all the effort
of boiling the water and filling the teapot was enough to cause
him acute distress.

The phone rang in the hallway.

'That'll be my daughter ringing,' Mrs Eccles said. 'I've been
expecting her to call.'

Most women in her position would have felt the need to add
something like, 'So if you'll excuse me for a minute . . .' but Mrs
Eccles merely left the room, closing the door firmly behind her.

Hall chuckled. 'This is the warm Northern welcome that I've
been told so much about, is it?' he asked. 'Still,' he continued,
more seriously, 'if she really does believe that her father didn't kill
Lilly, she was never going to take us to her bosom, now was she?'

The photographs had fascinated Paniatowski since she'd first
entered the room, and now – just as her mentor, Charlie Woodend,
would have done in her situation – she stood up and walked
over to the fireplace.

The photographs appeared to have been deliberately arranged
from left to right in strict chronological order.

The one on the extreme left was of a man and a young girl.
The man had his hand resting lightly on the girl's shoulder. The
girl herself stared at the camera with a look of dissatisfaction.

So even back then, before the family had been turned upside
down by her father's arrest, Elizabeth had had a sour view of
life, Paniatowski thought.

There were a few more photographs of Elizabeth's childhood,
and in each of them she displayed the same look of peevishness.

Then, in the centre of the mantelpiece, there was her wedding
photograph. Elizabeth looked older than she had in the earlier
pictures, but not *that* much older. Nor could she have been
described as a radiant bride, for though she had all the trappings
necessary – the white dress, the bouquet – she still managed to
appear as if life had somehow cheated her.

What was most noticeable about the photograph, however, was the groom. He was dressed appropriately – in a smart suit – and was standing as close to his bride as men are supposed to when marrying the woman of their dreams, but it was impossible to say how he *actually* felt about the occasion, because his whole face had been neatly cut out of the picture.

Elizabeth Eccles was certainly not the first woman to cut her partner's face out of a picture, just as she had cut the partner himself out of her life, Paniatowski thought. It was a very natural reaction in the first wave of anger.

But once the anger had cooled a little, most women in Elizabeth's place would surely have torn the photograph up. Or – at the very least – have put it away at the bottom of a deep drawer.

Yet she had done neither of those things. Instead, she had placed the photograph at the very centre of her display, where she could not fail to see it every time she looked in the direction of the mantelpiece.

Beyond the central wedding picture, there was a series of photographs of an older Elizabeth and a girl who, as the pictures progressed, grew from a child into a young woman.

This would be the daughter, Paniatowski thought – the one who was on the phone at that moment. She looked rather like her mother, though she was prettier, and did not have the same haunted look. So perhaps, after all, *some* good had come out of what had clearly been a disastrous marriage.

The parlour door clicked open before Paniatowski had time to return to her seat.

'What are you doing, snooping around by the fireplace?' Elizabeth Eccles demanded from the doorway.

'I'm sorry, I just . . .' Paniatowski said, caught off-guard.

'There's no need to apologize, Monika,' Tom Hall said firmly.

'Monika, is it?' Mrs Eccles asked, pouncing on the words. 'So that's how it is – you're all mates together.'

'Why don't you sit down, Mrs Eccles?' Hall suggested.

'Because I don't want to,' Elizabeth Eccles replied.

And, instead of sitting, she crossed the room and positioned herself with her back to the fireplace, as if to protect her precious photographs from Paniatowski's unwanted attention.

'I wish you'd sit down, Mrs Eccles. It really *would* be much more comfortable,' Hall said.

'I'm comfortable enough where I am,' Elizabeth said.

Echoes of the Dead

But she didn't look as if she'd ever been comfortable in her entire life, Paniatowski thought.

'Have you any idea of what the kind of investigation you want us to undertake will involve?' Hall asked, in a soft tone.

'Of course I haven't. How could I?' Elizabeth Eccles said aggressively, almost as if it were *their* fault that she didn't know.

'The reason I ask is that you seemed to be offended that DCI Paniatowski was looking at your photographs just now.'

'Why shouldn't I be? It's none of her business.'

'Ah, but, you see, it is. Once the investigation's underway, we'll be taking your family's *whole life* apart – because that's how we'll establish whether your father was guilty or innocent.'

'Everything your father ever did – and everyone he ever talked to – will be examined in the most minute detail,' Paniatowski said. 'Now maybe you don't want that, Mrs Eccles – and I could quite understand it if you didn't – but it's the way we have to work, and if you think you'll find that too much of a strain, you'd better say so before the investigation goes any further.'

And she was thinking, Pull back now, Elizabeth. You've buried your father – now let's bury the case.

'I really don't see why it should be necessary to rake through all the ashes of my father's life,' Elizabeth Eccles said.

'Of course you don't,' Hall agreed. 'But then you're not a police officer, are you? Take it from me, Mrs Eccles, there's no other way but the one we've outlined to you.'

For a full minute, the battle between her desires and her uncertainties was played out on Elizabeth Eccles's face.

Then she took a deep breath and said, 'All right.'

'All right?' Paniatowski repeated. 'Does that mean that you still want us to go ahead?'

'Yes.'

Paniatowski sighed. 'Then we'd better make a start,' she said. 'Now, am I right in thinking that at the time Lilly Dawson went missing, you were—'

'Lilly Dawson!' Elizabeth Eccles interrupted bitterly. 'Lilly Dawson! I'm sick of hearing her name! Everybody talks about what a tragedy her murder was – how *poor little Lilly* suffered so much. But nobody wants to know about what the murder did to *my* life, do they? Nobody wants to hear how much *I* suffered.'

'*We* do,' Hall said. 'Why don't you tell us?'

'When they shut my father up in that terrible prison, I thought

that things couldn't get any worse. But I was wrong! Some of
the neighbours – people I'd known all my life – stopped speaking
to us. But they weren't as bad as the ones who *did* speak –
because I wouldn't repeat to anybody the things that *they* said
to us.'

Hall nodded. 'You have my sympathy. Some people can be
very cruel,' he said.

Charlie Woodend might have said the same thing, Paniatowski
thought. But if *he* had said it, he would have *meant* it – and she
was not sure that Tom Hall did.

'My mother's nerves were completely shot to pieces by it all,'
Elizabeth continued, in full bitter flow now. 'And one day,
she decided she just couldn't take it any more and drowned
herself.'

'Terrible,' Hall murmured.

'My grandfather and my Uncle Robert should have given me
the support that I needed in my times of trouble – but they just
didn't want to know,' Elizabeth Eccles whined.

Uncle Robert, Paniatowski thought.

Would he be the owner of the RJH 1 number plate?

'So, after it happened, the rest of the Howerd family cut you
off completely, did they?' she asked.

'Yes!' Elizabeth said angrily. Then she paused for a moment
before adding, with great reluctance, 'Not completely, no. After
my rat of a husband deserted me, their chief accountant came
to see me, and said that for the sake of the baby they'd decided
to pay me a small monthly allowance. But that was it! That was
as far as it went!'

'When *exactly* did your husband leave you?' Paniatowski
asked.

'Shortly after my mother killed herself. He said he couldn't
stand the shame of belonging to the family any more. The shame
of belonging to the family! As if *we'd* dragged *him* down! Well,
let me tell you, he was nothing before I married him – he was
less than nothing.'

'Are you still in contact with him?'

'I've not heard a word from him since the day he left me. He
might be dead, for all I know. I hope he is.'

'You really should try to put it all behind you,' Hall advised.

The comment seemed to do no more than enrage Elizabeth
further.

'I *had* put it behind me – at least, as much as I could,' she said in a voice that was almost a scream. 'And then my father – that poor, dying man – came to live with me. And it started all over again – the looks, the comments, the . . . the hatred. That's why I sent my daughter away – because I didn't want to put her through what I was going through.' She paused again, but only for a moment, as she drew breath. 'Do you see now what a wicked thing Chief Inspector Woodend did?' she demanded. 'And not only to my father, not only to me, but to my daughter – because God alone knows what effect all this has had on her.'

'If your father was guilty of the crime, then Mr Woodend was only doing his job in arresting him,' Paniatowski pointed out.

'But I know he *wasn't* guilty,' Elizabeth Eccles said.

Hall smiled, benevolently and reassuringly. 'You loved your father, so naturally you want to believe that that he could never have done anything as terrible as to take a young girl . . .'

'You're not *listening*,' Elizabeth told him. 'I didn't say I *believed* he wasn't guilty – I said I *knew* he wasn't.'

'How *could* you know?' Paniatowski asked.

'I know because he told me he had an alibi for the time that Lilly Dawson went missing. He spent the whole afternoon and evening of that day in Bolton, with a friend of his.'

'Did you check out this alibi yourself?' Paniatowski asked.

'Of course I didn't! I'm not a *policeman*!'

'Then we're back to belief again,' Hall pointed out, reasonably. 'He said he had an alibi, and you *believed* him. But think about it, Mrs Eccles. If he really *did* have an alibi, why didn't he produce it at the time? Surely, any man would – rather than go to prison for a crime he didn't commit?'

'He told me it wasn't as simple as that. He said that after what the policeman had told him, he didn't *dare* produce his alibi.'

Elizabeth Eccles looked down at the floor – as if she were ashamed of her father, not because he had committed the crime he was accused of committing, but because he hadn't had the courage to produce the alibi which would clear him.

'I don't want to sound at all discouraging, Mrs Eccles,' Hall said softly. 'Honestly, I don't. We will investigate the case, just as we promised we would. But I have to say that nothing you've told us so far has been of much help. You see, it's still a question of belief on your part – you *believe* your father didn't kill Lilly, and you *believe* he had an alibi. But, really, you don't have anything to back up either of those assertions.'

Elizabeth Eccles's head snapped back up again.

'I don't have anything to back it up – but *he* does,' she said angrily.

'Who?'

'The man my father was with – the one who can give him an alibi. Have you talked to him? Have you bothered to find out what *he* has to say?'

'No, we haven't talked to anybody but you at this stage of the investigation,' Hall admitted. 'And before we can talk to this man – if he exists – we really need a name. And you can't give us one, can you?'

'Who said that I couldn't?' Elizabeth Eccles asked.

'Well, no one,' Hall admitted, clearly knocked off balance. 'I just assumed that your father hadn't told you who he was, and so you couldn't tell us.'

'He told me the day before he died,' Elizabeth Eccles said. 'The man you need to talk to is called Terry Clegg. He has a stall on Whitebridge Market, close to where Dad's used to be.'

THIRTEEN

Paniatowski could have booked an unmarked vehicle out of the police car pool, but instead she chose a patrol car with a broad red stripe running around its middle and a metal grill separating the back seat from the front.

'I've noticed that most civilians – even the ones who are totally innocent of anything – feel very uncomfortable about travelling in the back of police cars,' she said to Tom Hall, as they drove towards the town centre.

'And that's just how you want Terry Clegg to feel?' Hall asked.

'That's right.'

Hall chuckled appreciatively. 'I can see the way your mind's working, Monika – and I like it,' he said. 'Twenty-two years is a long time. Clegg could lie about the alleged trip to Bolton, and we'd have no way of *knowing* that he was lying. So what you want to do – from the very beginning – is to put him in a position in which he thinks that lying simply isn't an option.'

'Yes, that *is* what I want to do,' Paniatowski admitted. 'But it won't be easy.'

'That's the understatement of the year,' Hall told her. 'Won't be easy? It'll be like skating on thin ice – with a blacksmith's anvil in your arms.'

They pulled into the multi-storey car park next to the market, and left the patrol car on the ground floor.

Just before they entered the market, Hall put his hand on Paniatowski's arm and said, 'Listen, Monika, this is your patch, not mine – so unless I think I've got real contribution to make, I'll keep quiet and leave the talking to you. Are you happy with that?'

They worked well together, Paniatowski thought. Maybe not as well as she'd worked with Charlie Woodend – but well enough. They were two of a kind.

'I'm happy with it,' she said.

Clegg's Pork Butchers was in the centre of the market, a few stalls away from where Howerd's Electrical Goods had once been. There were two men standing behind the stall. One was in his early twenties, and had a thin moustache. The other was in his mid-fifties and had a receding hairline, a skin which was almost as pink as some of the meat he was slicing up, and huge forearms.

'There are no prizes for guessing which one of them is Terry Clegg,' Hall said. 'What do you think, Monika? Will he be a tough nut to crack?'

'I don't know,' Paniatowski admitted. 'But there's only one way to find out, isn't there?'

They waited until the customer Clegg had been serving walked away, then moved in.

'Mr Clegg?' Paniatowski asked.

The butcher looked up, but even then the cleaver in his hand did not stop slicing.

'That's me,' he said, with a broad smile. 'Terry Clegg – your friendly neighbourhood family butcher, servin' the general public with top quality meat since 1949.'

He was the sort of man who really liked to be liked, Paniatowski decided – the sort who would do almost anything, even something he didn't particularly want to do, rather than cause offence.

Paniatowski produced her warrant card. 'We're police officers. We'd like you to come down to the station with us, Mr Clegg,' she said.

Clegg's smile melted away like rendered-down fat.

'Why?' he asked. 'What have I done?'

'We don't *know* you've done *anything*,' Paniatowski told him. 'But there is a little matter we think you could help us to clear up.'

'*What* little matter?'

'I'd rather not discuss that here.'

'But . . . but this is my busy time,' Clegg protested. 'Ten minutes from now, I'll be swamped with women wantin' to buy sausages for their husbands' teas.'

'Your lad should be able to handle that,' Hall said.

'What?'

'We've been watching the way he works. He'll have no trouble dealing with the rush.'

'You've been *watchin'* him?' Clegg asked worriedly.

'We've been watching *both of you* – very carefully,' Hall said. 'And we've noticed at least three breaches of the Health and Safety Act that we could arrest you for right now, were we of a mind to.'

'I . . . I . . .' Clegg spluttered.

'It really would be much easier if you came with us voluntarily,' Paniatowski said.

'All right, I'll come,' Clegg said, defeated.

They left the market through the main exit – Paniatowski and Hall pointedly flanking Clegg – and headed towards the multi-storey car.

'Look, I really need to know what this all about,' the butcher protested, as they crossed the street.

He was nervous, Paniatowski thought.

And that was a good thing, because – though they rarely realized it themselves – nervous men were already doing part of their interrogators' job for them.

'I mean, I'm a law-abiding citizen,' Clegg babbled.

'Are you really?' Paniatowski asked. 'Have you *never* done anything wrong, Mr Clegg?

'No, I . . .'

'Not even in the distant past? Not even in *1951*?'

'1951?' Clegg croaked.

'Would it help you if I was more specific?' Paniatowski wondered. 'All right then, let's say, you didn't do anything wrong in *April* 1951.'

They had reached the lower floor of the car park, and Hall broke rank to open the back door of the vehicle. Then, with his hand already on the handle, he seemed to change his mind.

'What's the point of going all the way down to the station when we can do the interview here?' he asked.

'Here?' Paniatowski repeated, puzzled.

'Well, not *right* here,' Hall said. 'But somewhere close. We could go up the steps to the top of the car park. I should think you get a lovely view of the whole of Whitebridge from there.'

What the bloody hell did he think he was doing? Paniatowski wondered. If he wanted to change their plans – and she couldn't see why he *should* want to change them – then he should have discussed it with her first.

But she couldn't argue with him – not in front of Clegg – so she said, 'I suppose the top of the car park is as good a place as any.'

As they climbed the stairs, Tom Hall maintained an almost breathless monologue.

'Do you like going to the pictures when you have a bit of spare time on your hands, Mr Clegg?' he asked, as they passed the first floor.

Clegg said nothing, but that did not seem to deter Hall in the slightest.

'I love it myself,' the chief inspector continued, as they reached for the second floor. 'I saw this film with Michael Caine in it. What was it called, now? *Get Carter*! That's it! It was marvellous. Have you seen that one, Mr Clegg?'

Clegg grunted, non-committally.

'Of course,' Hall cautioned, as they arrived at the third floor, 'you have to do what they call "suspend disbelief" when you're watching a film like that, because it isn't very realistic. I mean to say – there isn't any way that the police would have allowed a criminal like Carter to go on the rampage like he did. Still, it's only a bit of fun, isn't it?'

What was this? Paniatowski asked herself. What the sodding hell was he playing at?

Hall knew, as well as she did, that the only way they'd get Clegg to reveal whether or not he had been harbouring a guilty secret for twenty-years was by maintaining a united front – by signalling, through that unity, that they knew they were the ones in charge, and they would get their way in the end. And what

that meant, from her viewpoint, was that she had to seem to be
going along with whatever Hall was doing, because once Clegg
sensed disagreement – once he could see a crack in the united
front – they were finished.

They had reached the top floor of the car park.

'A wonderful view – just like I promised,' Hall enthused.
'That'll be the cathedral, won't it? And look, there's the bus
station.' He lit up a cigarette. 'The only thing that put me off in
the film was Michael Caine's accent,' he continued, when he'd
inhaled. 'He was supposed to be a Geordie – born and bred –
yet every time he opened his mouth, it was obvious he was a
cockney.'

'What's all this about?' Clegg asked nervously.

This was about as good an opportunity as she was likely to
get to take back control, Paniatowski told herself.

'It's about Fred Howerd,' she said.

'Fred Howerd?' Clegg licked his lips nervously. 'I don't know
the man.'

'You've heard that he's dead, haven't you?'

'Like I said, I don't know the man.'

'Everybody in Whitebridge has heard of Fred Howerd,'
Paniatowski said. 'He was all over the newspapers back in 1951.
Besides, your stall is in spitting distance of where Fred's used
to be.'

'All right, I might have known him,' Clegg admitted. 'But
just – you know – to say hello to when we happened to pass
each other.'

'That's not what *he* said. *He* said you were the best of mates.
He said you could give him an alibi for the afternoon that little
Lilly Dawson was abducted.'

'He was lyin',' Clegg mumbled.

Tom Hall stepped forward, put his arm around Clegg's
shoulder, and steered the butcher across the car park to the very
edge of the parapet.

What the hell was he doing *now*? Paniatowski wondered.

'It's a long way down, isn't it?' Hall said, looking over the
edge. 'Look at the cars on the street. They could be toys.'

Clegg twisted his head round, and gazed frantically at
Paniatowski. 'Help me!' he pleaded.

She had to intervene, Paniatowski told herself. However much
that might upset the delicate balance she had been trying to
establish, there was no choice *but to* intervene.

'That's enough, Tom,' she said.

But instead of releasing Clegg, Hall tightened his grip on the other man's shoulder.

'Do you know what my favourite part of *Get Carter* is, Terry?' he asked. 'It's when Carter is questioning one the local villains – Bunbury, I think his name is – at the top of a multi-storey car park, which, now I come to think about it, is rather like this one.'

Clegg had both his hands on the edge of the parapet, and was gripping it as tightly as he could.

'Get away from him, Chief Inspector!' Paniatowski said firmly.

'And what do you think happens when Carter gets an answer he doesn't like, Terry?' Hall ploughed on. 'He throws Bunbury over the bloody edge!'

Another few seconds and she was going to have to do more than intervene with just words, Paniatowski thought desperately – another few seconds and she was going to have to get physical.

'I told you to get away from him, Chief Inspector!' she said, giving Hall one last chance.

Hall removed his arm from around Clegg's shoulder, and took several steps backwards.

'Is that far enough for you?' he asked.

Ignoring him, Paniatowski turned her attention back to Clegg. The pork butcher's ruddy face had turned white with fear, and he was still holding tightly on to the parapet, as if he was frightened that Hall had not yet finished with him.

'Tell me about Fred Howerd's alibi, Mr Clegg,' she said.

'Look, you've got to understand my position,' the butcher moaned. 'It wasn't easy for me at the time. I was engaged to be married and . . .'

'Tell me about the alibi!' Paniatowski repeated.

'We . . . we went to Bolton that day, to see this girl that Fred knew.'

'A girl?' Paniatowski echoed.

'I . . . I don't mean a girl like Lilly Dawson. Nothin' like that. This one was a prostitute.'

'So the *two* of you went to see *one* prostitute?'

'Yes.'

'How did you arrange things? Did you take *turns* with her?'

'No, we . . . we both did her at the same time. She . . . she didn't mind. She said she liked it that way.'

You really sicken me, you loathsome piece of dog shit! Paniatowski thought.

'How long were you in Bolton?' she asked, in as level a tone as she could muster.

'We set off as soon as the market closed. We didn't get back to Whitebridge until ten o'clock at night.'

'If that's what really happened, why didn't you inform the police as soon as you'd heard that Howerd had been arrested?'

'I . . . I was going to,' Clegg gabbled. 'I swear I was. But then Dyson Trypp came see me.'

'Who's Dyson Trypp?' Hall asked Paniatowski.

'He's dead now, but he *was* a local solicitor,' Paniatowski told him. 'A very *bent* local solicitor. So Trypp came to see you, did he, Terry?'

'Yes.'

'And what did he have to say for himself?'

Terry Clegg is sitting in his kitchen, polishing his best pair of shoes. He has been working on them for over an hour. Five minutes would have been more than sufficient for the job. Ten minutes' work would have produced a shine which even a regimental sergeant major could not have found fault with. He knows that. But, even so, he cannot stop polishing.

News of Fred Howerd's arrest has quickly spread around the town, and Clegg knows he'll have to come clean about what they did together on Saturday afternoon – if only because Fred is bound to come clean about it himself.

But somehow he can't bring himself to do it quite yet. It's almost as if the further away from the actual event they get, the less the effect of the revelation will be, so that to reveal it a few days later would be very shocking, but after a couple of weeks it would perhaps not sound quite so bad.

Besides, he needs time to prepare the story he will feed to his fiancée. His current plan is to tell her that he'd had no idea why he and Fred were going to Bolton that day, that once he realized it was to see the girl, he'd wanted to back out, and that the only reason he didn't *back out was because he was afraid that Fred would make fun of him.*

It's not a good story. It wouldn't fool even the most naive of girls – and Edith is anything but that. Yet he still clings to the hope that – given time – he'll come up with something better. Because he knows he has *to come up with something better!*

He hears a tap on the kitchen window, and looks up to discover that Dyson Trypp is standing in the yard. He feels his stomach turn to water. On shaky legs, he gets up and opens the door for the man who, he knows, can only be bringing him trouble.

Trypp takes the seat he has been offered at the table, reaches into his pocket, and produces a half-bottle of cheap whisky.

'Got any glasses?' he asks.

Clegg finds a couple of Woolworths' tumblers, and Trypp pours a generous slug of Scotch into each one.

'I represent Fred Howerd, who, as you probably know, has been arrested for the murder of Lilly Dawson,' Trypp says.

'Yes,' Clegg agrees, hardly daring to breathe.

'But what you also *know is that Fred was with you all Saturday afternoon and most of the evening.'*

'I was just planning to go the police when you arrived,' Clegg lies. 'That's why I was polishing my shoes.'

'I don't think that going to the police would be at all a good idea,' Trypp says.

'I beg your pardon?'

'You remember the girl who you and my client "entertained" yourselves with that afternoon?'

'Yes.'

'How old do you think she was?'

'I don't know – eighteen or nineteen?'

'She was fifteen, *Mr Clegg. You could go to prison for merely touching her – never mind all the disgusting things you prob-ably* actually *did during your sordid little session.'*

'I swear I didn't know . . .'

'In the eyes of the law, ignorance is no excuse at all,' Trypp says harshly. 'But it is *an excuse in the eyes of my client,' he continues, in a much softer tone. 'Fred didn't tell you how old the girl was . . .'*

'That's right – he didn't. If he had, I'd never have touched her with a barge pole.'

'I wonder if that's true,' Trypp says reflectively. 'But no matter,' he continues. 'Whatever you would have done – or not done – if you'd known the truth, is irrelevant. Fred now he feels that he was wrong to keep you in the dark, and he does not wish to see you suffer because of his own misjudgement. He has therefore decided that he would prefer you not to come forward.'

'But if I don't give him alibi, he could be convicted,' Clegg says.

'If you don't give him an alibi, he is very likely *to be convicted,' Trypp says. 'But that is the price he's prepared to pay to keep you out of prison.'*

It doesn't make sense, Clegg tells himself.

Fred Howerd is a mate, but he's not that much of a mate. In fact, nobody is that much of a mate. There can't be any other man in the whole of Whitebridge who would be prepared to go to prison for thirty or forty years, just to save his friend from being put away for two or three.

And then he is suddenly engulfed in a huge wave of relief.

It doesn't matter why Fred's doing it, he thinks.

It might well be through a sense of duty to his friend, as Trypp claims.

It might be that he's gone completely off his head.

But none of that is important!

What matters – the only thing that matters – is that he himself is now off the hook!

'If that's what Fred really wants, then I've no choice but to go along with it,' he says to Trypp.

The solicitor favours him with a thin smile.

'Do you know, I thought that's what you'd say,' Trypp tells him.

'And that's the story you're sticking with, is it?' Hall asked sceptically. 'You're saying the only reason you didn't come forward is because Howerd – through his solicitor – asked you not to?'

'It's the truth,' Clegg said. 'I swear to you it is.'

'You can go,' Paniatowski told him.

'Now just a minute, Monika,' Hall said. 'I'm not sure that I've finished questioning—'

'You've finished,' Paniatowski interrupted him. She turned to Clegg again. 'Go on – piss off!'

Clegg edged his way along the parapet, and when he was a fair distance away from Hall, he turned and ran towards the exit.

Paniatowski watched him until he'd disappeared down the stairwell, then swung round to face Hall.

'Just what the bloody hell did you think you were doing?' she demanded angrily.

'You said you wanted to keep him off-balance. I was just following your plan,' Hall told her.

'He wasn't just off-balance, you bastard!' Paniatowski said. 'He was bloody *petrified*!'

'You're right, Monika,' Hall agreed contritely. 'You're quite right. I misjudged it, and I'm very sorry. But I really did think that by putting a bit of pressure on him, I might get him to tell us the truth.'

'And he *did* tell us the truth,' Paniatowski said, still in a blazing rage, 'but after the way you got that truth out of him, we'll never be able to use it in court.'

'Use it in court?' Hall repeated, mystified. 'Why would we *want* to use it in court? You surely don't *believe* any of that rubbish, do you?'

'Don't you?' Paniatowski asked, incredulously.

'Not for a second. Come on, Monika, the man simply spewed out the first story that came into his head.'

Her rage bubbling over, Paniatowski realized, for the first time in her life, what people meant when they said they could see red. She felt an almost overwhelming urge to do to Hall what he had been suggesting he might do to Clegg. He was a strong man – he'd shown that by the way that he had manhandled the butcher – but she had a Judo black belt, and she was prepared to take her chances.

The madness passed, and she turned and walked towards the exit.

'Where are you going?' Hall called after her.

'Away from you – before I do something I might enjoy,' she said, over her shoulder.

Colin Beresford took a deep swig from his pint glass, then said, 'So where's DCI Hall now, boss?'

'I don't know, and I don't bloody care!' Paniatowski replied. 'Right up until we went to the top of the car park, I thought he was my kind of bobby. But he's not. The way he handled Clegg was a disgrace. It was almost as if he was trying to sabotage the investigation.'

'Maybe that's just the way they *do* things down in London,' Beresford suggested.

'Well, it's not the way we do things up here,' Paniatowski said. 'And this is *my* patch.'

'Putting aside how the statement was obtained for the moment, am I right in thinking that you believe what Clegg said?' Beresford asked.

'Yes, I do believe him,' Paniatowski admitted. 'I don't want to, Colin – but I do.'

'Then if he *is* telling the truth, why did Fred Howerd decide to confess to killing Lilly Dawson? Why didn't he just say where he'd been that afternoon?'

'Because he was afraid to,' Paniatowski said dully. She took her notebook out of her pocket, and flicked it open. 'When I asked Elizabeth Eccles what you've just asked me, she said, "He told me it wasn't as simple as that. He said that after what the policeman told him, he didn't *dare* produce his alibi."'

'Which policeman is she talking about?' Beresford asked. 'Was she referring to Mr Woodend? Or did he mean Sergeant Bannerman?'

'It could be either of them, couldn't it?' Paniatowski said.

'And what exactly *was it* that this policeman – whoever he was – told him?' Beresford wondered.

'I haven't got a bloody clue.' Paniatowski said dispiritedly. She drained the last of her vodka. 'And there's only one way that I can find out, isn't there? I'll have to ask.'

'Ask who?' Beresford said. 'If what DCI Hall told you about Bannerman is even halfway true, there's not a chance he'll run the risk of saying anything that might besmirch his precious reputation.'

'You're right,' Paniatowski said. 'So if Bannerman won't cooperate, who does that leave us with?'

'It leaves us with Charlie Woodend,' Beresford said.

FOURTEEN

'Another afternoon in paradise,' Charlie Woodend thought, looking down from his terrace at the fruit trees in his garden.

And he meant it, he told himself. He really didn't miss the cold winters and the wet summers. He was managing very well without the Drum and Monkey. He was even – and this took a *little* more self-persuasion – quite happy not to be investigating murders any more.

He heard a roaring noise in the distance, and, looking down the winding, single-track road which ran down the hill to the sea, saw that a car was approaching.

'I wonder who that bugger is,' he said aloud.

'What bugger?' asked Paco Ruiz, who managed to find a reason to drop in on Woodend most afternoons.

'Him,' Woodend said, pointing to the vehicle. 'It's a new car – and there's not many of them round here. And whoever's drivin' it isn't used to this road. You can tell that from the cautious way he's approachin' the bends.'

Paco laughed. 'Always the detective,' he said.

Woodend grinned, self-consciously. 'Well, there are some habits which *are* a bit hard to break,' he admitted.

The car turned another bend in the road, and was now close enough for them to see the driver.

'It's a woman!' Woodend said, surprised. 'A blonde!'

'Perhaps it is your old friend, Sergeant Monika Paniatowski, come to pay you a visit,' Paco suggested.

'Can't be,' Woodend said, 'because that would mean she was takin' a holiday – an' Monika *never* takes a holiday.'

And yet, despite his words – and the logic which undoubtedly lay behind them – Woodend felt a slight surge of hope that perhaps it was Monika, after all.

The car pulled up in front of the house, and Monika Paniatowski climbed out. Woodend was by her side immediately, flinging his arms around her and hugging her to him.

'By, but it's grand to see you, Monika,' he gushed.

'It's grand to see you, too, Charlie,' Paniatowski said.

And maybe she *did* think it was grand, Woodend thought, as he felt a slight disappointment stab into him – but from the hint of restraint in her voice, she certainly didn't seem quite as enthusiastic about it as he was.

He led her on to the terrace of his little palace.

'How's that for a view?' he asked, sweeping his hand grandly across the panorama.

'It's lovely, Charlie,' Paniatowski replied.

But again he detected that something was missing – that Monika was not quite herself.

'This is my good friend, Paco Ruiz,' he pressed on. 'I may have mentioned him to you, once or twice.'

'It was a lot more than once or twice,' Paniatowski told Ruiz, as they shook hands, 'and once he *did* start talking about you, he found it very hard to stop.'

'It is the same with me – when he talks about you,' Ruiz said.

Something's wrong, Woodend's instinct told him. Something's *very* wrong.

'Where's Joan?' Paniatowski asked, with a casualness that sounded just a little *too* casual.

'She's gone over to England to spend a couple of weeks with our Annie,' Woodend said.

And he could not fail to see the look of relief which came to Paniatowski's face.

'What's this all about, Monika?' he asked.

'Trouble, Charlie,' Paniatowski said bluntly.

'Trouble?' Woodend repeated worriedly. 'For you?'

'I wish it was, Charlie,' Paniatowski replied. 'I think I could handle that easier. But it's you who's in trouble this time.'

The sun still shone benevolently down, the sea glistened just as it had done half an hour earlier, but the magic had been sucked out of Woodend's day, and it might as well have been the bleakest midwinter.

He sat with Ruiz and Paniatowski on the terrace, and listened, almost without interruption, while Paniatowski told her tale.

'An', in your opinion, this Terry Clegg feller is tellin' the truth?' he asked when she'd finished.

Paniatowski nodded. 'I've rarely been surer of anything in my life.'

Woodend shook his head slowly from side to side. 'You're wrong,' he said finally. 'The alibi's a fake.'

'Why would Clegg *want* to fake the alibi, after all this time?' Paniatowski asked. 'He can't have done it to help Fred Howerd – Fred Howerd's dead. And, by providing it, he's only building up grief for himself, because if there's an official inquiry, everybody he knows will learn that their friendly neighbourhood butcher used to visit under-age prostitutes.'

'Do you think that there *will be* an official inquiry?' Woodend asked anxiously.

'When you put Clegg's alibi together with Howerd's dying declaration, I don't see how it can be avoided,' Paniatowski said.

'But I was there, remember,' Woodend protested. 'I was in that interview room with him, and I *know* he was guilty.'

'It was early days. You'd just been made up to chief inspector,' Paniatowski said softly.

'And what's that supposed to mean?' Woodend demanded.

'It means, Charlie, that you hadn't had the experience you'd gained by the time that I started working with you. It means that you're going to have to come to terms with the fact that, just that once, you might have been wrong.'

'I wasn't wrong!' Woodend told her. 'If Howerd had an alibi

– a real alibi, one that would have stood up in court *back then* – why didn't he produce it?'

Paniatowski sighed. 'I've already explained that. There was something that either you or Bannerman said which made him afraid to.'

'So you're seriously askin' me to accept that he was more scared by somethin' we *said* than he was of the thought of goin' to prison for *life*?'

'We've started going round in circles, Charlie,' Paniatowski said. 'Why don't we approach the whole thing from another angle?'

'What other angle?'

'I want you to go through that whole interrogation for me. I know it was a long time ago, but you need to tell me as much of what was said and what was done as you can remember – however little that may be.'

'I remember a lot,' Woodend said. 'In fact, I remember the whole bloody thing.'

Paniatowski looked at him almost pityingly. 'I understand that this is important to you, Charlie, but it won't help us if you're not brutally honest about what you do remember and what you don't.'

'I remember the whole bloody thing,' Woodend repeated firmly. 'Because it wasn't just *any* case, it was my *first* case as a DCI,' he prodded his forehead with his big index finger, 'and it's all up here.'

'Let's hear it then,' Paniatowski said.

As he and Bannerman walk along the corridor to the interview room, Woodend keeps repeating the same phrase over and over to himself.

'You're a professional, Charlie, you can do this . . . you're a professional, Charlie, you can do this . . . you're a professional, Charlie . . .'

Because however much he despises Fred Howerd – however he might want to crush the man's skull to powder – he knows that he is a detective chief inspector, and that he has a job to do.

The two detectives enter the interview room, and sit themselves down opposite their suspect.

Fred Howerd is looking very nervous indeed – like a frightened rat trapped in a corner.

'It's time to come clean, Fred,' Woodend says, and is pleased to note that he almost *sounds sympathetic.*

'I . . . I don't know what you're talkin' about,' Howerd replies.
There is a quiver in his voice, but that's only to be expected.
'Tell us about Lilly,' Woodend suggests.
'Who?'
'Come on, lad, don't give me that. You know perfectly well
that it's Lilly Dawson I'm talkin' about. Lilly Dawson! The girl
whose face has never been off the front pages of the newspapers
for the last week.'
'Oh, her,' Howerd says weakly. 'I thought you were talkin'
about some girl I actually knew.'
'Are you sayin' that you didn't know Lilly?'
'That's right.'
'But you both worked on the market.'
'It's a big place, the market.'
'So you really don't know her?'
'That's what I said.'
'You've never even seen her?'
'Not that I can remember.'
'Then tell us about your pigeons, instead, Fred,' Woodend
suggests.
'What about them?'
'You spend a lot of time with them, don't you?'
'I have to. They're champion birds, you know. They need a
lot of looking after.'
'Did Lilly like pigeons?'
'How would I know? I told you, I've never even met the
girl.'
'Because, you see, she liked all kinds of dumb creatures –
rabbits and hamsters, guinea pigs and—'
'I don't see what this has to do with me.'
'I haven't finished talking yet,' Woodend says firmly.
Howerd looks down at the table. 'Sorry.'
'And hamsters and cats and dogs. She liked them, too,'
Woodend continues. He pauses for a second. 'So it wouldn't be
at all surprisin' if she also liked pigeons, now would it?'
'I suppose not,' Howerd admits.
'In fact, I think she'd positively jump at the chance of seein'
some pigeons close to. Don't you think I'm right?'
'Maybe.'
'We found a pigeon feather in Lilly's clothes,' Woodend says.
'And another one in the potting shed where we discovered her
body.'

'So what?' Fred counters. 'Have you ever been down to the Boulevard? There's hundreds of the buggers there. Queen Victoria's statue is covered in pigeon shit.'

Woodend leans forward, so that his face was almost touching Fred Howerd's.

'Covered in pigeon shit?' he repeats, with a new menace in his voice. 'That's swearin', Fred. I don't like people swearin' at me – especially when they happen to be toe-rags like you.'

'Sorry,' Fred Howerd mumbles.

'Sorry what?' Woodend demands.

'Sorry, sir,' Howerd says, looking down at the table again.

'There's nothin' wrong with that, is there?' Woodend asked. 'Yes, I shifted ground occasionally, to keep him on his toes, an', yes, I slapped him down once or twice. But it was all well within the guidelines – all standard procedure.'

Paniatowski looked distinctly uncomfortable.

'Am I right about that, or not?' Woodend asked.

'You're right,' Paniatowski admitted.

'Well, there you are then.'

'But . . .'

'But what?'

'I must have sat there and listened to you interviewing dozens of suspects over the years—'

'Scores of suspects,' Woodend interrupted.

'. . . and none of those interviews sounded even vaguely like the one you've just described.'

'Well, of course they didn't. By the time you started working with me, I'd developed my own style. But you have to remember, back then I was just startin' out, an' feelin' my way as I went.'

'I know, Charlie,' Paniatowski said. 'That's exactly the point *I* was trying to make earlier.'

'What do you think, Paco?' Woodend asked, appealing to his old friend.

'If what you have given us is an accurate description of what actually occurred, Charlie . . .' Ruiz began cautiously.

'It is accurate! It's bloody spot on!'

'. . . then I would have to say that, from what we've heard so far, I can detect nothing that would have made Howerd afraid to produce his alibi.'

Well, that wasn't exactly a *ringing* endorsement, was it, Woodend thought gloomily.

'Carry on, Charlie,' Paniatowski said.

'The thing is, any fool can tell the difference between a common pigeon's feather and one that comes from a Sheffield tippler,' Woodend continues. 'But we can do even better than that. The boffins who work for us in the police laboratory have got this new technique called the Feather Identification Process. It can not only tell us what kind of pigeon the feather came from, it can pinpoint the exact pigeon. Did you know that?'

'I don't see what that's got to do with—'

'Did you know *that?'*

'No, I . . .'

Of course he doesn't know it, because no such technique exists – but Howerd doesn't know *that, either.*

'But we don't even need to use the FIP,' Woodend says, 'because we've got a witness.'

'A witness?' Howerd repeats.

'That's right. A witness who says he saw you take Lilly Dawson to your pigeon loft!'

'I never . . .' Howerd protests.

He is lying. It's obvious he's lying. But Woodend is lying too, because though the witness – 'Tinker' Bell – is sure it was a girl that Howerd took to his loft, he cannot definitely say that it was Lilly Dawson.

'And to top it all – to put the icin' on the bloody cake, as it were – we've got the pencil,' Woodend says.

'What pencil?'

'A Lakeland coloured pencil. A red one, as a matter of fact. It has bite marks on it which we can prove came from Lilly's teeth, and we found it right there in your pigeon loft.'

'No!' Howerd gasps.

'Yes,' Woodend says firmly. 'Lilly liked to draw things. She must have wanted to draw your pigeons – with the red feathers – which is why she took her pencils out of her satchel and—'

'She never opened that satchel,' Howerd interrupts. 'I'll swear she didn't.' A look of horror crosses his face. 'I mean, she couldn't have opened it, because she was never there,' he adds, unconvincingly.

*   *   *

'So there you have it!' Woodend said. 'The questioning had hardly begun, and Howerd had already as good as admitted that he took Lilly Dawson to his loft the night before she was abducted.'

On the face of it, he sounded confident – almost *triumphant* – Paniatowski thought.

But she'd known him a long time – had *worked* with him a long time – and she could see below the surface.

Whatever he might say, he was worrying about the alibi Terry Clegg had provided.

And he had other concerns, too. He was starting to question why – at the time – he had been so confident that Howerd was the right man.

'*I was confident because I had an airtight case,*' he would be arguing to himself.

But somewhere, at the back of his mind, there must be a nagging doubt. He had *needed* a result from that investigation, because it was his first major case and because his home town seemed to demand one. And perhaps it was that – rather than the facts – which had fuelled his conviction.

'*You* see what I'm gettin' at, don't you, Paco?' Woodend asked Ruiz, pleadingly.

'It may have been established that Howerd did take Lilly to his pigeon loft the night before she disappeared . . .' Ruiz said sombrely.

'That's what I'm sayin'!'

'. . . but that is still no proof that he killed her, is it?'

'There's more,' Woodend said, with just a hint of desperation in his voice.

'Then let's hear it,' Paniatowski said.

FIFTEEN

Now that Howerd has all but admitted he took Lilly to the pigeon loft, he is probably expecting his interrogator to keep hammering away at that point. But Woodend doesn't do that. Instead, he moves on to the afternoon of the abduction.

'It's a lot harder to kidnap somebody than most people think,' *the chief inspector tells his suspect. 'An' it's especially difficult at busy times of day – say, for example, when the market has just closed and everybody's rushing home for their Saturday dinner.' He pauses for a moment, to give Howerd time to consider the implications of what he's just said. 'So how do you grab a kid off the street, against her will, without anybody noticing?' he continues.*

Howerd says nothing.

'I asked you a question!' Woodend barks.

'I don't know,' Howerd replies, in a cracked, croaking voice.

'The answer is – you can't. *The kid will scream and kick and bite, because she knows you're up to no good, and the last thing she wants is to get into your car.' He pauses again. 'Oh, I'm sorry, you don't have a car, do you? You run a stall on the market, so you have a van. And, at this very moment, the forensics team are scrupulously examining that van for traces of Lilly Dawson.'*

'They won't find any,' Howerd says – and, for once, he sounds sure of himself.

'Didn't it bother you that Howerd seemed so confident you would find no evidence that Lilly had been in the van?' Paniatowski asked.

'No,' Woodend said firmly.

'Not even for an instant?' Paniatowski persisted.

'I said no!' Woodend replied, with a trace of anger in his voice. 'Look,' he continued, in a more reasonable tone, 'we all know that civilians have no real idea of just how good the forensic boys can be, so what I told myself at the time was that what Howerd was displayin' was not *innocence* but *arrogance*. He'd probably done a thorough job of cleanin' out the van, an' so he thought he was safe.'

'And how did you square that idea with the fact that he'd been sloppy about concealing the other evidence?' Paniatowski asked.

'What other evidence?'

'The evidence you found in the pigeon loft – the lemonade bottle with Lilly's fingerprints on it. Why hadn't he got rid of *that*?'

'At that point, we didn't know that Lilly's fingerprints *were* on the lemonade bottle, because the lab hadn't finished checking it.' Woodend said. 'But you're right, Monika,' he conceded, 'it's certainly something I should have taken into consideration.'

'*Did* the lab find traces of Lilly's presence in the van?' Paco Ruiz asked.

'No,' Woodend admitted, 'they didn't.'

'I see,' Paco mused.

'So maybe Howerd was right about that, and I was wrong – maybe he *had* done a good enough job to remove all the evidence,' Woodend said heatedly. 'Then again, maybe he'd used some other vehicle for the abduction.'

Or maybe it *wasn't* Fred Howerd who abducted Lilly, they all thought – though nobody actually said it.

'So, we've established that if Lilly had put up a struggle, some-body would have noticed,' Woodend presses on, seemingly impervious to Howerd's confidence about his van. 'That means she didn't *struggle, doesn't it? And why was that? It was because she wasn't being picked up by a complete stranger at all, but by someone who she regarded as a friend.' He counts slowly up to five. 'You* were *one of her friends, weren't you, Fred?'*

Howerd licks his lips. 'I wouldn't exactly say that.'

'Then what would *you say?'*

'I . . . I felt sorry for the kid.'

'Of course you did,' Woodend says, hating himself for sounding so sympathetic.

'I mean, I've got a daughter of my own,' Howerd amplifies, encouraged by this new tone.

'She's called Elizabeth, isn't she?' Woodend asks.

'That's right.'

'An' she's older than Lilly.'

'Not much. A few years.'

'A few years,' Woodend repeats. 'So that would make her seventeen or eighteen. Now *I understand!'*

'Understand what?'

'I've got a young daughter of my own. I worship her – an' I think she worships me. When she cuts her knee, it's me she comes to for comfort. When the boys bully her at school, I'm the one who she wants to tell her everything will turn out all right in the end. And sometimes, when I think about the future – her all grown up an' independent, an' not really needin' me very more – I feel sad. An' it'll be even worse when she finally gets married – when another man becomes the centre of her life.' Another pause. 'Your daughter Elizabeth got married recently, didn't she?'

'Yes.'

'*So you've lost her for ever, but you're still not ready to give up the role of the all-comfortin', all-knowin' dad. And that leaves an achin' void deep inside you. Am I right?*'

'*Something like that,*' Howerd mumbles.

'*And then, one day on the market, you notice Lilly, and you can immediately sense how miserable she feels about not having a dad of her own.*'

'*Yes, that's it! That's just how it happened!*' Howerd says, grasping at this wisp of understanding like a drowning man might grasp at a straw.

'*You* did *take her to see your pigeons, didn't you?*' Woodend says, and though it is phrased as a question, there is no longer anything questioning about it.

'*She said she'd like to see them,*' Howerd explains. '*She said she really loved birds.*'

'*So, just to get things perfectly clear in my mind, am I right in assumin' that not only did you take her to the loft, but you actually took her on the Friday night before she went missing?*'

'*That's right.*'

'*By why did you go after dark?*' Woodend asks, the sympathetic listener he has become disappearing and the inquisitor temporarily taking his place.

'*Pardon?*'

'*If you wanted to show her your pigeons, wouldn't it have been better to do it in the daylight?*'

'*I . . . er . . . I was busy at the market earlier. And I've got a storm lamp in the loft.*'

'*Ah, that explains it,*' Woodend says. '*An' was it on that Friday night that you first touched her?*'

'*I never touched her!*'

'*Not at all?*'

'*No.*'

'*It must be quite cramped in the pigeon loft. Surely you brushed against her once or twice – purely accidentally, of course.*'

'*I might have done.*'

'*And maybe you patted her on the shoulder.*'

'*I . . . err . . .*'

'*Did you or didn't you?*'

'*Yes.*'

'*And gave her a hug?*'

'*Only like one I might have given to my own daughter, when she was much smaller.*'

'And then, on Saturday afternoon, you went out with her again, only this time you didn't take her to the pigeon loft, you took her to the allotment.'

Fred Howerd begins to scratch, almost desperately, at his lower right arm. 'No, I . . .' he croaks.

'Is there something bothering you about that arm?' asks Bannerman, speaking for the first time.

'No.'

'Well, it certainly seems *to be bothering you.'*

'It's just an itch. That's all.'

'Are you sure?'

'Just an itch,' Howerd repeats hauntedly, as if he is beginning to feel the trap start to close its jaws on him.

'I know a bit about first aid, so why don't you let me take a look at that arm of yours?' Bannerman suggests.

'I don't want—'

'I said, let me take a look at it!'

Reluctantly, Fred Howerd rolls back his sleeve to reveal a large sticking plaster.

'So it's not just an itch, after all,' Bannerman says.

'No.'

'Then what is *it?'*

'I . . . cut myself.'

'Where?'

'On the side of the stall. There's a lot of rough edges. It's easy to do, if you're not careful.'

'You should always be careful, Fred,' Bannerman advises.

'I will be in future,' Howerd says, and there is an element of relief in his voice which suggests he thinks the crisis is past.

But it isn't!

'Shall we take a look at the wound, then?' Bannerman suggests.

'There's no need,' Howerd tells him.

'I think there is,' Bannerman counters, and before Howerd has time to realize what is happening, the sergeant has reached across the table and ripped the plaster off.

Howerd howls and clutches the arm to his chest.

'He should never have done that,' Paniatowski said.

'Probably not,' Woodend agreed. 'But you had to be there, Monika. I think, by that point, Bannerman was gettin' such a buzz from the way the interrogation was goin' that he didn't even think about would he should or shouldn't do – he just acted on instinct.'

'That doesn't make it right,' Paniatowski said firmly.

'What do you think, Paco?' Woodend asked.

Ruiz shrugged awkwardly. 'I saw much worse in my time with the police.'

'Maybe you did, but that was in Spain before the Civil War, and this was in England in the 1950s – and Bannerman *shouldn't have done it*,' Paniatowski said.

'Don't be such a baby! Put your arm back on the table, so we can look at the injury,' Bannerman orders Howerd.

'I don't want—'

'Now!'

Howerd lays his arm on the table.

The wound, which has almost healed, is perhaps three inches long and an inch and a half wide. And it is not so much a scrape or a cut – it is a gouge.

'It looks self-inflicted to me,' Woodend says.

'I told you, it was an accident,' Howerd protests.

'You say you cut yourself on the stall?'

'Yes.'

'Then the boffins from the forensic department should be able to find traces of blood on the stall, shouldn't they?'

'I don't know.'

'We found bits of human skin under Lilly Dawson's nails,' Woodend says. 'How do you think they got there?'

'I don't know.'

'What a lot of things you seem not to know,' Woodend ponders. 'You don't know how Lilly was snatched from the street without anybody noticin'. You don't know whether forensics will find blood on your stall. There are so *many* things *you don't know that it would take me all day to list them.' He slams his hand down hard on the table. 'You're either very stupid or just pretending to be very stupid. It's obvious to us that there's skin under her nails because Lilly scratched her attacker. So what is the attacker to do? And don't you dare say you "don't know", you bastard!'*

'I don't . . .' Howerd mumbles, before falling silent again.

'He has two choices,' Woodend says. 'He can leave the scratch marks to heal naturally, hopin' that nobody will notice until they do. Or he can disguise them by cutting them away – which is what you did.'

*   *   *

'There comes a moment in any interrogation when you can sense it's all over, bar the shoutin',' Woodend said. 'Do you know what I mean?'

Paniatowski and Ruiz nodded. On this point, at least, they could agree with him – because they knew *exactly* what he meant.

'The suspect may keep on protestin' his innocence for hours after that – perhaps even for days – but he knows, just as clearly as you do, that the game's up. An' in that particular interrogation, the moment came when I accused Howerd of cuttin' away the scratch marks. I could *see* him collapse. I could *see* him give up all hope. An' though I didn't expect a confession right away, I was convinced we'd get one in the end.'

Bannerman looks up at the big clock on the wall.

'Do you know, I'm really feeling quite hungry, sir,' he says to Woodend. He turns to the suspect. 'Are you feeling hungry yourself, Fred?'

'A bit,' Howerd lies.

'Well then, let's get this wrapped up, so we can all have something to eat, shall we?' Bannerman suggests. 'Mind you,' he continues, almost as an afterthought, 'after I've told you what's going to happen to you, I rather think you'll lose your appetite.'

'Happen to me?' Howerd repeats.

'The government claims that hanging's a painless process, you know, but they have to say that, don't they? And do you know why *they have to say it? It's because if the ordinary decent people on the street knew what it was* actually *like, they'd demand it was stopped immediately,' Bannerman says.*

'I don't want to hear this,' Howerd tells him, clamping his hands firmly over his ears.

'Your neck's broken in the first second after the drop,' Bannerman says – shouting, but, at the same time, managing to sound almost clinical. 'That's when your bowels open and you shit yourself.'

'Please . . .' Howerd begs.

'But it's at least half an hour before all signs of life are extinct,' Bannerman continues. 'Sometimes it's much longer than that. I've looked at those hanging men myself, and I'll swear to you that though they couldn't move or say a word, they were suffering.'

Howerd starts to cry.

'And it seems so unfair that you *should hang, because I know*

you didn't mean to do it,' the sergeant says, dropping his voice again, so that now it is almost gently hypnotic.

Howerd lowers his hands from his ears.

'What did you say?' he asks fearfully.

'I know you didn't mean to do it,' Bannerman repeats.

'You let Bannerman seize control of the interrogation,' Paniatowski said.

'I wouldn't exactly say that,' Woodend replied. 'He'd hit on a good line, and I decided to let him run with it. I've done the same with you, any number of times.'

'Yes, but I'm not Bannerman,' Paniatowski said, unyieldingly.

'All you wanted to do, Fred, was to give her a bit of the loving she was missing,' Bannerman says. 'She probably encouraged you – maybe even led you on. And then, at some point, she changed her mind – which is just what women do. She decided that she'd been raped – though both of you knew that wasn't true. You thought about going to prison and losing the family – and all because you'd tried to help the girl, to give her a little comfort. You panicked, which is perfectly understandable in the circumstances. Before you even knew what was happening, your hands were round her throat. All you wanted to do was shut her up. It never occurred to you that you might be strangling her. And then, suddenly, she was dead – and you'd certainly never meant that to happen for a minute.' Bannerman pauses again. 'Well, you can't hang a man for that, can you? It simply wouldn't be right.'

'I'd still go to prison, wouldn't I?' Howard asks.

'Oh yes, you'd still go to prison,' Bannerman agrees. 'And I won't lie to you, Fred, you'd get quite a stiff sentence. But that's still much better than the rope, isn't it? With a bit of luck, you'd be out in time to play with your grandchildren – and that's got to be worth something, don't you think?'

'That's it!' Paniatowski exclaimed.

'That's what?' Woodend asked.

'That's what we've been looking for! Up to that point, you see, Howerd had been holding back his alibi – but he'd always been *ready* to produce it, if that should prove necessary.'

'So what changed?' Paco Ruiz asked.

'What changed is that Bannerman painted him a picture of what death by hanging was like.'

'I'm not following you,' Woodend said.

'The reason he didn't want to say where he'd been that Saturday afternoon was that he knew it would show him in a very bad light. Remember, it was *Howerd* who took *Clegg* to see the young prostitute in Bolton, not the other way round.'

'So what?'

'So it probably wasn't the first time he'd used her services – or those of some other girl who was quite like her. And once he'd produced his alibi, that would all come out into the open.'

'Maybe that's true,' Woodend agreed, 'but it would have got him off the murder charge.'

'That's how *you* see things,' Paniatowski said.

'That's how *anybody* would see things,' Woodend countered.

'No, it isn't,' Paniatowski argued. 'Put yourself in Howerd's shoes for a minute. He's convinced that you and Bannerman have him marked down for the murder, and that whatever he says is going to make no difference. So why should he give you more ammunition – why should he reveal to you what a nasty little pervert he really was?'

'Because it would get him off,' Woodend said stubbornly.

'But he doesn't *believe* that. He thinks that you'll find some way to discredit the alibi, but still have all the damning information you've collected *as a result of the alibi* at your fingertips.'

'You can't possibly know what he was thinkin',' Woodend said.

'He's convinced he's going to be convicted, whatever happens,' Paniatowski pressed on. 'So he's faced with two choices, isn't he? He can continue to deny he killed Lilly – in which case he'll probably be hanged. Or he can make a false confession, which will mean, according to Bannerman, that he could be released in time to play with his grandchildren. Which of those two alternatives would you choose?'

'*He told me it wasn't as simple as that,*' Elizabeth Eccles had claimed. '*He said that after what the policeman had told him, he didn't dare produce his alibi.*'

'I don't buy it,' Woodend said.

'You mean that you don't *want* to buy it!' Paniatowski countered. 'Look at the facts, Charlie. There was no evidence that Lilly had ever been in his van, Terry Clegg has given him an alibi that no man in his right mind would ever have made up, and – most important of all – with his dying breath, and in the presence of a priest, he swore that hadn't killed Lilly.'

Woodend stood up and walked over to the edge of the terrace. He stood staring at the sea for perhaps five minutes, and when he turned round again, he seemed to have aged ten years.

'Oh, my God,' he moaned, 'we really *did* get the wrong man!'

SIXTEEN

Anyone watching the woman, who was slowly labouring up the steep street with a heavy shopping bag in each hand, could not have been blamed for assuming that she was at least seventy. In fact, she was much younger than that, and if her back was bowed, it was due more to the burden she had had to carry for much of her life than it was to the inevitable ageing process.

The woman laid her bags on the ground, and rested for a moment. She should shop more often, she told herself. But the truth was that she didn't want to shop *at all* – didn't want to leave the house *at all* – because every time she saw the look of pity in the eyes of those who knew her history, it was like going through the whole terrible ordeal again.

As she approached her own house, she noticed that a man was standing patiently outside her front door.

Perhaps it was a reporter. But surely, after all this time, the journalists had bled everything from her daughter's tragedy that they possibly could. Besides, he didn't *look* like a reporter. He wasn't dressed in a smart suit, but instead was wearing a shabby jacket and grey flannel trousers.

All these thoughts passed through her mind, as thoughts will do, but none of them really interested her. Nothing that she saw or heard had *really* interested her for almost a quarter of a century.

'Can I help you?' she asked, when she had finally drawn level with the waiting man.

'Mrs Dawson?' the man asked.

'Yes.'

'I didn't know it was you. If I had, I wouldn't have just stood there and watched you struggle, I'd have come down the hill and helped you. I really am *so* sorry.'

'Who are you?' she asked.

The man smiled. 'Didn't I say?' He reached into his pocket

and produced his leather-bound warrant card. 'Detective Chief Inspector Hall. I've come all the way from Scotland Yard to see you.'

'Scotland Yard,' Mrs Dawson repeated. 'I haven't spoken to anyone from Scotland Yard since . . . since . . .'

'I know – since poor little Lilly died,' Hall said sympathetically. 'Look, why don't you hand me your bags while you look for your key, and then we'll go inside, shall we?'

Once they were both in Elsie Dawson's kitchen, Hall insisted that the woman should sit down.

'You need a bit of a rest after all your efforts,' he said cheerily.

'But the shopping needs putting away and . . .' Mrs Dawson began.

'That can wait for a few minutes,' Hall assured her. He paused for a moment. 'Tell me, Mrs Dawson, just how long is it since Lilly was murdered?'

'Twenty-two years.'

'That's a long time ago.'

'Is it?' Mrs Dawson asked, as a tear leaked from the corner of her eye. 'It doesn't seem like a long time ago to me. It seems like it was just yesterday.'

'Of course it does,' Hall agreed readily. 'In some ways, time stopped still for you when Lilly was killed, didn't it?'

'It did,' Mrs Dawson said, suppressing a sob. 'It really did.'

'And here I am, upsetting you all over again,' Hall said, with what sounded like genuine regret. He reached forward and laid his hand gently on the woman's shoulder. 'You know what you need now, Mrs Dawson? You need a nice hot cup of tea. Wouldn't that be nice?'

'I don't know,' Elsie Dawson said weakly. 'I'm not sure I want to . . .'

'Well, I can see the kettle, and I can see the pot,' Hall told her. 'All I need now is the tea caddie. Where do you keep it?'

'What's this all about?' Mrs Dawson wondered.

'Is it in the cupboard over the sink?'

'Yes, but . . .'

Hall took the caddie out of the cupboard, opened it, scooped out three spoonfuls of tea and deposited them in the earthenware pot.

'One for me, one for you and one for the pot, as my old mum

used to say,' he told the woman, as he worked. 'You wanted to know what this was all about, didn't you?'

'Yes, I . . .'

'Well, to be honest with you, I'm here on a very painful mission.' Hall filled the kettle and switched it on. 'You'll be aware, won't you, that the man who went to prison for killing your little girl has recently died?'

'Yes – and I hope he's burning in hell for all eternity,' Mrs Dawson said passionately.

'After what he did, I'm more than certain in my own mind that he'll be doing just that,' Hall said. 'But did you know there are some people around here who are starting to say he didn't do it after all?'

'How *can* they say that?' Mrs Dawson gasped. 'He confessed!'

'So he did,' Hall agreed. 'He killed Lilly – your poor, sweet, helpless little Lilly – and he *confessed* to having killed her. That's why, before these vicious rumours have time to spread any further, we want to nip them in the bud. And that – in a nutshell – is why I'm here now.'

'I don't understand,' Mrs Dawson said.

She felt hot, as if she had caught a fever. And then, suddenly, she was she was so cold that she was shivering.

She was confused. She was upset. She was sure the policeman from London meant well, and didn't realize how much distress he was causing her, but it was awfully hard to bear and she was not sure how much more she could take.

Steam appeared in the spout of the kettle.

'Goodness, didn't that water boil quickly?' Hall said. He laughed. 'You must have better electricity up here than we have in the south.'

He poured the boiling water on the tea leaves, replaced the lid on the pot, and sat down opposite Mrs Dawson.

'We'll just give it time to brew,' he said. 'What I'm doing, you see, is re-investigating the case, just to make sure the evidence is as watertight as we think it is – which, of course, we both know it will be. So would you mind if I asked you a few questions?'

'It couldn't do any harm, I suppose,' Mrs Dawson said uncertainly. 'What happened was that Lilly went to the market that morning . . .'

'Oh, I don't want to distress you by making you go over all that again.' Hall stood up. 'The tea should be just about ready by now.' He laid out two cups, poured the tea and added milk. 'Sugar?' he asked.

'No, thank you.'

Hall grinned. 'Me neither. My wife says I'm fat enough as it is.' He sat down again, and took a sip of his tea. 'Delicious,' he pronounced. 'What brand is it? PG Tips?'

'Yes.'

'Thought so. I don't have many talents, Mrs Dawson, but I do pride myself on being able to tell one make of tea from another.' Hall took another sip. 'As I said, I don't want to drag you through all the painful details again. What I'm really interested in is the visit that the Scotland Yard men made to you back then. There were two of them, weren't there?'

'That's right,' Mrs Dawson agreed. 'One was Chief Inspector Woodend. I thought he was a nice man. I used to see him around town, after he moved back here, but somehow I could never bring myself to go up and speak to him.'

'Too painful for you, I expect,' Hall suggested.

'Yes, that must have been it,' Mrs Dawson agreed. 'The other man was Mr Woodend's sergeant. He *wasn't* so nice.'

Hall grimaced. 'Sergeant Bannerman. And you're quite right, he's not nice at all,' he said. 'Now, what I wanted to ask you, Mrs Dawson, is did they ask to see Lilly's things?'

'Yes, they did.'

'And I'll bet it was that nice Mr Woodend who actually went to look at Lilly's room, wasn't it?'

'It was.'

Hall grinned. 'Thought so. Bannerman was never much of one for the personal touch. So, tell me, Mrs Dawson, did Mr Woodend bring anything down from Lilly's room with him?'

'Yes, he brought a couple of her drawings. They always made me so sad, those drawings.'

'And did he take them away with him?'

'No, he apologized for bringin' them downstairs at all – said he couldn't think how it had happened. And then he went up to Lilly's room and put them back where he found them.'

'So he didn't take the drawings away with him,' Hall mused. 'Did he take anything else?'

'I don't think so,' Mrs Dawson said, uncertainly.

'You don't *think* so – but you're not entirely sure, are you?'

'No,' Mrs Dawson admitted. 'I'm not entirely sure. Is it important?'

'Not really,' Hall said. He paused again. 'What I'd like do now, Mrs Dawson, is ask you about some of the things that you bought for Lilly.'

What's the etiquette for greeting a friend who also happens to be your boss? Colin Beresford wondered, as he stood in the arrivals' lounge of Manchester's Ringway Airport, waiting for Paniatowski to clear customs and passport control.

Should he kiss her on the cheek? Should he kiss her on the lips? Should he offer to shake her hand? Or should he do nothing at all?

The moment he caught sight of her walking towards him, he knew that the best course would be to do nothing at all, because – clearly – the trip to Spain had not gone well.

'That's the trouble with booking your flights at the last minute – you don't get to choose where you sit,' Paniatowski complained when she drew level with him. 'I had to spend the whole of the return flight in the bloody non-smoking section.'

'Why don't you tell me about it?' Beresford suggested, sympathetically.

'I've already told you – I was nearly three hours without a cigarette!'

'I don't mean that,' Beresford said.

'I know you don't,' Paniatowski agreed.

By the time they reached Beresford's car, she had outlined the whole of the conversation which had taken place on Woodend's sunny terrace.

'I was looking forward to my first visit to Spain,' she said. 'I was going to take Louisa with me. She really loves her Uncle Charlie and Auntie Joan.'

'Yes, I know she does,' Beresford said.

'And now the whole thing's been spoiled for me – I can never go there again without remembering *this* visit.'

'How's Mr Woodend taking it?' Beresford asked, as they both climbed into the car.

'He's devastated at the thought of having sent an innocent man to jail. If it was anybody else, I'd say he'd get over it in time – but you know Charlie.'

Beresford fired up the engine, and pulled away.

'How much damage is the whole business likely to cause?' he asked.

'Scotland Yard and the Mid Lancs Constabulary will have to

pay out a fairly hefty sum in compensation to Howerd's daughter between them, so I imagine Charlie won't be exactly popular with the top brass in either of those places,' Paniatowski said. 'But as far as the rest of the Force is concerned – well, mistakes are made, even by the most diligent and scrupulous of police officers, and there's not a bobby who's ever pounded a beat who doesn't know that.'

'None of Mr Woodend's old colleagues will want to cast the first stone at him – if only for fear that the next one might well be aimed in their direction,' Beresford said. 'What about the news-papers?'

'They might kick up a stink for a couple of days, but it will soon die down, and nobody who's ever known Charlie Woodend personally will pay much attention to them, anyway.'

They were clear of the airport now. In less than an hour, they would be back in Whitebridge, Paniatowski thought, and as soon as she got there, she would ask to see the chief constable and report to him on what she and Hall had discovered.

And what would happen then?

Baxter would begin the process which would probably eventually lead to Fred Howerd's exoneration and pardon. Lilly Dawson's murder would be filed away on the cold case shelf. DCI Hall could go back to London, and she herself could return to active duty. And Charlie Woodend could sit under a blue Mediterranean sky and work on forgiving himself.

It was not the ideal end to an investigation, she told herself – so few things in life ever ended ideally – but, given the circum-stances, it was about as good as it could be.

She would not have taken such a philosophical view if she had known about the time bomb which, even then, was slowly ticking away back in Whitebridge. But she *didn't* know about it. Nobody did – for the moment – except DCI Tom Hall.

SEVENTEEN

The man sitting across the chief constable's desk from George Baxter was in his fifties, and had a naturally florid face which turned even redder when he was angry – as he was now.

'Don't *you* think that what happened to my poor brother was terrible?' the man demanded.

'The case is still being investigated, and I wouldn't wish to prejudge it by making any comments at this time,' Baxter said carefully.

'For God's sake, Fred protested his innocence – in what was almost his dying breath – to a priest,' Robert Howerd said.

'And, given those circumstances, what he said must be taken very seriously indeed,' Baxter agreed, 'but it's still not evidence.'

'My family has been going through hell for the past twenty-two years,' Howerd said. 'And it's *continuing* to go through hell – in fact, it feels worse than ever – because even though you have Father O'Brien's statement, your incompetent, corrupt police force is *still* dragging its heels.'

'Incompetent?' Baxter said, gripping the corner of his desk tightly. 'Corrupt? *My* police force?'

'That's what I said, and I stick by it,' Howerd told him.

'Oh, do you?' Baxter asked, as he felt an anger at least as strong as Howerd's begin to bubble to the surface. 'I wouldn't go making that kind of accusation if I was you. And I certainly wouldn't use my family's distress as an argument for wanting to see things done.'

'And why not?'

'Because, as I understand it, you'd already pretty much cut Fred adrift at the time of his arrest.'

'That's not true!' Robert Howerd protested.

'Oh, come on! Have you forgotten what it was like? There was you and your father, wandering around your big impressive shop on the High Street – fingering your watch chains and looking important – and what was Fred doing? Fred was slaving away at a tatty little stall in the covered market!'

Robert Howerd swallowed. 'My father did that to teach him a lesson,' he said. 'Fred had been rather wild in his youth, and Father felt that by denying him some of the privileges which went with our position, it might lead him to see the error of his ways. But it was always his intention to welcome Fred back into the bosom of the family. He had always planned to make Fred joint managing director when he himself retired. And that's just what *would have* happened, if your bungling policemen hadn't arrested him – on practically no evidence at all.'

'What a cosy family picture it is that you're painting for me,' Baxter said sceptically. 'And, do you know, it might even be a

convincing one – if I wasn't aware of the *complete* picture, with
all its blemishes.'

'Blemishes?'

'You didn't make much of a song and dance about Fred being
innocent when he was first arrested for the murder, did you?
And why didn't you? Because – along with the rest of
Whitebridge – you firmly believed that he'd done it – that he'd
raped and killed that little girl. Am I wrong?'

'We . . . we made a mistake,' Robert Howerd admitted.

'And there was another way in which you and your father
were like the rest of Whitebridge, too – you didn't want to have
anything at all to do with his immediate family!'

'You're quite wrong about that. We paid his wife's and
daughter's expenses from the moment he went to prison –
and we're still paying Elizabeth's to this day.'

'That's only *money*!' Baxter said, contemptuously.

'I beg your pardon!'

'It's easy to be free with your money – especially when you've
got plenty of it. But did you make any *real* effort with his family?
Did you show them any of the warmth or compassion they must
so desperately have needed? Did you, for example, invite them
round on Christmas Day?'

'No, we didn't actually . . .'

'And what about the way that you treated your brother himself?
Did you ever visit him while he was in prison? Did you even
bother to call on him when he was dying?'

'Well, no,' Howerd admitted, awkwardly.

'Because you still thought he was a murderer. But now, when
it turns out there's a chance he *didn't* kill Lilly, you're starting
to feel guilty about the way you've behaved towards him and
his family,' Baxter pressed on. 'And instead of taking responsibility for that guilt yourself – as a real man would, as a *Christian*
would – you're trying to pass it on to someone else. You want
me to crucify each and every officer involved in the case – and
you want me to do it even before my investigation is completed.
Well, let me tell you here and now, Mr Howerd, I simply won't
do it.'

'I think you're being highly impertinent!' Howerd blustered.

'I'm afraid you're wrong about that, sir,' Baxter said. 'An
ordinary constable may perhaps be impertinent, but I'm the *chief*
constable, and I'm just being as bloody rude to you as you've
been to me.'

'I . . . I . . .' Howerd choked.

'If there is a case to answer, then it will be answered,' Baxter promised. 'If I find that your brother is entitled to a posthumous pardon, then I will work unceasingly to see he gets one. But what I will *not* do is just sit here while you tell me how to run my police force.' Baxter looked down at his watch. 'I think we've said all there is to say to each other, so I'll wish you good day,' he continued.

Robert Howerd stood up, and stormed over to the door. Only when he was already in the corridor did he turn round and say, 'Let me assure you, you've not heard the last of this.'

No, he probably hadn't, Baxter thought – because when a man wouldn't face his own guilt, there was no telling *what* he might do next.

Howerd disappeared from the doorway, and the space was immediately filled by Lucy, the chief constable's secretary.

'Now *that* certainly didn't sound like one of your more successful meetings, sir,' she said.

'One of these fine days, they'll finally give me a secretary who knows how to mind her own business,' Baxter said. He grinned. 'Are you *just* here to gloat, Lucy, or was there something you actually wanted?'

Lucy smiled back at him. 'I've got Chief Inspector Hall in my office, sir. He says he knows he hasn't booked an appointment, but if you could just spare him a few minutes, there's something rather urgent he needs to discuss with you.'

'Is Chief Inspector Paniatowski with him?' Baxter asked.

'No, sir, she isn't.'

'Now that is strange,' Baxter said, almost to himself. 'They're supposed to working together – and if it *is* really important, then I'm surprised Monika hasn't come too.'

'Do you want me to send him away with a flea in his ear, sir?' Lucy asked innocently.

Baxter sighed. 'No, now that he's here, I suppose I'd better see him,' he said.

It was not the first time that Paniatowski had had to face an angry George Baxter. During their stormy on–off relationship, he had frequently lost his temper over her unwillingness – or inability – either to commit fully or to put an end to it altogether. And since then – since she had been a DCI and he had been her boss – there had been arguments over the way she conducted her investigations.

So Baxter's anger was not new to her – but she didn't think she had ever seen him quite so angry before.

'I've been trying to get in touch with you for over two hours – but nobody knew where you were!' Baxter said. 'In fact, Chief Inspector, nobody had seen you for *two days*! Now why was that?'

'I've been to Spain,' Paniatowski said.

And from the look on his face, she could see that not only had he already guessed that, but that the visit was the source of his anger.

'Been to Spain,' Baxter repeated. 'Without my permission!'

'I was following up on a lead in the *unofficial* investigation which you'd kindly foisted on me, and I wasn't aware I needed your permission to do that,' Paniatowski countered.

'Following up on a lead?' Baxter repeated incredulously. 'What you mean is that you've been to see your old mate Charlie Woodend.'

'That's correct, sir,' Paniatowski agreed. 'My old mate Charlie Woodend *was* the lead.'

Baxter shook his head slowly from side to side, and she could see the anger draining away from him and being replaced by something much closer to worry.

'If you won't work *with* me, Monika, then I can't protect you,' he said.

And, as so often happened, she was unsure whether he was now the chief constable (talking to one of his senior officers), or gingery George Baxter (in whose muscular arms she'd once lain).

'Why should I need protecting?' she asked.

'Because, while you've been away, the course of the investigation has taken a turn for the worse,' Baxter said gravely.

How *could it* have taken a turn for the worse? Paniatowski wondered.

What could possibly be worse for the investigation than the discovery that Charlie had probably sent the wrong man to prison for twenty-two years?

'Go on,' she said.

'While you were away on your little Spanish jaunt, DCI Hall went to see Elsie Dawson – Lilly's mother.'

'Why?'

'Why do you think? To see if he could throw any new light on the case.'

Paniatowski felt her stomach somersault. 'And did he?'

'Yes, I'm afraid he did.'

'*Afraid* he did?'

'In Charlie Woodend's report on the case, it is clearly stated that he found one of Lilly Dawson's coloured pencils in Fred Howerd's pigeon loft. You remember reading that, don't you?'

'Yes.'

'The assumption at the time was that Lilly had dropped it there herself, on the Friday night before she disappeared.'

'And it's a perfectly sound assumption. She was only there once, so that *must have been* when she dropped it.'

'Did *you* own a set of Lakeland coloured pencils when you were a child, Monika?' Baxter asked.

'Yes, I did.'

'And how did you feel about them?'

Paniatowski found her mind travelling back to a different time – a time when kids couldn't have all they wanted just when they wanted, when pennies had to be counted and gifts were treasured.

Her stepfather has made one of his unwelcome visits to her bed the night before, and perhaps her mother knows about it – or at least suspects – because, this morning, she hands her a totally unexpected gift.

Monika takes the small rectangular parcel, wrapped in reused wrapping paper, and feels her heart start to beat a little faster. She thinks she knows what is inside, but she tries not to hope too hard that she's right, in case those hopes are dashed.

She fingers the edges of the parcel. They are hard. It feels like tin! So maybe – just maybe – she has finally been given what she has admired in the stationer's window for what feels like a whole lifetime.

'Well, aren't you going to open it?' her mother asks – and there is a hint of sadness in her voice which suggests she does *know.*

Monika wants to rip the paper off, but that will mean it can never be used again, so instead she forces herself to carefully peel back the sticky tape.

When she removes the paper, she sees the lake on the front of the tin. It is a beautiful lake, with the bluest water surrounded by the greenest trees.

*She doesn't open the box immediately. For the moment, it is
enough to just absorb the picture. But eventually she does,
and inside are pencils which are every colour of the rainbow and
more.*

Sitting in Baxter's office, more than thirty years later, the memory
was enough to bring a smile to her face, despite the unease she
was still feeling.

'How did you feel about them?' the chief constable repeated.

'I thought they were most wonderful things that there'd ever
been,' she admitted.

'And did your mother ever let you take them out of the house?'
Baxter asked, deceptively innocently.

Paniatowski laughed. 'Of course not! They were far too valuable for that. I kept them in my bedroom and—'

Oh my God, she thought. Oh my God, oh my God, oh my
God . . .

'DCI Hall asked Mrs Dawson if Lilly was allowed to take
her pencils out of the house, and she said, no, she wasn't,' Baxter
told her. 'And you know what that means, don't you, Monika?'

She did!

She bloody did!

But she didn't want to admit it.

'Perhaps you'd better explain it to me, sir,' she said.

'If Lilly didn't leave the pencil in the pigeon loft, then someone
else did – someone who'd been into her bedroom and picked it
up. And that someone could only have been Charlie Woodend.'

'Or Bannerman!' Paniatowski said fiercely.

'Woodend left Bannerman downstairs while he went to search
Lilly's bedroom.'

'I don't believe it,' Paniatowski said flatly.

'You mean, you don't *want* to believe it,' Baxter countered.

'If what Mrs Dawson *now* says is true, why has she kept quiet
about it all this time?' Paniatowski asked. 'Why didn't she
mention the fact that the pencils were never allowed to leave
the room at the trial?'

'The question of the pencil never came up at the trial,' Baxter
said. 'There was no need to enter it into the evidence, because
Howerd had already confessed to the crime.'

'I need to talk to DCI Hall,' Paniatowski said frantically.
'Where is he?'

'Gone.'

'Gone?'

'He was here to establish whether or not Howerd was guilty as charged – and he considers that he's done that, so he's returning to London.'

Returning, Paniatowski thought. Not *has returned*, but *is returning*.

'Is he taking the two o'clock express train?' she asked.

'He didn't say, one way or the other, but that would certainly be the logical train for him to take.'

Paniatowski looked at her watch. It was twenty-five to two.

'I have to go,' she told the chief constable.

'This interview is not over, Chief Inspector,' Baxter said sternly. 'It will not *be* over until I decide it is.'

'I'm sorry, sir, but I have to go,' Paniatowski replied.

Then she turned and rushed out of the room.

EIGHTEEN

He was standing on the central platform, a cigarette in one hand and plastic coffee cup in the other. He did not look quite so chunky as the last time she had seen him, but that could have been accomplished – she now realized – by a simple change of posture. He had abandoned the scruffy sports jacket and flannel trousers, too, and was wearing a sharp blue suit.

He saw her approaching him, and smiled.

'I've not exactly been *expecting* to see you here, Monika,' he said, 'but I always knew you *would* turn up for a fond farewell if you possibly could.'

'How could you do it?' Paniatowski demanded angrily.

'It was easy,' Hall said complacently.

'That's not what I mean, and you know it,' Paniatowski told him. 'How could you treat a fellow officer like that?'

But Hall was not interested in discussing the ethics of policing, she thought, looking into his eyes. He had his script for this possible encounter well prepared, and he was determined to stick to it.

'The trick I pulled on you wasn't a very complicated one,' Hall said. 'All I did was talk to some old hands at the Yard who still remember Charlie Woodend – Bannerman amongst them – and then adopt a few of the characteristics of your old mentor. It was a weak disguise, at best, and I doubt it would have fooled most people. But it took you in, because you *wanted* to be taken in – because, in times of crisis, you really miss your Uncle Charlie.'

He was right on both counts, of course, Paniatowski told herself. It probably *wouldn't* have taken in most people – and she *did* miss Charlie.

'So, when it boils down to it, you were never anything more than one of Bannerman's arse-crawling lackeys?' she said.

'I'm nobody's lackey,' Hall replied, with a sudden edge to his voice.

He was angry that she wasn't sticking to the script that he'd envisaged, she thought – angry that, instead of basking in her grudging admiration, he was being showered with her contempt.

'So if you're not a lackey, just what *are* you?' she asked.

'I'm a man who played it straight for over thirty years, and never rose above the rank of chief inspector. I'm a good cop – a *very good* cop – who would like to retire soon, and would prefer to do it on a superintendent's pension.'

'And Bannerman can make that possible?' Paniatowski said.

'And Bannerman can make that possible,' Hall agreed.

'So it was *always* your intention to nobble Charlie Woodend, was it?' Paniatowski said.

'Of course it wasn't,' Hall replied, and now he was managing to sound a little hurt. 'Give me credit for a little human decency.'

'You'll have to earn it first,' Paniatowski told him. 'So if the plan wasn't to nobble Charlie, what was it?'

'The original plan was to prove Fred Howerd was guilty as charged,' Hall said. 'That would certainly have been the best solution all round. Or, failing that, I intended to bury any evidence which pointed in the other direction. Which is why, as you'll appreciate, I was rather knocked off balance by Mrs Eccles's revelation that her father actually had an alibi.'

'Yes, I can see that must have been something of an inconvenience for you,' Paniatowski said.

'I badly miscalculated the way I handled Terry Clegg,' Hall admitted, 'but, in my own defence, I have to say it would have been a tricky situation for *anybody* to handle.'

'When did you decide to pull that stunt on the top floor of the car park?'

'As we were leaving the market. It was obvious to me that Clegg would crack the second you started questioning him, and I couldn't have that, because I knew that once he had told you Howerd *did* have an alibi, you'd feel obliged to investigate it further.'

'So what was the point of threatening to throw him over the edge?'

'I didn't threaten to throw him off – not in so many words. I was very careful about that.'

Paniatowski sighed. 'All right – what was the point of *implying* you might throw him off the edge?'

'I thought it might scare him into demanding to see a lawyer. If he'd done that, everything would have worked out fine, because any lawyer worth his salt would have told our friend Clegg that as long as he kept his mouth shut, we wouldn't be able to touch him.'

'Wouldn't it have been much easier simply to *suggest* the idea of a lawyer to him?' Paniatowski asked.

'Much,' Hall replied. 'But you'd have overheard, and wondered why I was doing it. And at that stage of the game, the last thing I needed was for you to have doubts about me.'

'But now that doesn't matter,' Paniatowski said.

'But now it doesn't matter,' Hall agreed. 'Still, things did look distinctly sticky for a while, and I could see my superintendent's pension disappearing right down the plughole. The problem is, you see, that Bannerman's had something of a rocky ride recently, and he can't afford any more slip-ups.'

'And that's why it's just not enough for him to be seen as part of an investigation which made the perfectly understand-able mistake of getting the wrong man?'

'Exactly! What *he* wants – what he *needs* – is complete exoner-ation from any wrongdoing.'

'Which means there was no choice but to set up Charlie Woodend to take the fall?'

'I knew you'd get there in the end, Monika! Well done! He needed exoneration, and I've got it for him – because the only thing he looks guilty of now is naively trusting his superior.'

'How long have you known about the red pencil?'

'Oh, right from the start. It was the one thing that Bannerman was really worried about.' Hall clamped his hand over his mouth, and when he removed it again, he was grinning. 'Oh dear, I should never have said that,' he continued, in mock horror. 'Still, this is no more than a bit of idle banter between colleagues, so what's the harm in it?'

'Everything's a joke to you, isn't it?' Paniatowski demanded.

'That's right,' Hall agreed. 'And if you're intending to keep on wading through this lake of shit that we fondly call a career, you'd better start treating it as a joke, too.'

'Tell me about what happened to the pencil,' Paniatowski said.

'Can't do that, because I don't know myself, with any certainty,' Hall said, not even trying to sound convincing. 'But I can *hypothesize*, if you like.'

'Hypothesize then,' Paniatowski said, stony-faced.

'Picture the scene, if you will. A newly appointed chief inspector and a hungry detective sergeant visit the mother of a murder victim. The chief inspector – who fancies himself as a dab hand at solving crimes by simply soaking up the atmosphere – goes up to the murder victim's room. Once he's left, the sergeant says something which upsets the mother – he has a natural talent for that kind of thing – and the woman has to go outside for a breath of fresh air. Are you still with me?'

'I'm still with you,' Paniatowski said.

'The chief inspector, meanwhile, is looking around the girl's room, and he sees something there that upsets him so much that he has to rush to the toilet and spew up his ring.' Hall paused. 'Bannerman and I had a good laugh at that, back at the Yard.'

'You would.'

'Anyway, the sergeant, hearing the disturbance, goes upstairs to see what's happened. Then, when he realizes that what his boss is doing is throwing up, he thinks he might just have a look in the girl's bedroom himself. That's when he sees the pencils – and what particularly attracts him to them is that they have the girl's teeth marks on them. "Hello, that might come in useful," he tells himself. He pockets the pencil, and goes back downstairs before his boss has finished his business in the lavvy. Then later, when they're in – for example, and still hypothetically speaking – a pigeon loft, he takes the opportunity to drop the pencil on the floor. Perfectly sound police work, you might say . . .'

'I wouldn't,' Paniatowski interrupted.

'. . . except that, years later, it turns out that he's planted it on the *wrong* man. Well, you can't expect him to take the blame for it, can you – not when his old boss has retired, and so has nothing more to lose, while he's still got a bright future ahead of him.'

'Nothing more to lose?' Paniatowski repeated. 'Charlie could go to jail for this!'

'Theoretically, I suppose he could,' Hall agreed airily. 'But it's not likely, is it? I would imagine that, even now, your chief constable is looking for ways to cover the whole thing up.'

'You wouldn't say that if you really knew George Baxter,' Paniatowski told him.

'Well, even if he decides to institute legal proceedings, it could take years to bring it to court, and Woodend could be dead by then,' Hall said, as if he still saw no real problem. 'Besides, if the worst comes to the worst – and I don't for a minute think that it will – we don't have an extradition treaty with Spain, so all old Charlie has to do is sit tight.'

There had been something about the whole conversation – perhaps Hall's bravado, or perhaps his refusal to take things seriously – which had had a familiar ring about it to Paniatowski, and now she had finally managed to pin it down.

'I know why you're doing this,' she said.

'Doing what?' Hall asked.

Paniatowski said nothing.

For a moment, Hall just stood there, shifting his weight awkwardly from one foot to the other, then he said, 'I'm doing it because you asked me to – and a gentleman always tries to give a lady what she wants.'

'You're doing it because you're feeling bad – because you realize that there's no difference between you and all those scumbags you've spent your life glaring at across the interview table,' Paniatowski told him.

'I don't know what you mean,' Hall said.

But he did!

She could *see* that he did!

'What do you normally say to those scumbags when you're trying to get them to come clean?' she asked. '"Come on, lad, tell us you did it. You know you'll feel much better once you've got it off your chest." *Is* that what you say, Tom?'

'Maybe,' Hall admitted.

'And they often *do* feel better, don't they? And why is that? Because you've convinced them that you'll understand! Because, though you don't actually say it, you've given them the impression that, in their place, you might have done exactly the same thing!'

'So what?'

'Can you picture that look of guilty relief in their eyes, as they're making that confession that you've coaxed out of them, Tom? And do you know that if I held a mirror in front of you now, you'd see that same look in your own eyes?'

In the distance, they could hear the sound of a klaxon, as the train approached the station.

'You're talking a load of bollocks, Monika!' Hall said. 'Complete and utter bollocks.'

But he knew that he did not sound convincing – even to himself.

'I'm sitting across that table from you right now, Tom – listening to your confession, seeing that look in your eyes – and *I* don't understand at all,' Paniatowski continued. 'I'd *never* have acted as you did. I wouldn't bend the rules for a *decent* bobby who'd done wrong, let alone for a piece of offal like Bannerman.'

'You can say that now – I might have said the same thing at your age – but just you wait until you get bit older,' Hall said weakly.

'I'll never get *that* old, Tom,' Paniatowski told him. 'I'll never get that *rotten*.'

The train pulled into the station and juddered to a halt. Hall did not offer her his hand, because he knew she would not have taken it if he had done. Instead, he simply reached out and opened the carriage door closest to him.

He stepped on to the train, then swivelled round to see if she was still there. He seemed almost surprised that she was.

'I really had you fooled, though, didn't I, Monika?' he asked, rallying a little. 'I had Charlie Woodend down to a "t". I was *so much* like him that I think you might have agreed to sleep with me – if I could have been bothered to ask.'

'Is that the best you can do?' Paniatowski asked with a mixture of pity and contempt – both genuine – in her voice. 'After all the time you've had to prepare your parting shot, could you *really* not come up with anything better than that?' She shook her head. 'I suppose I shouldn't have expected anything else,' she conceded. '*It's* pathetic because *you're* pathetic. You've sold your soul for your pension. And not even to the Devil – who at least has some terrible dark satanic majesty about him – but to a worm of a man who's not fit to lick Charlie Woodend's boots.'

A sense of loss filled Hall's eyes. 'You'll see,' he said weakly. 'Give it a few more years on the job, and you'll see it for yourself.'

Hall closed the door, the guard blew his whistle, and the train began to pull out of the station.

Paniatowski stood watching until it was out of sight. Slowly, she noted, her vision was becoming more blurred, and supposed that was because she was crying.

NINETEEN

The boss looked rough, DI Colin Beresford thought – rougher than she'd looked when there seemed to be no light at the end of the tunnel in the bakery murders investigation; rougher, even, than when, whatever they did, they were making no headway at all in the hunt for the serial killer who stripped his victims naked and posed them on their hands and knees. But then, on those cases, it had only been her own future on the line – and now it was Charlie Woodend's.

Beresford took a sip of his pint, which was probably just as good as the Drum and Monkey's best bitter always was, but tasted – at that moment – like old engine oil.

'It's not your fault, Monika,' he said.

'It really isn't, boss,' agreed DC Jack Crane. 'From what you've told us about him, DCI Hall was so good at pulling the wool over people's eyes that he would have fooled anybody.'

Paniatowski looked around the bar which was almost her second home – at the dedicated darts players engaged in a fierce competition in the corner, at the inveterate gamblers hungrily feeding coins into the one-armed bandit.

It was kind of her lads to say she wasn't to blame, she thought – but was it really true?

Or was the truth actually that there had been some point at which she *could* have penetrated Hall's 'honest' disguise and thereby had at least a chance to limit the damage?

'We have to fight back,' she said aloud. 'We have to find a way to protect Charlie.' She took a drag on her cigarette. 'I'm not including you in this, Jack, by the way.'

'And why's that?' Crane demanded angrily. Then he swallowed – twice – before adding, 'Sorry, boss, I seem to have got a bit carried away there. But *why* am I not included?'

'Because you didn't know Charlie Woodend,' Paniatowski

said. 'You never worked for him like we did, so you don't owe
him a thing. And if there's any fallout from whatever we decide
to do, I don't want it landing on you.'

'I'm part of the team, aren't I?' Crane asked.

'Of course you are.'

'Then if there's any fallout, I'll take my fair share.'

Paniatowski reached across the table and patted his hand.

'Thank you, Jack,' she said.

And then she thought, Jesus, I just patted his bloody hand.
Now he'll think I'm either treating him like a baby, or – worse
– that I bloody fancy him.

'If you want your share of the fallout, you've got it,' she said,
trying to sound crisp and efficient – trying to sound, in fact, like
a DCI who had the best part of two decades on the young detective constable. She turned her attention back to Beresford. 'The
thing is, Colin, what *can* we do?'

'If we can get Mrs Dawson to say that Bannerman had the
opportunity to go upstairs while she was outside, we can at least
establish the *possibility* that it was the sergeant who took the
pencil,' Beresford suggested.

'And if wishes were horses, then beggars would ride,' Crane
murmured to himself.

'What was that you just said?' Beresford asked.

'She remembers Mr Woodend going upstairs, because he'd
asked to see her daughter's things – which will have mattered
to her. But how likely is it, after nearly a quarter of a century,
that she'll not only remember that she went outside for a breath
of air, but *how long* she was outside for?'

'It's very *unlikely*,' Paniatowski said.

'And even if – against all odds – she did have *vague* mem-
ories of it, you can be certain that DCI Hall will have scrambled
them up during his cosy little chat with her,' Crane concluded.

Right again, Paniatowski thought. Whatever they managed to
squeeze out of Mrs Dawson – if they could squeeze anything at
all – the finger of suspicion would remain pointing almost entirely
at Charlie.

So just what the hell *could* they do?

'Phone call for you, Chief Inspector,' the barman called across
the room. 'Do you want to take it here, or should I put it through
to the other phone?'

But even though he'd gone through the ritual of asking the
question, he already knew the answer. None of DCI Paniatowski's

team – nor DCI Woodend's team before it – had ever taken their calls on the bar phone, because there were too many flapping ears close to it.

The Drum's 'other' phone was in the corridor, midway between the ladies' and gents' toilets.

It looked like every other wall-mounted telephone in the world, Paniatowski mused, as she navigated her way between the crates of empty beer bottles to reach it. But it wasn't – at least, not to her.

Important milestones in her life had been marked out by *this* phone. It had been from this phone that she had received the information which had helped crack several major cases. And it had been on this phone, too, that George Baxter – then still only a DCI himself – had finally forced her to admit that their relationship was going nowhere.

There should be a brass plaque over it, she thought – though if there had been one, she had no idea what it ought to say.

She picked up the receiver, and heard a faint click as the barman transferred the call.

'Detective Chief Inspector Paniatowski?' asked the man on the other end of the line.

It was a harsh voice. She didn't recognize it – but that was not surprising, because she was almost certain that the man was doing his best to disguise it.

'Yes, this is Paniatowski,' she said. 'Who am I speaking to, please?'

'Is anything bad going to happen to those policemen of yours who investigated the Lilly Dawson murder back in 1951?' asked the caller, ignoring her question.

Jesus, how does he know anything about *that*? Paniatowski thought.

'What policemen are you talking about?' she asked, stalling for time.

'Don't play games with me,' the caller said. 'You know the ones I mean – DCI Woodend and his sergeant.'

'Sergeant Bannerman.'

'That's right. Will they be punished for arresting the wrong man?'

'You must realize I can't possibly discuss that with you,' Paniatowski said.

'I take it that means they will be,' the caller said. 'Doesn't it bother you that your old boss will be getting a raw deal?'

'Of course it bothers me,' Paniatowski said, before she could stop herself.

'And would you do anything that you possibly could to help him out of the mess he's in?'

'Yes.'

'Then what you have to do is to find out who *really* killed Lilly Dawson.'

'Do *you* know who did it?'

'Yes, I do.'

'Then give me a name.'

'I can't do that. But if you want me to, I'll tell you something that will point you in the right direction.'

'*Why* can't you give me a name?' Paniatowski insisted.

'If you ask me that again, I'll hang up,' the man threatened, and now the harshness in his voice was more than just a disguise. 'Just give me a yes or no to my question – do you want pointing in the right direction or don't you?'

'Yes, I want pointing in the right direction,' Paniatowski confirmed.

'Then if you're ever to find out who *really* killed Lilly, you first need to find out who *really* killed Bazza Mottershead,' the man told her.

The name rang a bell – but not a loud one.

'Who's Bazza Mottershead?' Paniatowski asked.

But by then, the line had already gone dead.

Most of the lights in Whitebridge police headquarters had long since been extinguished, but the one in Monika Paniatowski's office – to which the team had returned straight after the phone call – still valiantly blazed on.

'The moment the anonymous caller mentioned Bazza Mottershead's name . . .' Paniatowski began. She paused for a second. 'We can't go on referring to him as "the anonymous caller",' she continued. 'We need to give him a name.'

'How about "Looney Tunes"?' Beresford suggested.

Paniatowski glared at him. 'That's really not very helpful, Colin,' she said. 'If no one has any objections, I'll call him "Mr X".'

'I've no objections,' Beresford replied, indifferently.

'The moment Mr X mentioned Bazza Mottershead's name, I knew it sounded vaguely familiar,' Paniatowski said, picking up her thread again. 'And, of course, that was because I'd read it in the papers, while I was researching Lilly's death.' She opened the file which was lying on her desk. 'Bazza Mottershead was killed a few days after Lilly's body was discovered. He was a small-time criminal, and the bobbies back then soon arrested another minor thug, who went by the name of Walter Brown, for his murder. Brown pleaded not guilty at his trial, but he was duly convicted and sentenced to fifteen years.'

'Which means he was out in ten,' Crane said.

'No,' Paniatowski replied. 'He wasn't out in ten. In fact, he served his full sentence.'

'Probably couldn't keep his nose clean, even when he was inside,' Crane said dismissively. 'Some people never learn.'

'You're making an assumption – and it's a wrong one,' Paniatowski told him. 'Far from causing trouble, Brown was an almost exemplary prisoner.'

'So why didn't they let him out on licence?'

'You tell me.'

Crane thought about it. 'The likely reason is that Brown would never admit his guilt,' he said finally.

'Correct!' Paniatowski agreed. 'After he'd served ten years, he became eligible for release. All he had to do was say he was sorry for what he'd done, but he wouldn't – because he still claimed he *hadn't* done it.'

Beresford had been twitching awkwardly for some time, and now he said, 'I think that we may be wasting our time here, boss.'

'Do you?' Paniatowski asked, in a voice which suggested she wouldn't welcome further discussion on the subject.

'Yes, I do,' Beresford said determinedly. 'I think we're desperate to find something we can do for Mr Woodend . . .'

'You'll get no argument from me on that score.'

'. . . and because we're desperate, we're more than willing to go off on any wild goose chase that presents itself to us.'

'What you really mean is that *I'm* more than willing to go off on any wild goose chase, don't you?' Paniatowski asked.

'Well, yes,' Beresford admitted.

'And what makes you think this *is* a wild goose chase?'

'Look at the facts,' Beresford said. 'Some feller rings you up in a pub, and tells you that neither the real killer of Lilly Dawson nor the real killer of Bazza Mottershead has ever been found. Now, under any normal circumstances, you'd just dismiss him as a nutter, wouldn't you?'

'No,' Paniatowski said firmly. 'I'd carefully examine the call on its own merits, and then decide what action to take.'

'Right,' Beresford said, unconvinced. 'And having carefully examined this anonymous call on its own merits, you've decided that it's opened a whole new line of inquiry for us?'

'Yes, I have,' Paniatowski agreed. 'Mr X said it would help Charlie if we found out who really killed Lilly—'

'But I don't see how it possibly could,' Beresford interrupted. 'Even if we *did* find the real killer, it wouldn't alter the fact that someone dropped the pencil in the pigeon loft in order to frame Fred Howerd – and though we know that wasn't Mr Woodend, the evidence certainly points to him.'

'I don't understand how it would help, either,' Paniatowski admitted. 'But Mr X says that it would – and I believe him.'

'You don't understand, but you still believe him,' Beresford said. 'And why is that? Because you *need* to believe him!'

'No, that's not it at all,' Paniatowski countered. 'I believe him because he knows things that most people don't.'

'Like what?'

'That we've reopened the murder investigation, for a start. How many people do you think are aware of that?'

'Half the town, by now,' Beresford said, with what was *almost* a snort of derision. 'Look, boss, DCI Hall talked to Mrs Dawson, Mrs Dawson will have talked to her neighbour, the neighbour will have discussed it in the shops, the people who heard the neighbour will have told their friends . . . Do I need to go on?'

'He also knows that Charlie's in trouble.'

'That's no more than can be worked out by exercising a bit of simple logic. If we're re-investigating the case, then we think mistakes have been made. And if mistakes have been made, somebody's *bound* to be in trouble.'

Everything that her inspector had said made perfect sense, Paniatowski thought, and yet . . .

And yet . . .

'You didn't talk to Mr X, Colin,' she said. 'But I did, and if you'd heard the way he spoke, you'd be as convinced as I am.'

'With respect, Ma'am . . .' Beresford began, in a stilted, wooden voice.

'Respect is what it's all about,' Paniatowski interrupted him. 'Either you respect my gut on this matter or you don't. And if you *don't*, then – no hard feelings, Inspector – you're of no use to me in this investigation.' Her face suddenly softened and she smiled sadly at him. 'Really, Colin, I *do* mean that – no hard feelings at all.'

Damn the woman! Beresford thought angrily. Why did she seem to have so much power over him? Why was it always so easy for her to pull him in the direction in which she wanted him to go?

And then he shrugged, smiled back at her, and said, 'Well, if it's one of your famous gut feelings, I suppose there's no point in arguing with it, is there? So where do we start?'

'We start with Walter Brown. He's always said he didn't kill Mottershead – let's find out who he thinks did.'

'Wouldn't it just be easier to track down Mr X, boss?' Crane asked tentatively. 'He says he knows who did the killings, and you say you believe him. So if we can just get our hands on him, we'll have the answer to all our questions.'

'And if wishes were horses, beggars would ride,' Paniatowski said, throwing his earlier comment back at him. 'Sorry, Jack,' she continued, looking guilty. 'You're right, of course – he would be able to answer all our questions. The only problem is, as you've already pointed out, he's *anonymous*.'

'We should still be able to narrow down the number of people it *could have* been,' Crane pointed out.

'Or we could put someone else on that particular line of inquiry,' Paniatowski replied.

'Who?' Beresford asked.

'Who do you think?' Paniatowski replied.

And then she picked up the phone, and dialled a number in Spain which she knew by heart.

TWENTY

It was a chill early morning, but Monika Paniatowski's brisk pace, as she walked down Whitebridge High Street, had less to do with the temperature than with the fact that she knew that if she once lost her self-imposed sense of momentum on this case, she would never get it back.

She turned off the main road, and was soon swallowed by a series of lanes which were just wide enough for two horses and carts to pass each other. This was the old part of town, the few remaining blocks of historic Whitebridge which the developers had yet to get their itchy hands on.

Browns' Second-Hand Books was located on Primrose Lane. To its left there was a joke shop – or joke *emporium*, as the faded sign above it proclaimed – which had severed rubber hands, devil masks and itching powder on display in the window. On the other side was a tobacconist's, which had as its display a large – and sun-bleached – cardboard model of a brand of cigarettes which the manufacturers had stopped making years earlier.

The bookshop itself presented a pleasing contrast to the quiet desperation of the two businesses that it was sandwiched between. Its window, unlike theirs, had been cleaned in the recent past, and the books on display had clearly been placed there with care, if not with a great deal of presentational skill.

When Paniatowski entered the shop, a brass bell jangled, and the door to the back room opened to reveal a large man in his late fifties.

He was wearing an old cardigan with leather patches on the elbows, and a pair of trousers which were probably not new at the time of the Queen's Coronation. It was the perfect uniform for a seller of old books, and it blended in like a dream with the rest of the shop.

The man's *face*, unfortunately, was not quite such a good match. It was obvious that his nose had been broken at some time in the past, and his cheeks, chin and forehead bore numerous scars of ancient battles. It was the sort of face that had old ladies nervously reaching for the communication cord in railway carriages – the sort of face that mothers would hold up to their children as an example of what might happen to them if they continued to run wild.

And yet when he smiled – as he did now – the harshness melted away, and a much gentler soul was revealed.

The man peered myopically at Paniatowski for a second, then said, 'Mrs Gaskell?'

'No, I'm . . .'

'You're quite right, and I'm quite wrong,' the man said firmly. 'Mrs Gaskell wouldn't suit you at all. You'd be much happier with something a little less stylized – something with a bit more zing to it. *The Mill on the Floss* by George Eliot, perhaps? I'm getting closer, aren't I? I can always tell what people will like – even when they're not quite sure themselves.'

'I'm sorry, but I'm not a customer,' Paniatowski said, producing her warrant card. 'I'm looking for Walter Brown.'

'Ah!' the man said, disappointedly. 'And which Walter Brown might that be? Walter Brown the lover of old books? Or could it be Walter Brown the convicted murderer?'

Paniatowski grinned, despite the macabre nature of the question. 'Which one are you?' she asked.

'I'm both, as you've probably already realized,' Brown said. 'But I imagine it's the latter, rather than the former, that you're interested in.'

'I'm afraid it is,' Paniatowski admitted.

Brown nodded, perhaps a little sadly.

'In that case, you'd better come into the back room, and we'll have tea and biscuits,' he said. 'Tea and biscuits *always* make interrogations just a little more bearable.'

'I was a real thug at the time I was sent down for Mottershead's murder,' Walter Brown said, as he poured Paniatowski a cup of Earl Grey. 'A thoroughly nasty piece of work – and a semi-literate one, to boot. Back then, I'd as soon have cut off my own arm than open a book. Prison changed all that. At first, I only took the reading classes they offered because it was a soft option. Then something magical happened. I started to enjoy it. And by the time I came out, I'd read everything in the prison library at least three or four times. But I didn't mind that, because there's always something new to find in a book, however well you think you know it.'

'You always maintained your innocence,' Paniatowski said.

'I still do,' Brown told her.

'So why did the police fix on you as their prime suspect?' Paniatowski wondered.

'Oh, they had reasonable enough grounds, I suppose,' Brown admitted. 'As I said, I was a thug. I gloried in violence. It excited me, back then, almost as much as books do now. I may not have killed anybody, but I put a number of men in hospital, and one of them could *easily* have died.' He paused, and looked Paniatowski straight in the eyes. 'I didn't murder Bazza Mottershead – but, given more time, I might well have done.'

'If it's true that you were wrongly convicted, I'm surprised you don't sound bitter,' Paniatowski said.

'What would be the point of that?' Brown asked. 'It's over and done with, and we can't change the past, however much we

might want to. Besides, in some ways, being wrongly convicted
was the best thing that ever happened to me. In fact, I think you
might say it made me free.'

'Could you explain that?' Paniatowski asked.

'Willingly. I've paid my debt to society – not for killing
Mottershead, but for all the other terrible things I did – and now
I can look the world squarely in the face. And prison made me
a new man – a better man, I hope. If I'd gone on as I was, I'd
probably have ended up dead in some back alley, without ever
having experienced the joy of books, so, on one level at least,
everything that happened, happened for the best.'

'The police must have thought they had enough evidence to
arrest you,' Paniatowski said. 'What sort of case did they actually have?'

'A circumstantial one,' Brown said. He chuckled. 'Back then,
of course, I didn't know the word "circumstantial".'

'Why don't you fill in the details for me?' Paniatowski suggested.

*'There was really bad blood between you and Bazza, wasn't
there, Wally?' Chief Inspector Paine demands.*

'No, I liked the feller,' Walter Brown says unconvincingly.

*'You worked with the feller – he was your fence – but you
didn't like him at all,' the chief inspector replies. 'Tell me, Wally,
when exactly did it finally penetrate that thick skull of yours that
Bazza had been cheating you for years?'*

A few days before he died, Brown thinks.

'I don't know what yer talkin' about,' he says aloud.

*The chief inspector laughs. 'He always told you that the stuff
you took to him was far less valuable than it actually was – and
you were too stupid to know any different. But somebody must
have finally tipped you the wink – and when they did, you went
bloody mad.'*

*Yes, Brown thinks, I went bloody mad. I cornered Bazza in
the lounge bar of the Pig and Whistle, grabbed him by throat,
an' told him if he didn't pay all the money he owed me, I'd slit
his bloody throat.*

*'I don't know what yer talkin' about,' he says, for the second
time.*

'You really are *thick, aren't you?' the chief inspector jeers.
'We've got half a dozen witnesses – decent, respectable people
– who are willing to swear they heard you threaten to kill him.'*

*   *   *

'So you had a motive for murdering him,' Paniatowski said. 'What else did the police use to build up their case against you?'

'I'll make a deal with you, Wally,' the chief inspector says. 'You give me an alibi for the night Bazza was killed, and I'll let you go immediately.'

But Brown has no alibi. He remembers nothing of the period between six o'clock on the evening of the murder, when he was drinking heavily in the Lamb and Flag, and eight o'clock the next morning, when he woke up among the bushes in the Corporation Park, with an empty whisky bottle at his side.

'Come on, Wally, if you didn't do it, just give us your alibi,' the chief inspector says.

'I can't,' Brown admits. 'I don't have an alibi.'

'So they had motive and opportunity,' Paniatowski mused. 'What else did they have on you?'

'Nothing,' Walter Brown told her.

Paniatowski frowned. 'Well, if that's *really* all they had, I'm surprised they thought they had enough to charge you,' she admitted.

'Maybe they wouldn't have charged me if it hadn't been for the race,' Brown said.

'The race? *What* race?'

'The race with Scotland Yard!'

'I'll be honest with you, Wally, a lot of the younger lads in the division are really pissed off that the chief constable called in Scotland Yard on the Lilly Dawson murder,' the chief inspector tells Wally Brown.

Brown, who has no idea of what any of this can possibly have to do with him, says nothing.

'It's true we hadn't made a lot of progress in that case,' the chief inspector admits, 'but, given time, we'd have cracked it, wouldn't we?'

Wally Brown is obviously expected to say something, so he says, 'I don't know.'

'Oh, we'd have cracked it, all right,' the chief inspector asserts. 'But we've lost our chance, because the "experts" have arrived and taken over. Now, I've nothing against Charlie Woodend – apart from the fact that he's from the Yard – but that poncey sergeant of his is really getting up my nose.' He reaches into his

pocket, and takes out a packet of cigarettes. 'Fancy a smoke, Wally?'

'Please,' Brown says.

The chief inspector lights up their cigarettes. 'Now the question you're probably asking yourself is, are we just going to take this lying down?' he continues. 'And my answer is that we're not. You see, if we can solve our murder before they solve theirs, it'll be obvious to anybody who are the real *detectives and who are just big girls' blouses. Are you following me, Wally?'*

'No,' Brown says.

'The way I see it, we can do each other a bit of good here, you and me. You can help me by confessing to the murder, and I can help you by putting in a good word for you with the judge. What do you say to that?'

'I didn't do it,' Brown tells him.

The chief inspector's eyes harden. 'Think carefully, Wally,' he advises, 'because there's a time limit to how long this offer will be on the table. If they catch their man before you confess, we'll be left with egg on our faces, and you've no idea what kind of a rough time we'll give you then.'

'I wouldn't confess, but they charged me anyway,' Walter Brown told Paniatowski. 'Funnily enough, it was shortly after that when I met Chief Inspector Woodend.' He smiled. 'They were taking me to the cells, and Mr Woodend was standing in the corridor. I asked him to help me, and when he said he couldn't, I reacted like I always did in those days. I tried to hit him – and he, quite rightly, flattened me.'

Paniatowski was hardly listening to him any more.

It couldn't be as simple as Brown had described it, she told herself. It simply couldn't be.

'Isn't it possible that you were so drunk on the night Bazza Mottershead was murdered that you might have killed him, and then remembered nothing about it?' she asked.

'No,' Brown said emphatically.

'But if you had a complete memory loss about that evening . . .'

'If I'd have killed him, I'd have known. However drunk I'd been, I'd have *known*.'

'When you woke up that morning, did you have a wound you couldn't remember getting?' Paniatowski asked.

'I was always getting injured,' Brown told her. 'Like I said, I was a rough bugger. A lot of the time, I hardly even noticed it.'

'But I'm not talking about any old injury – this would have been a *new* wound, wouldn't it?'

'I don't know,' Brown said. 'In fact, I have no idea what you're talking about.'

'The police found two types of blood at the Mottershead murder scene,' Paniatowski explained. 'Their theory was that one of them belonged to the killer. Actually, they didn't regard it as a *theory* at all – they took it as a rock-solid certainty.'

'I didn't know that,' Brown said.

'You must have done,' Paniatowski replied sceptically. 'It was in all the papers.'

'I didn't read the newspapers back then. To tell you the truth, I *couldn't* read them.'

'And you're sure you had *no* new wounds when you woke up in the park that morning?'

'I'd got cut a couple of weeks earlier – I'd had a slight disagreement with another of my associates – but that particular cut had all but healed.'

But not in the eyes of the police, Paniatowski thought – not if they didn't *want* it to look healed.

'The main reason I'm here is that a man rang me last night to say that you didn't kill Bazza Mottershead,' she said. 'Do you have any idea, Mr Brown, who that man might be?'

'It could have been the real killer?' Brown suggested.

'It wasn't,' Paniatowski said.

'Are you sure?'

'As sure as I can be. He *said* he wasn't – and I believe him.'

'Well, if it wasn't the real killer, I haven't got a clue who it could be,' Brown admitted. 'I don't see how anybody else *could* know, with absolute certainty, that I didn't murder Bazza.'

'I want you to help me,' Paniatowski said.

'Help you?' Walter Brown repeated, suddenly wary. 'How could *I* help you?'

'You could give me a list, with the names on it of everyone else you can remember who associated with Mottershead – especially anybody who might have had a grudge against him.'

Brown laughed. 'It'd a long list,' he said. 'Bazza had a real talent for making enemies – and some of them *really* hated him. That's how he got to be Bazza the Claw.'

'Bazza the Claw?'

'It's what some of the lads used to call him in the old days.'

'Why? Because he'd claw every penny out of you that he possibly could?'

'Oh, he'd do that right enough, but that wasn't the reason. They called him the Claw because his right hand *did* look a bit like a claw.'

'Arthritis?' Paniatowski asked.

'That's right – but what started the arthritis off in the first place was that somebody had broken every bone in that hand.'

'Who?'

'I don't know. It happened a long time before I even met him. I'm only mentioning it now to give you some idea of just how popular he was.'

'Will you give me the names I want?' Paniatowski asked.

Brown fell silent for a moment, then he said, 'Maybe.'

'Why the reluctance, when all I want to do is clear you?'

'*Is that* all you want to do?'

'No,' Paniatowski admitted – because she knew that with this man, she would never get away with lying. 'I have some other purpose as well. But I really *do* want to see justice done in your case.'

'Why?' Brown asked, his suspicion deepening. 'Because that's part of your job?'

'Yes, but if it *wasn't* part of my job, it wouldn't be the kind of job I'd have wanted in the first place.'

'I like you, Chief Inspector Paniatowski,' Brown said. 'I really do. And I think I trust you.'

'Thank you.'

'But after everything that I've been through, you'll understand why I don't trust you *that* much, won't you?'

'Yes,' Paniatowski agreed. 'I do understand.'

'The last thing I want to do is to get some other poor innocent sod into trouble – and I'm afraid that if I give you a list, that's just what will happen,' Walter Brown told her.

'It won't,' Paniatowski said firmly. 'I promise you it won't.' She waited for a moment, before adding, '*Will* you give me the names?'

'I need time to think about it,' Brown told her. 'Come and see me again tomorrow.'

It would be a mistake to push him too far, she realized.

'All right,' she agreed.

'Have a look at what I've got on my shelves on your way out,'

Brown said, 'and if anything catches your fancy, take it as a gift.'

It was morning in Spain, too, though a far warmer, more caressing kind of morning than the one in Whitebridge.

Charlie Woodend was sitting on his terrace, a large sheet of plain paper spread out on the table in front of him, and a box of coloured pencils – bought specially for the occasion – lying next to his ashtray.

In the centre of the sheet, he'd written the single word 'Who?' and around the edges of the page were a list of names, most of them crossed out with a violence that said much about the frustration he was feeling.

'Still no luck on working out who your anonymous friend might be?' asked Paco Ruiz, who'd been for a walk around the garden, in the hope that a change of scene might stimulate his brain.

'No luck at all,' Woodend replied. 'All we really know is who it *can't* be. It *can't*, for example, be that slimy shit from Scotland Yard, DCI Hall, can it?'

'No, that doesn't seem likely,' Paco agreed.

'*His* aim was to save Bannerman by stitching me up, an' after he's made such a good job of it, there's no way that he'd suddenly decide to throw me a lifebelt.'

'Who else have you eliminated?' Paco asked.

'It can't be one of the local Whitebridge police, either.'

'Why not?'

'Because of the way this Mr X spoke to Monika. As near as she can remember it, he said, "Is anythin' bad goin' to happen to those policemen of yours who investigated the Lilly Dawson murder." You get the point?'

Paco nodded. 'If he'd been a cop, he'd have said something like, "Are they going to be pulled up in front of a disciplinary board?"'

'Exactly.' Woodend agreed, lighting up a Ducados. 'An' he wouldn't have talked about "those policemen of yours", either. He'd have said, "our lads".' He took a drag on his cigarette. 'Then there's the fact that he claimed to know who actually *did* kill Lilly. Now that doesn't necessarily mean that he was around at the time – an' the time was *twenty-two years ago*, remember – but it certainly makes it a strong possibility.'

'So the man who you're looking for is at least in middle age?' Paco Ruiz asked.

'I think he must be.' Woodend frowned. 'But what's really got me bothered – above all else – is that when Monika asked him to name the killer, he said, "I can't do that." Not, "I won't do that", but "I can't". Now *why* can't he?'

'It is possible that the reason he "can't" is because he's implicated in the murder himself?' Ruiz suggested.

'That was the first thought that came into my head,' Woodend admitted.

'But now you've rejected it?'

'Yes, an' I'll explain why in a minute. But first, I want you to think back to the days when you were a homicide bobby in Madrid.'

Ruiz did as he'd been instructed. And immediately, he could feel the stifling heat of summer envelop him as he crossed the Puerta del Sol on the trail of a killer, and the freezing cold of winter as he stood on the bank of the Manzanares River, chatting to the shivering prostitutes while he waited to meet a contact.

'Are you there?' Woodend asked.

'I'm there,' Ruiz told him.

And in some ways, he thought, it was almost as if he'd never been away.

'Can you remember how many murder cases you had to deal with, while you were in Madrid?' Woodend asked.

'Far too many,' Paco replied.

'An' do you remember any of them?'

'I remember them all.'

'Me, too,' Woodend said. 'So this is my question – did you ever, in the course of any of those investigations, come across somebody who was implicated in a murder himself, but whose main concern seemed to be to point the investigation in a direction which might get one of the policemen involved out of trouble?'

'Of course not,' Ruiz said. 'None of the criminals I had to deal with ever bore the police anything but ill-will.' He grinned. 'But then, perhaps your English criminals are of a somewhat gentler nature than our Spanish ones?'

'If they are, I never noticed it,' Woodend replied, returning the grin. 'But this feller – this anonymous caller – really *is* on my side,' he continued, growing more serious again. 'I can sense he is, even from this distance. An' that must mean that while he knows about the murders, he had nothin' to do with them himself.'

'That makes sense,' Ruiz agreed.

'So what are we left with?' Woodend asked. 'We've got a

man who's probably in late middle age. He knows about not *one* murder but *two* – an' murders, furthermore, which have absolutely nothin' in common, because one's a sex crime an' the other's a typical underworld killin'. An' this man – this Mr X – seems willin', possibly at some risk to himself, to come to my aid.'

He looked out towards the sea, as if he hoped to see some inspiration gently floating towards the shore.

'Knowin' all that,' he continued, 'it should be easy enough to narrow it down, shouldn't it? Even if we can't come up with a specific name, we should at least be able to produce a profile of the kind of person who'd be willin' to help me in these circumstances. An' we can't.'

'That's true,' Ruiz agreed. 'As you would say yourself, Charlie, "We simply haven't got a bloody clue".'

'But it's far from bein' an *insoluble* puzzle,' Woodend said, with a hint of self-anger in his voice. 'I'm absolutely convinced of that. We only have to ask the right questions, an' everythin' will become clear. The problem is, we've no idea what the right questions are.'

TWENTY-ONE

'It has been announced that Rex "Rubber Legs" Norton has died peacefully at his home in Blackpool, aged eighty-three,' said the local newsreader, speaking from the wall-mounted television in the chief constable's office. 'Rex, who was born and raised in Whitebridge, had an uncanny ability to bend his legs into seemingly impossible – and amazingly comic – positions, which made him a great favourite of audiences on the pre-war music hall circuit.'

The very fact that George Baxter even *had* a television in his office was a sign of the times, Monika Paniatowski thought. When she'd joined the Force, the telly was something you watched to relax, when you were off duty. If you needed to contact the media back then – and they hadn't even *called it* 'the media' in those days – you did it over a pint in their favourite pub. But it wasn't like that any more – local television had started flexing its muscles, and any officer in charge of a major investigation ignored it at his or her peril.

'Accrington's new home for stray animals admitted its first two guests today,' the newsreader said, going all misty-eyed, 'and the fox terrier puppies, Bobby and Billy, already seem to be making themselves at home.'

Paniatowski shifted uneasily in her seat as a grinning kennel maid held up the two puppies for the camera's inspection.

'Would you mind telling me exactly why I've been summoned here, sir?' she said.

'Just be patient for a moment, Chief Inspector, and all will be revealed,' Baxter replied.

Chief Inspector! He'd called her 'Chief Inspector'. And that wasn't a good sign.

'We like to think we can have confidence in the police, but is that confidence really justified?' asked the newsreader, as her facial expression instantly transformed itself from sentimental to serious. 'In the past few years, a number of criminal cases in which there has been a miscarriage of justice have come to light nationally. And today, Mr Robert Howerd, the managing director of the Howerd Electrical chain of shops, has made allegations which may well lead to the re-investigation of yet another case – this time, very close to home.'

The scene changed to another studio, in which three people – Robert Howerd, Elizabeth Eccles and another, younger woman – were sitting stiffly side by side on a sofa, and gazing into the camera.

'Tell us what happened to your brother, Mr Howerd,' said a soft off-screen voice.

'My brother Frederick was arrested twenty-two years ago for the rape and murder of a little girl who he hardly knew,' Robert Howerd said in a voice edged with anger.

'But surely, he confessed to committing the crime, didn't he?' the off-screen voice asked provocatively.

'He did indeed confess,' Howerd replied. 'But we have reason to believe that the confession was coerced from him by the policeman who was in charge of the investigation.'

'And are you willing to name that policeman?'

'I am. It was Detective Chief Inspector Charles Woodend.'

'Is that the same Chief Inspector Woodend who, until recently, was a well-known – and, many would say, well-respected – figure around Whitebridge police headquarters?' the off-screen voice asked.

'The very same Chief Inspector Woodend,' Howerd agreed.

'Though, at the time he wrongly arrested my brother, this "well-respected" figure was not based in Whitebridge, but was working for New Scotland Yard.'

The three of them together presented an interesting tableau, Paniatowski thought.

Robert Howerd kept looking at his niece after almost every sentence, as if he were continually seeking her approval. Elizabeth, for her part, barely seemed to be acknowledging him, preferring, instead, to stare fixedly at the camera with angry eyes. But however much she might *appear* to be ignoring him, she was still acutely aware of her uncle's close proximity, Paniatowski decided, because every time he shifted his position, however slightly, her body instinctively shrank away. And if it was true that she did not wish to be too close to her uncle, it was even truer that the other woman on the sofa – the younger one, who was almost certainly Elizabeth's daughter – didn't want to be in the studio at all.

'What are your reasons for believing your brother was innocent?' the off-screen voice asked.

'The certainty that he was not a man who would wish to face his Maker with a lie still on his lips,' Howerd told her.

The Devonshire Arms was one of those Manchester pubs which catered for all tastes but the most refined. It had a public bar, in which shop workers and students would feel most at home. It had a best room, where men could take their wives and girl-friends, and be served by a waiter in a white – if sometimes slightly stained – cotton jacket. And it had the vault.

The vault was where the manual labourers congregated after a hard day swinging a pick or wielding a shovel. They were men of simple ambitions, the two main ones being to drink as much as they could afford and speak their minds without restraint. The air inside the vault was always blue with cigarette smoke and cursing, and ladies – of all kinds – were encouraged to steer well clear of it.

At lunchtime, the vault was a much quieter place. Then, its customers were not men who earned their living by the sweat of their brow, but men who didn't have jobs at all – and showed absolutely no inclination to find one. These men spent less and scrounged more than the manual workers. They had hair which was not stylishly long but merely uncared-for long. They smoked hand-rolled cigarettes, and ran up debts – with a clear conscience

– wherever they could. And some of them, it had to be said, stank.

The man sitting in the corner of the vault at that moment was typical of the type of customer who he was forced to deal with at lunchtime, the barman thought, with some disdain.

His name was Mike, and if he had a second name, no one knew what it was. He was probably in his late forties, though the barman could point to some seventy-odd-year-olds who were in much better shape. He had been coming to the pub for as long as any of the current staff could remember, and was generally agreed to have turned being bone idle into an art form.

Normally, Mike would just sit there and gaze into space – as if contemplating a life which might have been – but today he was watching the regional news programme on the television.

No, he was doing more than just *watching* it, the barman decided – he seemed *absorbed* by it.

The barman looked up to see what the fuss was about. A man and two women, sitting side by side on a sofa, were being interviewed, though it seemed to be the man who was doing most of the talking.

'I didn't know you were interested in current affairs,' the barman said jovially, but the other man ignored him.

Well, sod you, the barman thought. If you can't be pleasant to me, I see no need to be pleasant to you.

The weather girl appeared on the screen, and Mike immediately seemed to lose interest. He drained what was left of his drink, then stood up and shambled over to the bar.

'You couldn't lend me the odd twenty quid, could you, Ralph?' he asked hopefully.

'Couldn't lend you *what*?' the barman repeated, in disbelief.

'The odd twenty quid,' Mike repeated.

'No, I most certainly couldn't,' the barman said firmly.

'Or ten quid, if things are a bit tight for you right now. I suppose I could manage with ten.'

'Not ten quid, either.'

'I'll pay you back,' Mike said. 'I promise you I will.'

'No chance,' the barman replied.

Mike licked his lips, and ran his hand thoughtfully across the stubble on his chin.

'I'll tell you what,' he said, 'lend me ten quid now and I'll pay you back a hundred next week.'

The barman chuckled. 'Course you will.'

'I mean it – honest,' Mike said. 'I've to get to Whitebridge – but once I'm there, I'll be rolling in money.'

'I wouldn't doubt that for a minute,' said the barman, and moved quickly across to the other end of the bar.

'What do you hope will happen next?' the off-screen interviewer asked Robert Howerd.

'What I trust will happen next is that there will be a full official inquiry which will both exonerate my brother and bring to book those guilty policemen who, by their actions, caused my niece and her daughter so much unnecessary distress,' Howerd said.

'Thank you, Mr Howerd,' the off-screen voice said. 'And now we return to the studio for the local—'

'But the police are not the only ones who are guilty of committing great wrongs,' Robert Howerd said.

He was going off-script, Paniatowski realized – and, from the wild look in his eyes, it was likely that even he hadn't planned that.

'I have done great wrong myself . . .' Howerd continued.

'We've run out of time, Mr Howerd,' the interviewer said, *sotto voce*.

'I have sinned, and now I must pay the penance,' Howerd said, ignoring her. 'There must be restitution for what I have done. The Lord, my God, will settle for no less!'

Robert Howerd disappeared from the screen, and was replaced by a weather girl with chubby cheeks, who announced that there was a strong chance of rain later in the day.

The chief constable switched off the television.

'Well?' he asked.

'Well what?' Paniatowski replied.

'Mr Howerd is demanding action and, much as I dislike the man personally, I think he has every right to. Don't you agree?'

Of course she agreed, Paniatowski thought. Fred Howerd had been sent down for a crime he hadn't committed, and something should be done about it. The only problem was that doing the *right* thing by Howerd would also involve doing the *wrong* thing by the man she most admired in the whole world.

'I'm willing to submit a report which admits that mistakes have been made and clears Fred Howerd,' she said.

'That's not enough,' Baxter said.

'Charlie Woodend didn't plant that pencil,' Paniatowski said. 'You know he didn't!'

'No, I don't know that at all,' Baxter contradicted her.

She had a cassette tape in her pocket – one that even Beresford and Crane didn't know about – and, for a moment, she was tempted to play it to Baxter.

But what would be the point – what would be the *bloody* point?

'I think it's time we put the inquiry on an official footing with another officer in charge – one who is not so personally involved,' Baxter said.

'Give me two days,' Paniatowski pleaded. 'Two days and you'll have a full report on your desk.'

'And what am I expected to do in the meantime?' Baxter demanded. 'How am I supposed to handle the media? Hell, forget the media – how am I supposed to handle the police authority, several members of which, I happen to know, are close personal friends of Robert Howerd?'

'You'll find a way,' Paniatowski said. 'You always do. You'll run rings round them.'

'So now you're so desperate that you're resorting to flattery, are you?' Baxter asked.

Yes, I *am* that desperate, Paniatowski thought.

'Two days,' she repeated. 'Please, *George*.'

She was exploiting the relationship they had once had. She knew it – and she hated herself for doing it. But what choice did she have?

'Two days,' Baxter said, weakening. 'But suppose that, during those two days, you find even more damning evidence against Charlie Woodend? What will happen then?'

She wouldn't find any such evidence, because there would be no such evidence to find, Paniatowski thought

'Anything I find will be in my report,' she said.

But what if she was wrong, a sudden panicked voice asked from somewhere in the dark recesses of her mind. Charlie would never lie to her, but what if he *had* cut corners, and then been so ashamed of it that his memory – for self-protection – had completely blanked it out?

'Do I have your word that *nothing* will be excluded?' Baxter asked.

'Yes,' Paniatowski promised.

And even as she spoke, she wasn't entirely sure that she would have the strength of character to see that promise through.

Colin Beresford was gloomily examining his pint when his boss entered the public bar of the Drum and Monkey, and sat down opposite him.

'Did you see Robert Howerd being interviewed on television?' Paniatowski asked.

'Yes, I saw it,' Beresford replied. 'And I wasn't the only one. *Everybody* saw it – at least, everybody who *matters*.'

It was time she did a bit of morale boosting, Paniatowski decided.

'I established a real rapport with Walter Brown, and I'm almost certain that he's going to come through with that list of names for me,' she said brightly. 'Of course, I'll put the pressure on him if I have to – but I really don't think that will be necessary.'

The statement did nothing to improve Beresford's mood.

'But even if you *did* manage to arrest the real killer – and you'll admit that, after all this time, the prospect's unlikely – that still won't get Mr Woodend out of trouble, will it?' he asked.

'Mr X says it will,' Paniatowski replied stubbornly.

'Oh, well that's all right then,' Beresford countered. 'If *Mr X* says it, it must be true.'

'Another phone call for you, Chief Inspector,' the barman shouted. 'You're gettin' to be right popular.'

Paniatowski felt her body tense.

'It's him,' she said to Beresford.

'It could be anybody,' the inspector replied.

'It's him,' Paniatowski said firmly.

When Paniatowski picked up the phone in the corridor, she heard the same harsh, disguised voice on the other end of the line.

'How's the investigation going, Chief Inspector?' it asked.

'It's official police business,' Paniatowski replied. 'I can't talk to you about it – and you know that!'

'Have you talked to Walter Brown?'

'Yes, I have.'

'And has he told you anything useful?'

'Like what?'

'Like, for instance, who Bazza Mottershead's friends were?'

'His friends?' Paniatowski repeated. 'Did you *mean* to say his friends? Or were you talking about his *enemies*?'

'I can think of at least one man who would easily qualify to be both,' the caller said.

'And what's his name?'

There was a short pause, then Mr X said, 'There are some things you say you can't tell me because it's official police business. Right?'

'Right.'

'Well, there are some things I can't tell *you* because . . .'

'Because of what?'

'Because I can't!' Mr X said.

He sounded angry, Paniatowski thought. Perhaps that was because he had said more than he meant to, and almost revealed his secret – whatever *that* was.

'Are you still there?' she asked, though she could hear his breathing and knew that he was.

Silence.

'Speak to me,' she pleaded.

The man cleared his throat.

'You have to accept that this is not an equal partnership,' he said, finally.

'What do you mean by that?'

'I mean that you need me more than I need you.'

It wasn't true, Paniatowski thought. She could sense a desperation at the other end of the line which was at least as deep as her own – but she knew it would be a mistake to argue with him.

'What do you want from me?' she asked.

'I want you to stop hiding behind "official police business" and tell me how the investigation's going.'

'It's not going anywhere,' Paniatowski said – and realized that in admitting it to him, she was also admitting it to herself. 'But maybe it would – if you'd only give me more to work with.'

'I have to think!' the man said worriedly. 'I need time to think.'

'Take all the time you need,' Paniatowski told him, in a soothing voice.

She began to count silently to herself . . . one elephant, two elephants, three elephants . . .

She had reached 'thirty elephants' when the man said, 'You need to talk to Michael Eccles.'

'Who's he?'

'You're the detective – *you* work it out.'

He sounded furious, and she thought she understood why that was. He had been agonizing over what he could he tell her and what he couldn't, and when, out of this struggle, he finally produced what he no doubt considered a precious pearl of information, she treated it – from his perspective, at least – as if it were nothing.

'I need you to guide me,' she said. 'Is this Michael Eccles you're talking about Elizabeth's estranged husband?'

'Yes, he is.'

'But he left her over twenty years ago.'

'I know he did.'

'And she hasn't heard a word from him since. For all we know, he could be dead by now.'

'He may indeed be dead,' the caller agreed. 'But if he *isn't*, you could learn a great deal by talking to him.'

'Are you suggesting that he might have killed Lilly Dawson or Bazza Mottershead?' Paniatowski asked.

'No, I'm not. In fact, I'm certain that he didn't kill either of them.'

'Then does he know who *did* kill them?'

'I can't be sure of that – but I don't think he does.'

'So how could he possibly be of any help to the investigation?'

'You'll know that when you find him,' the caller said.

And then he hung up.

'He's yanking your chain – giving you the runaround,' Beresford said, when Paniatowski had outlined the conversation with Mr X.

'He's not,' Paniatowski told him.

'Until you got that telephone call, wasn't your plan to cast a bigger net and see just what got caught in it?' Beresford asked.

'Nice analogy,' Paniatowski said, smiling. 'Where'd it come from? Have you just taken up fishing as a hobby or something?'

But Beresford did not smile back, and if she'd hoped to deflect him from what he wanted to say, it was clear that she had failed.

'The whole point in trying to persuade Walter Brown to talk was to widen the investigation, wasn't it?' Beresford asked.

'Yes, it was,' Paniatowski admitted – because she had little choice *but to* admit it.

'Yet now, instead of *widening* the investigation, your Mr X wants us to *narrow* it! He's throwing us back on the Eccles family, who – it's already been established – have nothing to do with the case.'

'Or, at least, they have nothing to do with it that we're *aware of*,' Paniatowski argued. 'Fred Howerd may have been innocent of the rape and murder he was charged with, but he wasn't as pure as the driven snow, you know.'

'No, I *don't* know,' Beresford said exasperatedly. 'And neither, if you're honest with yourself, do you.'

'We know that he liked to visit fifteen-year-old prostitutes.'

'Again, we don't. All we know is that Dyson Trypp told *Clegg* that the prostitute was fifteen. But he might have been lying. He might just have said it to stop Clegg from coming forward with his alibi.'

'And we know that Howerd confessed he'd taken Lilly Dawson to his pigeon loft, the night before she was murdered.'

'He confessed to a lot of things. He confessed to killing her, and we know that's not true – so maybe he was lying about her being in his pigeon loft too. Maybe he only said it because that was what Mr Woodend and Sergeant Bannerman *wanted* him to say.'

'Charlie is convinced Lilly *was* in the loft.'

'And Charlie could be as wrong about that as, it now turns out, he was wrong about so many other things.' Beresford sighed. 'Look, boss, Robert Howerd's already an extremely angry man – as anybody who saw his little performance on the news will tell you.'

'I know that.'

'And what you're planning to do – at the instigation of an anonymous caller, who *I* still think is off his head – will only make matters worse.'

'We can't let members of the public like Robert Howerd influence the way we carry out our investigation,' Paniatowski said.

'But he's not *just* a member of the public, is he?' Beresford demanded. 'He's a man who feels – entirely justifiably – that his family's been very badly treated by the police.'

'I just want to talk to Michael Eccles,' Paniatowski said soothingly. 'That's all, Colin. I just want to have a little conversation.'

Beresford shook his head in dismay. 'You're dancing barefoot round a steel trap – and, sooner or later, the jaws are going to snap shut and have your leg off.'

'Maybe they are . . .'

'If you know that, then why don't you walk away while you still have the chance?'

'. . . but I'd still like you to check with all the regional police
forces to see if they know where Michael Eccles is. And if they *don't*
know, I want you to ask them to keep an eye out for him.'

'So you want thousands of bobbies to be on the lookout for
Eccles?'

'That's right.'

'How long do you think it will be before one of them mentions
to a reporter that you're interested in finding Fred Howerd's son-
in-law? And when that happens – and it *will* – how long will it
be after that before Robert Howerd learns that you're still
conducting a vendetta against his family?'

'It's *not* a vendetta.'

'Maybe not – but it certainly looks like one, and it smells like
one.'

'I'm really not prepared to discuss this any further,'
Paniatowski said, waspishly. 'You know what I want doing –
see to it that it's done.'

Beresford sighed again. 'You're the boss,' he said.

'Yes, I am,' Paniatowski agreed.

'But how much longer that will be the case is anybody's
guess,' Beresford told her.

TWENTY-TWO

When the lorry driver had stopped to pick up a hitch-
hiker on the slip-road out of Manchester, he had not
known either that his potential passenger was drunk
or that he was a walking advertisement for the need for a
deodorant, but both these things soon became apparent once the
man had climbed into the cab. Still, the driver told himself
philosophically, even a drunk's rambling conversation could help
break up the monotony of the journey, and as long as he kept
smoking, the smell would not be too bad.

'So where are you going?' he asked his passenger.

'Whitebridge,' Mike Eccles told him.

'Do you live there?'

'I used to – but it was a long time ago.'

'So what made you decide to go back now? Do you have
family still living there?'

'Oh yes, I've got family, all right,' Eccles said, slurring his words more obviously now. 'I've got an evil bitch of a wife who I haven't seen for twenty-one years. But I'll be seeing her soon, won't I?'

'I imagine it'll be a bit of a shock for her, you just turning up like that,' said the lorry driver, who was beginning to wonder if he was doing the right thing in helping this man reach his destination.

'She made a *big* mistake by appearin' on the telly,' Eccles said. 'If she hadn't appeared on the telly, I'd never have known.'

'Known what?' the lorry driver asked.

But Eccles was clearly bored with this particular strand of the conversation, and wanted to move on to something else.

'Nobody would have her but me,' he said. 'Nobody *wanted* her but me. An' do you know . . . do you know why *I* wanted her?'

'No, I don't,' the lorry driver said, uncertain that he really needed to hear the answer to that particular question.

'I wanted her because of what I've got up here,' Eccles boasted, tapping his forehead with his dirty index finger. 'Brains,' he amplified, in case the lorry driver had missed the point. 'Oh yes, I knew which side my bread was buttered on – make no mistake about that.' Then his mood suddenly changed, as drunks' moods are apt to. 'But it all went wrong,' he continued, as tears began to trickle from his eyes. 'It all went wrong, an' it wasn't my fault.'

With fellers like him, whatever happened was *never* their own fault, the lorry driver thought.

'Listen,' he said aloud, 'if you *are* going to see your wife, it might be a good idea to smarten yourself up a bit first.'

'What d'ya mean?' Eccles asked aggressively.

'Well, to be honest with you, I don't think you can exactly expect a warm welcome home under any circumstances – not after you've been gone for twenty-one years,' the lorry driver said. 'But you'll stand a better chance if you look as if you've at least made the effort.'

'I don't need to make the effort,' Eccles told him. 'An' d'ya . . . d'ya know why?'

The lorry driver said nothing.

'An' d'ya know why?' Eccles repeated.

'No,' the lorry driver admitted. 'I don't know why.'

'Because that family owes me!' Eccles said. 'Because, by marryin' that bitch, I made them *respectable*.'

If he'd made them respectable by marrying her, it was hard
to imagine what they'd been like *before* the wedding, the lorry
driver thought.

'Stop!' Eccles said, with a sudden urgency. 'Stop right now!
I gotta . . . I gotta throw up.'

The lorry driver checked in his side mirror, and indicated he
was about to pull in.

'Quick,' Eccles gasped, as he swallowed in an effort to post-
pone the inevitable.

The lorry came to a halt.

Eccles opened the door, missed his footing halfway down, and
fell into a crumpled heap on the grass verge. For a moment, he
just lay there. Then he rolled over, forcing himself back on to his
knees, and the moment he'd done that, his body – finding itself
in the optimum position for vomiting – restrained itself no more.

The lorry driver watched, with increasing disgust, as Eccles
spewed up the results of his morning's drinking on to the vegeta-
tion. He considered himself a tolerant man by nature, he thought,
but, really, he'd had enough. He reached across and closed the
passenger door shut, then slid into first gear and pulled away.

Still on his knees, Eccles heard the sound of the lorry moving
off, and just managed, between bouts of retching, to gasp the
word 'bastard'.

Edward Wilberforce looked first at the man sitting opposite
him and then at the document which lay on the desk between
them.

'I have been your family's solicitor for a good many years
now, Robert,' he said.

'I know you have,' Robert Howerd agreed.

'Over those years, I have done my very best to offer you
advice which was both cautious by nature and in your best long-
term interest.'

'And you've made a splendid job of it,' Howerd told him.

'I have also, despite occasional misgivings about the wisdom
of a particular course of action you have chosen, always obeyed
the instructions you gave me to the letter.'

'Thank you.'

'And that is what I've done on *this* particular occasion, Robert,
though with more misgivings than I can ever remember before.'
Wilberforce tapped the document on the desk. 'This, in my
opinion, is neither prudent *nor* in your best interest.'

'It's what I want,' Howerd said firmly.

'But surely we can find some compromise – some middle ground,' the solicitor suggested.

'No.'

'I simply do not see why . . .'

'The Howerd family follows the teachings of the Holy Catholic Church,' Robert said. 'It always has.'

'I know that.'

'I have tried to be true to my faith, though I have sinned many times, because man, by his very nature, is imperfect—'

'Yes, well, I'm sure we're all guilty of a few sins, now and again,' interrupted Wilberforce, who – as a staunchly *social* member of the Church of England – was finding the whole direction the conversation was taking to be slightly uncomfortable.

'We must do penance for our sins,' said Howerd, not to be put off. 'And the greater the sin, the greater must be the penance.'

'I quite understand that.'

'And this,' said Howerd, tapping the document as Wilberforce had done earlier, 'is *my* penance.'

The sun was slowly sinking behind the mountains. Soon the twilight would descend, and with it would come the chorus of tiny insects whose job it was to close the day. Yet the day was far from drawing to a close for Charlie Woodend, who was still sitting on his terrace, gazing at the sheet of paper with the names written on it.

'Why don't you take a break, Charlie?' asked Paco Ruiz, concerned for his friend. 'We could both go down to Pedro's bar, and play dominoes with the boys for an hour or so.'

'I don't have time for a break,' Woodend replied, more curtly than he would normally have done. 'My reputation's at stake here.'

'I know,' Ruiz agreed. 'But perhaps, if you thought about something else for a while—'

'An' it's not just mine that's threatened,' Woodend interrupted him. 'It's Monika's. I know her. She'll go out on a limb for me – she always has – an' there's a good chance that if I go down, I'll drag her down as well. An' I simply can't have that, Paco.'

'She's not just an old colleague to you, is she?' Ruiz asked softly. 'You love the woman, don't you?'

'Aye, I do,' Woodend admitted. 'But don't get me wrong,' he added hastily, 'the kind of love that I have for Monika has nothin' at all to do with her bein' a *woman*.'

Paco snorted sceptically. 'Are you saying that you're not in the least attracted to her?' he asked.

'Well, of course I'm attracted to her,' Woodend replied. 'A man would have to be blind *not* to be attracted to her. But I've never let that get in the way of our relationship.'

'Never?' Paco asked – and the scepticism was still there.

Woodend sighed. 'All right, there was one time when I suppose it *might* have happened.'

The other man said nothing.

'Do you want to hear about it or not?' Woodend demanded.

Paco smiled. 'Go on,' he said.

'We were involved in a particularly unpleasant case. A young girl had been found dead in a moorland farmhouse, an' – for reasons I won't go into now – there were some powerful people in Whitebridge who didn't want the murder lookin' into too closely. So what they did to bring the investigation to a grindin' halt was to try an' fit me up on corruption charges. An', I have to say, they made a pretty good attempt at it. There was a real possibility that I'd go to jail.'

Paco nodded. 'I get the picture.'

'An' it was then, when things were at their nastiest, that we almost fell into bed together,' Woodend said.

'I see,' Paco said.

'It would have been an act born out of desperation – and nothin' more,' Woodend said firmly. 'It would have been Monika offerin' me the only comfort she still had left to offer me, an' me takin' it, because I was more frightened of goin' to prison than I'd ever been under enemy fire. But, by God, lookin' back, I'm glad we *didn't* do it – because it would have ruined everythin' that we'd worked so hard to build up between us.'

'I can see that,' Paco said – and now the scepticism was gone, and he was being deathly serious.

Woodend lit up a fresh Ducados. 'I want to tell you somethin' now that I've never told anybody before – an' the *reason* I want to tell you is so that you'll really understand Monika, an' how I feel about her,' he said.

'I'm listening,' Paco told him.

'Monika was abused as a child,' Woodend said heavily. 'Her bastard of a stepfather first started climbing into her bed when she was ten or eleven – she's not sure which – an' it went on for years. That experience would have destroyed most girls, but somehow Monika managed to summon up the spirit to overcome it. She had the balls to stick with her job in the Force, too, at a time when most bobbies thought that all female officers were good for was makin' the tea, filin' the reports an' talkin' to grievin' relatives. An' now she's a chief inspector.'

'Yes, she is,' Paco said.

'She's come so far,' Woodend said. 'That's why I can't let her down. That's why I've got to stick at this thing until I come up with an answer.' He gazed at the sheet of paper again – at the list of names he had written and then rejected. 'The anonymous caller – Mr X – told her he *couldn't* give her the killer's name,' he said for the fiftieth time. 'What was stoppin' him? What would stop *you*?'

'I suppose I might have made a promise to someone not to say anything,' Paco suggested.

'An' would you have felt bound by that, even if you knew it meant shelterin' a murderer?'

'Probably not. But I might have felt that way if the promise I'd made wasn't just an ordinary promise – if, say, it was an oath.'

'You're thinkin' of the Freemasons, aren't you?' Woodend asked.

'Yes.'

Woodend shook his head. 'Unlike a lot of bobbies, I've not got a lot of time for the funny handshake and bare bollock brigade, but I've still got enough respect for them to know they'd never try to hide somethin' like this. What else can you suggest?'

'I might have felt constrained if I thought it was for the general good.'

'An' what do you mean by that, exactly?'

'I'm not sure, Charlie,' Paco admitted. 'I'm still playing around with the idea.' He strode to the end of the terrace, then turned around and continued, 'Let us say, for example, that I was a member of the security service, and, as a result of that, I knew that the killer's continued liberty was essential for the good of my country. Under those circumstances, I think I might choose to sacrifice the one for the many, and hold my silence.'

'An' do you think Mr X is likely to be a spy?'

'No, I don't. In fact, the more I think about it, the less probable it seems.' Paco paced the terrace again. 'Could it be that Mr X is being limited by a professional code of conduct?'

'You mean like a lawyer or psychiatrist?'

'Exactly.'

'That's the best suggestion you've come up with yet, my old mate,' Woodend said. 'But it's still not very likely, because, under English law, both lawyers and psychiatrists are obliged to reveal any knowledge they have of a crime, and if they *don't* reveal it, they could go to prison themselves.'

'Then, if none of those ideas are of any use to you, I am at a complete loss,' Paco admitted.

'Aye, an' I'm at a complete bloody loss myself,' Woodend said despondently. He turned his attention back to the large sheet of paper. 'The anonymous caller said he couldn't tell Monika what she wanted to know,' he mumbled. 'Not that he *wouldn't* tell her, but that he *couldn't*.'

It was getting dark, and some of the vehicles speeding past Mike Eccles had already switched on their headlights. He had no real idea of how long he'd been standing on the spot where the lorry driver had abandoned him – he had pawned his last wristwatch, for drinking money, years earlier – but he thought it must be several hours at least.

'Why won't you stop an' give me a lift, you bloody swine?' he shouted after a motorist who had actually speeded up when he'd seen a vomit-stained man standing there with his thumb out.

None of them would give him a lift, he thought miserably – and it just wasn't fair.

It was just under twenty miles to Whitebridge, he calculated. If he started walking now, he could easily be there by morning.

But he didn't *want* to walk.

He didn't see why he should *have to* walk.

'Bloody bastards!' he said, to the world in general.

He needed to come up with some other plan of action, he told himself – one that didn't require quite so much effort on his part.

He put his hand into the pocket of his threadbare jacket, and felt his fingers brush against the half-bottle of cheap whisky that he had been hoarding for emergencies.

'I'll only have one little slug,' he promised himself. 'I'll drink just enough to help me come up with a plan.'

He glugged back most of what was left in the bottle, and immediately started to feel dizzy.

He didn't actually *need* to come up with a plan right away, he decided hazily. It was quite a warm night, and he still had a little booze left. What was wrong with bedding down by the side of the road until morning, when everything was bound to be clearer?

Yes, he would think the whole thing through in the morning, he told himself as he lay down on the verge and squiggled in search of a comfortable position.

And soon, when he'd got his hands on all that money which Elizabeth would be *forced* to give him, he wouldn't need to *think* at all.

Paniatowski had rung the team to call off the evening meeting at the Drum and Monkey.

'There haven't been any new leads since the last time we talked,' she'd told Crane and Beresford, 'so we might as well grab the opportunity to have an early night for once.'

What she'd said had been accurate – as far as it went.

The other police forces in the region had all been more than willing to cooperate in her search for Mike Eccles, but willingness was all they'd been able to offer so far, because none of them had the faintest idea where he might actually *be*.

She hadn't got the list of Mottershead's associates from Walter Brown yet, either. When she'd called at his bookshop, towards the end of the afternoon, she discovered that he'd closed much earlier than the sign in the window promised he would, and when she'd rung his home phone number, no one had answered.

But there was another reason for her reluctance to go to the Drum that night, and that reason – which she could barely bring herself to admit, even *to* herself – was Beresford.

She couldn't stand the thought that he might question her whole approach to the investigation again – might hold up all her arguments under the harsh light of logic, and expose them for the tattered, flawed remnants that they actually were.

And it would have been even worse if he *hadn't* done that – if, instead, he'd sat there like the loyal member of her team he was and pretended to be going along fully with everything she said.

And so, instead of spending the evening with her lads, she had spent it with her daughter – trying to show interest in Louisa's daily adventures and pushing to the back of her mind the thought that if she failed this time, then everything Charlie Woodend had worked for – everything Charlie Woodend *was* – would be destroyed.

She had just tucked her daughter in bed – and given her the goodnight kiss which she sometimes suspected Louisa secretly considered herself too old for – when the phone rang.

The caller was Dr Shastri, the police surgeon.

'And how are you, tonight, my dear Chief Inspector?' Shastri asked, in her usual chirpy manner.

Paniatowski pictured the good doctor, a beautiful coffee-coloured woman, swathed in a multicoloured sari and a wicked sense of humour.

'I'm fine,' she lied. 'I've never been better. Is there something that I can do for you, Doc?'

'Perhaps,' Shastri replied. 'My confidential sources tell me that you are re-investigating the Lilly Dawson case.'

Despite herself, Paniatowski could not resist a smile. 'Your confidential sources, in this case, being the local television news?' she guessed.

Shastri laughed. 'Just so,' she readily agreed. 'And having received that information, it occurred to me that you might possibly, in the course of your investigations, have talked to Mrs Elizabeth Eccles, the daughter of the man who was falsely convicted of killing Lilly.'

'Yes, I talked to her,' Paniatowski said, as an image of the sour-faced Elizabeth floated across her mind.

'And was it a long discussion you had with her, or no more than a few words?' Shastri asked.

'It was quite a long discussion.'

'In that case, my dear Monika, I wonder if you could find the time to visit the morgue some time tomorrow,' Shastri said.

'What's it all about?' Paniatowski wondered.

'It is a little difficult for a simple Indian doctor like myself to explain over the phone,' Shastri told her. 'It would be much better for us to talk face to face, if you can possibly spare the time.'

With the clock relentlessly ticking off the hours until she had to submit her report – and the chief constable breathing down her neck while it did so – time *should have been* the last thing she had to spare, Paniatowski thought.

Yet she could not honestly say – without any new leads – that this was the case at all.

Besides, even if she'd been busy, she would still have had to *make* time to see Shastri, because the doctor had been a good friend and a good colleague over the years, and had rarely asked for any favours in return.

'Monika?' Shastri said questioningly

'I'll be there,' Paniatowski promised. 'I can't say exactly when it will be, but I'll be there.'

'What a sweet little thing you really are,' Shastri said. 'I shall look forward to seeing you, then. And will you do one more thing for me?'

'Of course.

'Please give my love to Louisa, and say I look forward to seeing her, too, though in slightly cheerier surroundings than the police morgue.'

'I'll do that,' Paniatowski told her.

'Then there is no more to be said, except to wish you goodnight and sweet dreams.'

'Sweet dreams!' Paniatowski repeated to herself as she hung up the phone.

Dark nightmares would be closer to the mark, she suspected

TWENTY-THREE

Charlie Woodend awoke to the sound of seagulls engaging in a heated discussion on the roof of his villa.

There was something to be said for being a seagull – or any other wild creature for that matter – he thought. It wasn't an ideal existence, obviously – the diet was incredibly monotonous, it was almost impossible to get health insurance, and you were in constant danger of vicious little kids with airguns taking potshots at you as you flew over them – but at least, by being a seagull, you never ran the risk of having your reputation destroyed or of seeing your life's work turned to ashes before your eyes.

'It's nice that you can still be whimsical, Charlie,' he told himself, as he climbed out of bed. 'Well done, lad.'

But the whimsy, edged as it already was with a sense of grim reality, did not last him even as far as the kitchen.

'Think, Charlie, think!' he urged himself as he filled the kettle. 'Who *couldn't* tell you something, even if he wanted to?'

In the distance, he could hear the sound of the church bell tolling. It was a very un-English sound, he thought, as different from the church bells back home as it could possibly be. There, in Anglican England, a peal of six or eight beautifully constructed bells created a melodious sound which gently drifted across the verdant countryside and reminded the faithful that, if it was not too much trouble, God would rather like their presence in His house. Here, in Catholic Spain, it was a single bell – little more than an upturned bucket, in Woodend's opinion – which harshly and uncompromisingly called the worshippers to mass.

The kettle had boiled. Woodend poured the steaming water into the pot, and was just lighting up his first cigarette when he suddenly froze.

'Jesus!' he said.

Paco had been quite right to advise him to stop thinking about the anonymous caller and turn his mind to something else for a while – because he'd done just that, and it had worked.

Now he had the answer, it was so obvious that he almost couldn't believe it had taken so long to occur to him – because of all the answers he *could have* come up with, it was the only one which truly *fitted*.

He wished that he could be whisked back to Whitebridge in a second, so that he could follow up the sudden insight himself.

But since that was not going to happen, he thought, he'd better talk to Monika as soon as possible.

The bookshop door was open, and Walter Brown was sitting behind the counter, quietly reading. He was aware she was there, but did look up until he had finished the paragraph.

'I called you at home last night, but you didn't pick up the phone,' Paniatowski said reproachfully, before she could stop herself.

And then she thought, Don't pressurize him. For God's sake, don't *pressurize* him.

'I didn't answer the phone because I wasn't there to answer it,' Brown told her. 'I went for a long walk. I visited all the places that I knew as a younger man – as a *different* man. I thought doing that might help me to decide whether or not to give you the list you wanted.'

'And *did* it help?' Paniatowski asked calmly, though what she really wanted to do was grab him by his cardigan and scream, 'Give me the bloody list!'

'Yes, it helped,' Walter Brown said. Then he added, with a slight smile, 'I decided that I'm going to trust you to do the right thing – even though you *are* a police officer.'

The list! a voice in Paniatowski's head thundered. Hand over the bloody list!

Brown's smiled widened. 'I can see that you're more than eager to read it, so here it is,' he said, holding up a piece of paper which been lying on the counter.

As Paniatowski took the list from him, she could not fail to notice the slight tremble in her hand.

Calm down, she ordered herself. It's only a few names. It may not lead anywhere.

'Would you allow me to ask you about the people on this list?' she said to Brown.

'By all means, ask,' Brown replied, as if he'd been anticipating the question. 'But you must accept – right from the start – that if I don't want to give you answers, I won't.'

'That's understood,' Paniatowski agreed.

Walter Brown's handwriting was large, clear and almost child-like, and though she'd cautioned herself that it would be a few names, the list was, in fact, very long.

Paniatowski scanned the names. She recognized a few of them from the days when she'd been in uniform, and in regular contact with Whitebridge's petty criminal fraternity, but this list was history, rather than news, and most of the names were unknown to her.

This wasn't going to help, she thought with sickening realization. In her desperation, she'd pinned most of her hopes on this list – and it wasn't going to lead her anywhere!

And then she saw a name which made her heart beat a little faster.

'What's Fred Howerd doing on this list?' she asked, almost breathlessly.

'You asked me for the names of all Mottershead's known associates, and that's what I've given you,' Brown told her.

'But Fred Howerd was . . .'

'A little wild in his youth, but later a successful market trader who would one day inherit his half-share of his father's business?' Brown asked, with obvious amusement.

'Well, yes.'

'You've really no idea what Fred was actually like, have you, Chief Inspector?' Brown asked.

'Then enlighten me,' Paniatowski said.

'There are men who are just naturally bent – who couldn't resist the opportunity of stealing a penny from a poor orphan,

even if they already had a thousand pounds in their pocket –
and Fred Howerd was one of them.'

'Are you saying he was a thief?'

'Not exactly a thief. He was more of a fence, I suppose.
To be strictly accurate, he was the last stage in the fencing
process.'

'Could you explain that?'

'Fred sold electrical goods on the market, but they didn't
belong to him, they belonged to his father – and his father took
most of the profit.'

'Yes, it's natural that he would.'

'But let's just suppose that, as well as doing that, he used his
father's business to sell goods the old man *hadn't* provided him
with.'

'Stolen goods! You're saying Fred dealt in *stolen goods*?'

'That's exactly what I'm saying. If I nicked anything new
– or even nearly new – Mottershead would pass it on to Fred,
who'd sell it off at a slight discount.' He chuckled. 'And do
you know what's ironic – some of the stolen goods that Fred
sold from his father's stall had actually been stolen from his
father!'

'So Fred fenced the goods and then split the profits with
Mottershead?'

'Yes, and the real beauty of the racket was that Howerd
Electrical had a reputation in Whitebridge for absolute honesty
– the old man was a God-fearing Catholic, you know – so it
never occurred to anybody that some of the goods might be a
bit dodgy.'

And so Fred had abused his position and cheated his father,
Paniatowski thought.

Worse than that, he had risked his father's reputation, because
if he'd been caught, there would have been plenty of people who
would think the old man was in on it.

A sudden fresh wave of depression washed over her. She had
discovered a minor racket which had been played out nearly a
quarter of a century earlier – but where did *that* get her?

'Did Howerd ever have a falling out with Mottershead, like
the one you had?' she asked hopefully.

Brown shook his head. 'They never exchanged a cross word,
as far as I know.'

'But it's possible, isn't it, that Mottershead cheated Howerd
just as he cheated you, and that Howerd found out about it?'

'Mottershead would never even have dreamed of cheating Fred,' Brown said, with conviction.

'How can you be so sure of that?'

'Would *you* cheat your best friend?'

'They were *best friends*?' Paniatowski asked, incredulously.

'Maybe *friends* is the wrong word,' Brown admitted, 'but it's difficult to find the right one.' He waved his hands helplessly in the air, then grinned, and added, 'Do you know, there are some days when I really wish I was Tolstoy.'

And there are some days when I wish I was one of those detectives you read about in mystery novels, who always seem to know all the answers immediately, Paniatowski thought.

'You're doing fine,' she assured Walter Brown. 'Just take your time.'

'I used to know two fellers called Brian King and Eric Dewhurst,' Brown said. 'They were very keen fly-fishermen – almost fanatical about it, if the truth be told. They spent nearly all their free time together, but apart from the fishing, they had nothing at all in common. Do you understand what I'm saying?'

'I think so.'

'Brian liked dancing, but Eric had two left feet. Eric was a supporter of the Rovers, but football left Brian cold.' Brown chuckled. 'You'd only got to look at their wives to really see how different they were – they'd never have gone in for wife swapping, that pair, because each one thought his own wife was gorgeous and that his mate's wife wouldn't have looked at all out of place in a horror movie. And then there was—'

'I get the point,' Paniatowski interrupted. 'They'd never have been friends under normal circumstances, but their mutual interest – their mutual obsession – in fly-fishing held them together.'

'That's it!' Walter Brown agreed. 'It created a sort of invisible bond between them – a bond that outsiders, who didn't share their obsession, couldn't possibly understand.'

'And Howerd and Mottershead had the same kind of bond?'

'That's what I'm saying.'

'So what was it *they* were interested in?'

'To tell you the truth, I don't really know,' Walter Brown confessed. 'Whatever it was, they never talked about it when there were ever any other people around – which is more than you could say for Brian and Eric, with their bloody fly-fishing.'

'You must have some idea – even if it's only a very vague one,' Paniatowski pressed him.

'I do know is that they sometimes used to go off for half-day excursions together, if that's any help.'

'Where did they go, when they took these excursions?'

'Again, they never talked about it. But I remember them once lettin' it slip – accidentally like – that they'd been to Bolton.'

The message that the desk sergeant handed to Paniatowski said simply that Charlie Woodend had called from Spain and wanted to speak to her urgently.

'He asked me to underline "urgently" three times, so I'd imagine he means it,' the sergeant said.

Charlie must believe that he'd come up with the name of the anonymous informer, Paniatowski thought, too impatient to wait for the lift, and instead taking the stairs three at a time.

And maybe he had.

But even if he was wrong about that, she still wanted to talk to him, because – suddenly – the case was on new level.

Charlie had once told her that, in many ways, an investigation was just like a jigsaw puzzle, she remembered, as she rushed down the corridor towards her office. All you had to do was fit all the pieces of the puzzle together and you'd have the complete picture. But *unlike* a jigsaw, he'd cautioned, the pieces weren't all lying neatly in the box – they were spread all over the place, and before you could begin to slot them into place, you first had to bloody well find them.

Well, she'd scooped up a number of the pieces that morning. There were not enough for the complete picture, it was true, but at least she now had some idea of what *kind* of picture it was – and she wanted to find out what Charlie made of it all.

She had meant to hear what Woodend had to say before laying out her own discoveries in front of him, but when he answered the phone, Paniatowski just began talking.

She told him all about the fencing racket deal that Howerd had been running with Mottershead, and how, beyond that – or so it seemed to Walter Brown – the two men were united by a strong common interest. She talked about their half-day excursions, at least one of which had been to Bolton.

It was as she was talking that she suddenly realized she did not sound like the detective chief inspector who was in charge of the case at all, but much more closely resembled the eager young sergeant who she'd once been, in the process of reporting a triumph to her wise and all-seeing boss. She realized it – and she didn't give a damn!

When she'd finished, Woodend said, 'You've done well, Monika. Now let's talk about what it all means.'

And they did. They argued the case back and to, and inside out. They challenged each other's theories with a passion, and reached common ground with some relief. And when they had finished, Paniatowski felt exhausted.

'You've been a great help, Charlie,' Paniatowski said. 'No, more than that – you've been a bloody marvel.'

Woodend chuckled.

The chuckle annoyed Paniatowski for a second, because it seemed as if he was laughing at *her*. Then she told herself not to be so sensitive, that it was good that he *could* chuckle, because that meant that – at least in his opinion – the darkest days were possibly behind them.

'What's so funny, Charlie?' she asked.

'You were about to hang up the phone, weren't you, Monika?' Woodend replied – and he was still laughing at a joke that, as yet, she seemed unable to share with him.

'Well, yes, I was about to hang up,' she admitted. 'I thought we'd thrashed out pretty much all we *could* thrash out for the moment, and that I needed to brief my team next. Anything wrong with that?'

'Not really,' Woodend said, 'except that you seem to have forgotten that though *you* rang *me*, it was only because I asked you to.'

'That's true,' Paniatowski replied, a slightly perplexed frown crossing her brow. 'Why was that, Charlie? Was it because . . .' And then it hit her. 'Of course! You think you know who Mr X is!' she all but screamed.

'That's right,' Woodend agreed.

'So who the bloody hell *is* he?'

'What you're looking for is a man wracked by guilt and weighed down by his sense of responsibility,' Woodend told her.

He was teasing her, she thought, but after what he'd been through, she supposed he was entitled to.

'Go on,' she said.

'He knows the right thing to do, and he wants to do it. The only problem is that in doing the right thing, he will also be doing the *wrong* thing – because it will mean betraying the principles which have guided his life. So he looks for a compromise – a way of letting you know what you *need* to know, without breaking the confidences that have been entrusted to him.'

'A name, Charlie,' Paniatowski said, giving in to her exasperation. 'Give me a bloody name!'

And he did.

'Of course!' she said, banging her forehead with the flat of her hand. 'I was a fool not to have seen it earlier.'

'We were *both* fools not to have seen it earlier. But now we've got the information, you have to use it, an' if you want my opinion . . .'

'You know I do.'

'You have to use it *quickly*. This is one of them cases where you must strike while the iron is hot. If you don't crack it today, the people involved will soon start buildin' up walls between you an' the truth – an' then the chances are that you'll *never* crack it.'

'You're right,' she agreed.

'So bearin' that in mind, I'd better leave you to get on with it. Good luck, Monika.'

'Thank you, sir,' Paniatowski said.

As she hung up, it occurred to her that, for a while back there, they really *had* been the old team, with Charlie Woodend firmly in charge. But it wasn't like that any more, now that she'd put the phone down, she reminded herself. *She* was in charge – and whatever successes or failures the day brought would all be down to her.

The door opened, and Crane and Beresford entered the office. They looked first at her, and then at each other.

'Something's happened,' Beresford guessed.

'You're damn right something's happened!' Paniatowski agreed. 'Sit down, lads – but don't make yourselves too comfortable, because you've got a busy day ahead of you.'

'A busy day?' Crane repeated. 'What is it that you'll be wanting us to do, boss?'

'I don't know yet,' admitted Paniatowski, whose head was still spinning from her conversation with Woodend. 'I haven't had time to work out all the details, but give me five minutes and I'll get there.'

TWENTY-THREE

M ike Eccles had never walked with a bounce in his entire
life, but as he made his way up the steep cobbled street
he had last walked over twenty years earlier, there was
less of a shuffle to his step than usual.

In his own mind's eye, he was nothing less than a hero – for
how else could you describe a man who had made the epic
journey from Manchester to Whitebridge with unfailing courage
and determination?

It had not been easy. His first lift that morning – after he'd
woken up by the side of the road, still drunk – had been on a farm
tractor. The second had involved sitting on the back of a builder's
lorry, where his fellow passengers had been breeze blocks and bags
of cement. And the final stage, from the outskirts of Whitebridge,
had had to be made on foot, since an aggressive bus conductor
had refused to let him mount the bus on the totally unreasonable
grounds that, as well as having no money, he stank.

No, it hadn't been easy at all, but against the odds, he had
made it – and now, as heroes always do, he was about to claim
his reward.

It would have occurred to most men in his situation that, as
twenty-one years had passed since he'd left Whitebridge, his wife
might no longer live in the house they had briefly shared, but he
was not a great thinker, and the idea never crossed his mind. Nor,
as things turned out, had his mind *needed* to exercise itself unduly,
because as he drew closer to his old home, he saw Elizabeth
standing on the doorstep, watching workmen loading her furniture into a large van.

So she was moving, he thought. Well, given all that had
happened recently, that certainly made sense.

The furniture van was pulling away as he reached the house,
and his wife was just about to go back indoors when he called
out, 'Liz!'

She turned towards him, and a look of disgust – though not
of recognition – filled her face.

'It's me – Mike,' he said. 'Your husband.'

Disgust rapidly turned to shock.

'Just look at the state of you,' she said.

'You're not in such great shape yourself,' he told her. Then, realizing it would make things easier if he had her on his side, he added, 'It's been a long time, Elizabeth. We've both got older.'

'What do you want?' she demanded.

'My share,' he said simply.

'Your *what*?'

'We both know why you married me – and why I married you,' he said.

He had seen disgust in her eyes, and shock in her eyes, and now – for just an instant – he saw fear.

'Yes, we both *do* know why we got married,' she agreed, looking down at the pavement.

'Well, I've fulfilled my side of the bargain,' Eccles said. 'I'd done that the moment I put the ring on your finger. But you never came through for me, did you? And now it's time you did.'

Elizabeth raised her head again, and looked frantically up and down the steep street.

'Listen, I've only got a few pounds in the house at the moment,' she said urgently, 'but if you take them – and then leave straight-away – I'll get you some more later.'

'How *much* more?' he asked.

She ran her eyes over his threadbare clothes, and did a quick mental calculation. 'Five hundred pounds,' she said.

'It's not enough,' he told her.

'Not enough!' she repeated scornfully. 'It's more money than you've seen in your life.'

'You might be right about that,' Eccles agreed. 'But when you think about what I've been through—'

'What *you've* been through?' Elizabeth interrupted him. '*I'm* the one who's had to stay here. *I'm* the one who's put up with the neighbours sniggering at me and people crossing the road to avoid me.'

'He was your father, not mine,' Eccles pointed out.

'Yes, and if he *hadn't* been my father – if I'd had some *other* father – you'd never have wanted to marry me in the first place.'

'I want my share,' Eccles said, stubbornly reverting back to his original argument.

'I might perhaps be able to raise a *thousand* pounds, if you give me enough time,' Elizabeth said.

'That isn't enough, either,' Eccles said, sticking firmly to his guns. 'I want half of what you're getting.'

It was anger that blazed in Elizabeth's eyes now. 'You're totally insane!' she said.

And before he could stop her, she had stepped back inside the house, and slammed the door.

Eccles hammered on the door with his fists. 'Let me in!' he screamed. 'I want my share.'

A neighbour – a stocky middle-aged woman in a floral pinafore – opened her door.

'Will you please stop makin' all that dreadful noise,' she said. 'My husband's on shift work, an' he's tryin' to get some sleep.'

'Bugger off!' Eccles said.

'If you don't stop immediately, I'll call the police,' the pinafored woman threatened.

'Call 'em if you want to – see if I care,' Eccles told her, before resuming his banging.

More doors opened.

'Tell him you'll call the police, Edna,' shouted another woman, from across the road.

'I've already told him that,' the neighbour shouted back. 'He's taken no damn notice.'

'I'm surprised *she's* not already called them,' said a third woman, pointing at Elizabeth Eccles's house.

'Her!' said the first neighbour. 'She's as bad as he is.'

Eccles stopped flailing against the door and looked around him.

'I need a key,' he said. 'Has anybody got a key?'

The women all moved back from their steps into their hallways, and closed the front doors behind them.

'A key,' Eccles said, to the now empty street. 'Will somebody please give me a key?'

He searched around for a weapon, and found one in the shape of a half-brick that was lying in the road.

He walked back to the door, and called through the letterbox, 'This is your last chance, Liz.'

When there was no answer, he stepped back again, and hurled the half-brick through Elizabeth's front window.

The street was suddenly filled with the sound of shattering glass – and then it was filled with the sound of a police car siren.

The chief constable looked up from his pile of paperwork and said, 'Would you like to take a seat, Chief Inspector?'

Paniatowski shook her head. 'No, thank you, sir. I can see

you're busy and I don't want to detain you longer than I need to.'

Or to put it another way, she thought, the less time I'm here, the less chance you'll have of asking me questions I don't want to answer.

'So what can I do for you?' George Baxter asked.

'I think that perhaps I may have been acting a little unreasonably recently, sir,' Paniatowski said contritely. 'I think I—'

'You, Chief Inspector?' Baxter interrupted her. 'Acting unreasonably? I find the very idea almost impossible to comprehend.' He smiled. 'What do you actually *want*, Monika?'

'I want you to schedule a press conference in time for the midday news bulletin, sir,' Paniatowski said.

'Really!' Baxter replied. 'And is there anything specific you'd like me to say at this press conference – or shall I just make it up as I go along?'

'I'd like you to say that there is clear evidence of police misconduct in the Fred Howerd case, and that you expect to issue a more comprehensive statement by tomorrow morning at the latest.'

'Why?'

Paniatowski shrugged, as if the answer were obvious. 'That – or something like it – is what you've been wanting to say for some time, sir.'

'I know it is,' Baxter agreed. 'What I'm interested in now is why *you* want me to say it.'

'I'm hoping that by shaking things up a bit, I'll get the answers to several questions that have been troubling me, sir,' Paniatowski said, almost clinically.

'Oh, come on, Monika, that won't do at all,' the chief constable told her. 'You're going to have to be much more specific.'

Yes, Paniatowski thought, sighing inwardly, she supposed she was.

She outlined her reasons for wanting the press conference, and when she'd finished, Baxter said, 'It's a risky strategy, Monika.'

'Yes, sir.'

'You may not get the result that you're hoping for.'

'I know that.'

'And once I've promised the press a more comprehensive statement by tomorrow, I *will* deliver that statement – and you'll help me to prepare it.'

'I understand, sir.'

'And when I *have* delivered it, any chance you might once have had of protecting Charlie Woodend could be gone for ever.'

'I have thought it all through, you know,' Paniatowski said, only just containing her irritation. 'I do realize all that.'

'And do you also realize that not only may I have to serve up Woodend's head on a platter, but I might also have to use the officer who tried to protect him as garnish?'

'Like I said, I've thought it all through,' Paniatowski said.

And then she shivered.

It really bothered DC Crane that he found Dr Shastri so attractive, because though she was not quite old enough to be his mother, she was probably the same age as his Aunt Sarah, and a young man like him had no business fancying *anybody's* auntie. It bothered him even more that, as a trained doctor, she might possibly notice the *physical* manifestation of that attraction – which was even now straining against the trousers of his second-best suit – and, instead of being flattered, would merely laugh at him.

'You seem preoccupied, Detective Constable,' Shastri said, in a silky voice which didn't make the situation any easier for him.

Crane swallowed hard. 'I was . . . err . . . just running through the details of the case I've come to ask you about, Ma'am,' he said.

'Please call me "Doc",' Shastri said. 'Which case are you interested in?'

'The Barry Mottershead murder.'

Shastri frowned – which seemed to make her even *more* attractive, if that were possible.

'The name is not familiar to me,' she said.

'No, of course, it wouldn't be,' Crane agreed. 'It was long before your time, Ma'am . . . Doc. 1951, to be exact. But there will still be a copy of the autopsy report somewhere, won't there?'

'Of course there will,' Shastri agreed. 'And if you want to see it, all you have to do is go to the general office and ask one the clerks to take you down to the archives.'

'Thank you, Doc,' said Crane, finally getting it right this time.

Shastri smiled, and, but for the fact that she was a highly qualified doctor in a senior position, Crane would almost have called the smile a mischievous one.

'There is nothing wrong with it at all, you know, Detective Constable,' she said.

'Nothing wrong with what?'

'With what you are experiencing at the moment. Among men of your tender age, the rampant Oedipus complex is much more prevalent that you might imagine – but do not fear, you will no doubt grow out of it in time.'

'I . . . err . . . I'd better go and find your clerk, ma'am,' Crane said.

'Yes, I think you better had,' Shastri agreed.

And as he walked away, Crane was almost certain he could hear the sound of Shastri gently chuckling to herself.

The senior clerk was somewhere in her fifties – which Crane considered *really* old – but, even so, he simply could not stop himself from noticing that she still had rather shapely legs.

'Bloody hell, if I'm not careful I'll be fancying my own granny next,' he thought, as he followed her down the corridor.

The archive was a large, daunting room lined with metal filing cabinets which reached from floor to ceiling, but the clerk with the good legs – who said her name was Mrs Walton – seemed totally *undaunted*, and went straight over to a cabinet in the corner.

'When you've worked here for as long as I have, there's nothing you can't find,' she said, sensing his wonder.

'How long would that be?' Crane asked.

'Twenty-three years,' Mrs Walton told him, then added dryly, 'and, do you know, it's been such fun that it's just seemed like one long roller-coaster ride.'

Twenty-three years! Crane repeated silently. He'd been just a baby when she'd first started filing things away in this place.

Mrs Walton slid the cabinet door closed, and held the file up to the light.

'You're lucky,' she said.

'Lucky?'

'The police surgeon at the time this autopsy was carried out was called Heap. We used to call him *Shit* Heap.'

'Really,' Crane said, feeling himself start to blush.

'He was a pig of a man – forever looking for excuses to brush up against any woman who came close to him – and as a doctor he would have made a good hatstand,' Mrs Walton said.

'He wasn't very good?'

'He *might* have been good, if he'd made the effort, but he couldn't be bothered. You've never seen reports as sloppy as the ones he wrote.'

'Didn't anyone in the Whitebridge police ever complain about him?' Crane asked.

'No, they were as sloppy as he was,' Mrs Walton said. 'Actually, that's not quite true,' she amended. 'Do you know DCI Woodend?'

'Not personally, no.'

'*He* once gave Heap a right bollocking. He was working for Scotland Yard at the time, and he wasn't at all happy about the way Heap had written up some report or other. I don't think it was so much what he said to him as the way that he said it, but Heap crept around the place like a frightened mouse for a week after that, and I still have to laugh when I think about it.'

'And I'm *lucky* that he was the one who wrote the report, am I?' Crane asked, remembering why he was there.

Mrs Walton laughed. 'No,' she said. 'Quite the contrary – you're lucky he *didn't*.'

'I beg your pardon?'

'It was his assistant, Dr Wells, who sliced Mottershead up – and there was a man who *did* know what he was doing.' She walked across the room, and handed the file to Crane. 'I'll leave you to it, then. Happy reading.'

Bazza Mottershead had died as a result of having his throat cut – probably with a razor – but he had not given in without a struggle, as was clearly revealed in his autopsy report. The sleeves of his jacket had been slashed in several places, suggesting that what had occurred had been a fight, rather than an attack, and this was confirmed by the presence of another man's blood at the scene of the crime.

So what had happened had probably been unplanned, Crane thought, as he read the report. The murderer had not *intended* to kill Mottershead, at least not at that point in time – because if he had, he'd have chosen a method which involved him in much less personal risk. It was likely that they'd had an argument which had unexpectedly turned into the fight. Mottershead had either been the first to produce his weapon – which was probably also a razor – or had pulled it out when he saw the weapon in his killer's hand. They'd circled each other, and though it had been the killer who had struck the lethal blow, it could have easily been the other way around.

But the fight that had resulted in Mottershead's death was not
Crane's main concern. He was there to search for indications of
an injury which had been inflicted earlier than the fight – possibly
as much as several *days* earlier.

He scanned the main findings of the report, praying he'd find
the evidence on which much of Paniatowski's theory rested.

And there it was!

'*The subject also had several scratch marks on his left arm,
which are consistent with being inflicted by human nails,*' he read.

'Nice one, boss!' Crane exclaimed, holding up an imaginary
glass in salute to Paniatowski.

For years, Paniatowski had thought of her ex-lover as a great
big ginger teddy bear, and even during their meetings in his
office – as chief constable and chief inspector – it was sometimes a little difficult to banish the image. But watching him on
the television screen in her *own* office was a different matter,
she thought. On television, where there was none of their personal
history to cloud her vision, she could see him for what he really
was – a man whose authority and integrity were undeniable.

'So you're saying that by the end of the day, you expect
charges to be brought against ex-Chief Inspector Woodend?' one
of the reporters at his press conference was asking.

'Am I?' Baxter asked, looking slightly bemused. 'I didn't
know that.'

'But surely, you said—'

'I said that by the end of the day I hope to have satisfactory
answers to all the questions that you – and the general public –
have been asking,' Baxter interrupted. 'Following on from that,
it is possible that charges will be laid against certain police officers, but I am not prepared to go further at the present time.'
He stepped away from the podium. 'That's all, ladies and
gentlemen. Thank you for coming.'

There was no point in watching any more. Paniatowski stood
up, walked over to the television, and switched it off.

'Mr Baxter carried that off very well,' Beresford said, from
behind the desk.

'He carried it off brilliantly,' Paniatowski countered. 'And –
make no mistake – we owe him for it.'

'But will it do the trick?' asked Crane, pacing back and forth
in what little space the office allowed for pacing. 'Will it actually make our feller do what we *want* him to do?'

'I don't know,' Paniatowski admitted. 'But we'll soon find out.'

They lingered in the car park of the Drum and Monkey much longer than they would normally have done. They took their time over lighting their cigarettes, and then feigned an animated conversation, while all the time surreptitiously looking around them.

'Can you see him?' Beresford asked anxiously.

'No, I can't,' Paniatowski admitted. 'But he's not stupid, and the fact that we can't see him doesn't mean he's not there.'

He *had to be* there, she told herself. He simply had to be.

But what if he wasn't? What if he'd missed seeing the news conference? Or had seen it, and then decided there was simply nothing more he could do?

If either of those things had happened, then the gamble she'd made, using Charlie Woodend's already shaky reputation as her stake, hadn't worked, and all she'd actually succeeded in doing was to push that reputation even closer to the brink.

'If he *is* there, he's already had more than enough opportunity to see us,' Beresford said.

'There's no harm in giving it a while longer,' Paniatowski said.

'There bloody is,' Beresford countered. 'It's starting to look suspicious that we've been here even *this* long.'

He was right, Paniatowski was forced to admit to herself.

'Well, then, let's get this show on the road,' she said aloud.

They crossed the car park and entered the pub though the door which led straight into the public bar, but while Paniatowski then headed for the usual table, Beresford and Crane kept on walking towards the other exit.

Paniatowski sat down and looked at her watch. How long should she give it before accepting that the plan had failed, she wondered.

Fifteen minutes?

Half an hour?

She would give it a whole forty-five minutes, she decided – and if it still hadn't worked by then, it was *never* going to work.

'There's another phone call for you, Chief Inspector,' the barman shouted across the room.

She checked her watch again. Less than three minutes had passed.

She breathed a sigh of relief. 'He must really be feeling desperate,' she thought.

'I saw the press conference that the chief constable gave,' Mr X said angrily. 'He said he was going to have Chief Inspector Woodend arrested.'

'I didn't hear him say that,' Paniatowski replied.

'All right, he *as good as* said it,' the anonymous caller countered.

'I suppose he did,' Paniatowski agreed.

'Can't you stop it?'

'Not with the little you've told me.'

'Not with the little I've told you,' Mr X said bitterly. 'Do you know what anguish and soul searching it's taken for me to tell you even as much as I have done? Can you even begin to comprehend how I've had to wrestle with my own conscience – how I've woken in the middle of the night, bathed in sweat?'

'It's not my problem,' Paniatowski said bluntly. 'I'm not the one who's done wrong. I'm not the one who's looking for some way to atone for my sins. I'm just the poor bloody chief inspector who has to try and find a way to stop what *you* started.'

There were seven public phone boxes within easy walking distance of the Drum and Monkey. Crane had been assigned the four which were bunched close together, while Beresford had given himself the three outlying ones.

It was Beresford who found Mr X. It was not difficult. He would have stood out at any time – even in a crowd – and, alone in a phone box, he was no more than a sitting duck.

Beresford knocked on the window with his knuckles.

The caller turned around, and mouthed the words, 'I'm on the phone.'

That was pretty much what you'd expect someone in a phone box to say, Beresford thought, as he took out his warrant card.

He held up the card, and knocked again.

The caller, his hand over the mouthpiece of the phone, opened the door slightly.

'This is a very important call that I'm making, officer,' he said in a voice which had a slight lilt to it.

'Would you step out of the box, please, sir,' Beresford replied, in his best official tone.

'A very important call,' the man said urgently. 'In fact, it's a matter of life and death.'

'A matter of *death*, certainly,' Beresford agreed.

'What?'

'If you can prove to me that it's not Chief Inspector Paniatowski that you're talking to, I'll apologize and be on my way,' Beresford said. 'But if it is the chief inspector – and we both *know* it is – then I'd like you to step out of the box.'

The other man nodded his head in defeat. Then he opened his hand, and simply let the receiver fall, before finally stepping out of the box.

The phone was swinging back and forth like a pendulum. Beresford grabbed it, raised it to his mouth, and said, 'We've got him, boss.'

TWENTY-FOUR

The priest had not moved so much as an inch for some considerable time. His hands, resting uncomfortably on the interview room table, were so tightly clenched together that they had turned an almost deathly white. His mouth was determinedly closed. Even his eyes – focussed on the opposite wall, as if searching for inspiration or guidance – were still.

'You do know that you're way out of your league, don't you, Father O'Brien?' Paniatowski asked, conversationally.

O'Brien said nothing.

'Oh, I'll admit that you were smart enough to work out that if you kept ringing me at police headquarters, we'd probably have put a trace on the line,' Paniatowski continued, 'but it really *wasn't* very clever, once you'd seen me go into the Drum and Monkey, to make the calls from a phone box which was quite so close to the pub.'

'I have nothing to say,' the priest told her.

'Haven't you?' Paniatowski asked. 'Then I'll just talk to my inspector, won't I?' She turned to Beresford. 'As I was telling the good Father on the phone, just before you collared him, he has to take direct responsibility for this whole bloody mess – because *he* was the one who demanded that we re-open the Lilly Dawson investigation. Well, we gave in to his demands, and we *did* re-open it, so he should have been feeling very pleased with himself, shouldn't he?'

'He certainly should,' Beresford agreed. 'I know I would be, if I'd been in his place.'

'And perhaps, initially, he was. But the feeling didn't last. And do you know why that was?'

'I haven't got a clue,' Beresford said.

'Would you like me to tell you?'

'If it's not too much trouble, boss.'

'No trouble at all, Colin. The reason Father O'Brien stopped patting himself on the back was that soon after the investigation was launched, some new information came his way. And in the light of this new information, he realized that, rather than assisting the cause of justice – which is what he'd thought previously – he was doing the exact opposite. Ask me how he got this new information.'

'How did Father O'Brien get this new information, boss?' Beresford asked obediently.

'It was given to him in the *confessional*. And that was the source of his problem, you see, because he wanted to tell us what he'd learned, in order to prevent an *injustice*, but he couldn't do that because of the confessional seal. So what he *did* do was to try and set up a situation in which we'd find out the information for ourselves. Are you following all this?'

'Not really,' Beresford lied.

'Well, for example, he couldn't say anything as specific as "Joe Bloggs killed Lilly Dawson" because that would be breaking the seal. So what he had to do instead was to say, "Find out who killed Mottershead, and that will lead you to who killed Lilly." In that way, you see, he was *using* the information he'd been given in the confessional without actually having to *reveal* it. But even so, I'm not sure he was acting strictly within his vows.'

'And neither am I,' the priest moaned. 'If you knew what torment I have been in . . .'

'Yes, well, I might have some sympathy for you if I hadn't already used most of what I had available on a good man called Charlie Woodend, whose whole life is likely to be destroyed by what you did,' Paniatowski said dismissively. 'There's one thing I still don't understand, though, Father – one of your fussy little, conscience-stricken hints that I still haven't been able to completely unravel. And do you know what it is?'

'No,' the priest said, in a dull flat voice.

'You said we should talk to Michael Eccles. But however hard I think about it, I still can't see what he could possibly contribute to the investigation.'

'I want to tell you why it's important,' O'Brien said. 'Believe me, Chief Inspector, I *desperately* want to tell you. But I can't.'

'Well, that's not much use then, is it?' Paniatowski said, 'especially since we've no idea where Michael Eccles is.' She paused. 'Still, that doesn't really matter, because your main value to us, Father, is not actually what information you have – it's that you have it *at all*.'

'I don't understand,' the priest said.

'I told you that you were out of your depth,' Paniatowski countered. She turned to Beresford again. 'Explain it to him, Colin,' she said wearily.

'What really matters is where you got the information *from*,' Beresford said. 'In other words, when you learned all this in the confessional, just who was it who was confessing?'

'I can't tell you that,' O'Brien said.

'You don't need to,' Paniatowski told him. 'We already know it was Elizabeth Eccles.'

'In all the time he was here – and he served most of his sentence in Preston Prison – Fred Howerd only ever had one visitor,' the assistant governor said.

'And that would be his daughter?' Crane guessed.

'That's right.'

'How often did she come to see him?'

The assistant governor frowned slightly. 'Sorry, I must not have been expressing myself very well. What I meant, when I said he only had one visitor, was that he was only visited *once* – and that was by his daughter, just before he was released.'

'I'd like to talk to any warders who came into close contact with Mrs Eccles during the visit,' Crane said.

'None of them did,' the assistant governor replied. 'I handled the whole thing myself.'

'Oh!' Crane said, surprised. 'Was that because he was something of celebrity prisoner?'

The assistant governor laughed. 'Is that how you think of him, back in Whitebridge? Well, I suppose he might have been a bit of a celebrity when he was first admitted, but after nearly a quarter of a century, you know, he was merely looked on as just another of the old lags.'

'Fame is such a fleeting thing,' Crane said, almost wistfully.

The assistant governor laughed again. 'So it is,' he agreed. 'In actual fact, the reason I was so closely involved with Mrs Eccles's visit is that it was my job to arrange for Fred Howerd's transfer from the prison to some other accommodation – either a hospital or a relative's home.'

'How much do remember about the visit?' Crane asked.

'Probably more than you'd imagine I would,' the assistant governor said. 'It was a rather unusual visit, you see.'

'Was it? And what made it unusual?'

'Mrs Eccles did.'

In his time in the prison service, the assistant governor has observed all manner of visitors. Some have been so distraught at seeing their loved ones behind bars that they have almost had to be carried from the visiting room. Some have come wrapped in their own cloak of martyrdom, some clad in the armour of resentment. But he has never met one like Mrs Eccles before. She does not ask him how *her father is, merely* where *he is. And right from the start, she is all business – as cold and calculating as a butcher negotiating the price of a side of beef.*

The assistant governor takes the woman to the infirmary where her father is lying, and then tactfully withdraws to the other side of the room. From where he has positioned himself, he can't hear what they are saying – though he can see them clearly enough.

Mrs Eccles does not kiss her father – or even just touch him – though there is nothing to stop her from doing so. Instead, she looms over the bed like a vulture and talks in a low harsh whisper. Two or three times during her monologue, the dying man does his best to shake his head, but his daughter seems to simply ignore it. Finally, she stops speaking and just stands there – waiting.

One minute passes, and then two. In the end, Howerd gives her what could be taken for a nod, and she immediately wheels round and walks away from the bed.

'How long has he got to live?' she asks the assistant governor.

'I'm not a doctor,' the man says carefully.

'I know you're not,' Mrs Eccles agrees, with a hint of impatience – the first real emotion she has shown – in her voice. 'But you must have some *idea of how long he'll last.'*

'It's getting very near to the end,' the assistant governor admits.

'How near?' the woman snaps.

'He could last a month or two, or he could be gone in a few days.'

Mrs Eccles nods, as if that is what she expected to hear. 'I'll take him,' she says.

'That's *all* she said? "I'll take him"?' Crane asked, incredulously.

'That's all,' the assistant governor agreed. 'And then, without so much as a goodbye to her father, she turned and marched out of the infirmary.'

The puzzle was finally starting to fit together, and a much clearer picture was beginning to emerge, Colin Beresford thought, as he walked towards the main exit to police headquarters, intent on grabbing a breath of fresh air while he had the chance.

But that picture still wasn't clear *enough* to get cocky about, he cautioned himself. Some of the important details were missing, and that meant that not only were there questions they hadn't yet got answers to, but there were probably questions they hadn't even thought to ask.

He was so wrapped up in his own thoughts that he didn't even register the fact that the desk sergeant was waving at him as he walked past, and it was only when the man called out his name that he broke his step and turned around.

'Yes?' he said.

'I was looking for your boss, sir, and I wondered if you might know where she was,' the sergeant explained.

'She's gone to the morgue, to talk to Dr Shastri,' Beresford said.

Although *why* Shastri should want to talk to her, when she had no connection with the current case, was still a mystery.

'Oh well, it doesn't matter. It'll probably keep,' the sergeant said.

'What will probably keep?' Beresford asked.

'I read in the bulletin that she's on the lookout for a feller called Michael Eccles.'

'That's right, she is.'

'Well, we've got *a* Michael Eccles down in the cells. He was arrested this morning. Now, I couldn't say whether or not it's *the* Michael Eccles that you want to get your hands on, but—'

'What was he arrested for?' Beresford interrupted.

The sergeant consulted the notes on his desk. 'For throwing

a brick through the window of a house belonging to a Mrs Elizabeth Eccles,' he said.

There were days when God seemed to be in a good mood with you, Beresford thought – and this might just turn out to be one of them.

'He's down in the cells, is he?' the inspector asked.

'That's right,' the sergeant agreed.

'Then I think I might just go and have a word with him myself,' Beresford said.

TWENTY-FIVE

M ike Eccles was a real mess, Beresford decided, looking at him across the interview table – and the state he was in hadn't just happened overnight, but must have taken years to cultivate.

And *this* was the man who Father O'Brien had firmly believed could provide them with some of the answers to their questions, he thought. This *wreck* was supposed to give them insights into the whole sorry business.

It was hard to believe that he had anything to contribute – and even harder to work out what questions to ask in order to bring that contribution to the surface.

Well, he had to start somewhere, Beresford supposed – and the reason why Eccles was there in Whitebridge at all was as good a place as any.

'You threw a brick right through your wife's front room window,' Beresford said.

'Wasn't me,' Eccles replied, automatically.

'You were the only person on the street when the patrol car arrived. Besides, there were at least a dozen women, peeping from behind their curtains, who *saw* you do it.'

'She should have let me in,' Eccles said sulkily, abandoning all pretence of innocence. 'I was only there for what was rightfully mine.'

'Really?' Beresford asked. 'And just what *was* rightfully yours?'

'A lot of money. Thousands of pounds. Maybe hundreds of thousands of pounds.'

'And it was rightfully yours because . . . ?'

'Because I earned it.'

'How?' Beresford wondered.

'I married the bitch, didn't I? They said that was all I needed to do. After that, they told me, I could just sit back and wait till the money rolled in.'

'You still haven't said where the money was coming from?' Beresford pointed out.

'We were supposed to get part of the family fortune when her dad was made joint managing director of the firm. Only that never happened like it was supposed to, did it? Because her dad got sent to prison, and the rest of the family didn't want anythin' to do with us.'

'I thought that they agreed to pay you a small allowance every month,' Beresford said.

'An allowance!' Eccles repeated in disgust. 'An allowance was no good to me. I didn't want to live in a terraced house for the rest of my life. I wanted expensive cars an' a big mansion with its own swimmin' pool.'

'So you left your wife and set off to find your fortune elsewhere?' Beresford asked.

'That's right,' Eccles agreed – failing completely to see the obvious incongruity between his statement and his present condition.

'And now you're back in Whitebridge,' Beresford said.

'I am. I've come back to claim what's due to me.'

Just what kind of creature was this he was dealing with here, Beresford wondered angrily.

His own mother had been struck down with Alzheimer's disease in her early sixties, and for years he had tended to her, at whatever the personal cost to himself. It had been hard – very hard – but he had done it because he knew what was right. Yet Eccles felt under no such obligation to *his* family. The bastard had not got exactly what he wanted, so he had simply taken off. And now . . .

Calm down! Beresford told himself. When you're conducting an interview, you have to stay calm.

But even as one part of his brain was issuing this instruction, there was another part of it – outraged at Eccles's behaviour – which knew that he was fighting a losing battle.

'You've got a real brass neck on you, haven't you, Mike?' he asked, with a mixture of anger and contempt.

But both the tone and the nature of the words themselves seemed to go completely over the other man's head.

'What do you mean – a brass neck?' Mike Eccles asked.

'What I mean is that a proper man wouldn't expect *anything* if he'd behaved as disgracefully you have,' Beresford said, heatedly.

'Disgracefully?' Eccles said, with evident surprise. 'Me?'

He was beyond redemption, Beresford thought. He would never see himself as other men saw him, and it was pointless to even try to make him.

'A proper man wouldn't complain that the allowance he was getting from his wife's grandfather wasn't enough to keep him in the style he'd expected,' he said, trying – despite everything – to hold up a mirror in which Eccles could see his own worthlessness. 'A *proper* man would think it was his duty to get a job, so he could support his wife and daughter himself.'

'Say that last bit again,' Eccles told him.

'I said a *proper* man would think it was his duty to get a job, so he could support his wife and daughter himself.'

Eccles grinned, revealing a mouthful of rotting teeth.

'You've got it all wrong,' he said.

'I have a problem which I think you may be able to help me with,' Dr Shastri told her visitor.

Paniatowski grinned. '*You* have a problem? The great Dr Shastri has a *problem*?' she said. 'The age of miracles has come at last.' Then she saw that Shastri was looking unusually serious, and added, 'I'm sorry, Doc, what *is* this problem?'

'Did you know that I was the one who carried out a post-mortem on Frederick Howerd?' Shastri asked.

'No, I didn't. But now you've told me, I must admit I'm surprised that you didn't assign a straightforward case like his to one of your staff.'

'I decided to conduct the autopsy myself because I was told the cause of death was almost certainly lung cancer,' Shastri said.

'I'm not following you,' Paniatowski admitted.

'I had a number of students observing me that day, and several of them were already – totally foolishly, in my view – heavy smokers.'

'Ah, and the autopsy was more to do with them than it was to do with Fred Howerd,' Paniatowski said, understanding.

'Just so,' Shastri agreed. 'In fact, my dear Monika, I contemplated inviting you along, since you, too, could have done with a salutary lesson.'

Paniatowski lit up a cigarette. 'I don't know what you're talking about,' she said innocently.

'Since it was more a demonstration for the benefit of students than it was an examination to determine the cause of death, I was even more thorough than I normally am,' Shastri continued.

'I see,' Paniatowski said – though she didn't.

'Let us move on,' Shastri suggested. 'Let us widen the discussion, and talk in general terms.'

I wasn't aware it was a *discussion* we were having, Paniatowski thought, but she nodded anyway.

'I have carried out a number of autopsies on the cadavers of the terminally ill,' said Shastri, 'and I am often faced with the same dilemma.'

'And what dilemma might that be?'

'Though I have no personal experience of taking care of a dying relative, I can imagine how hard it must be,' Shastri said. 'The pain of those about to leave the world must, to a certain extent, be shared by those who are watching them leave it. And that is not the only problem. The dying often need constant attention, and those administering it are only too well aware that *whatever* they do, it is ultimately pointless, and death *will claim* his victory.' Shastri shook her head. 'The whole process must be completely exhausting. So it is hardly surprising, is it, that some of those loving carers eventually lose all perspective, and behave in a way which they would not normally even contemplate?'

'Go on,' Paniatowski said.

Shastri hesitated. 'This conversation is being held in confidence, isn't it?' she asked.

'Of course.'

'Very well, then. If there are any questions as to the actual cause of any particular death, I am required by law to report them to the appropriate authorities.' She hesitated again. 'Yes, that is what I am *required* to do, but sometimes, having considered the circumstances of those left behind, I ignore that requirement. Do you understand what I'm saying?'

'Yes, I do,' Paniatowski told her gravely. 'But I promise you that the moment I leave this room, I'll forget I ever heard it.'

'Thank you,' Shastri said. 'And now I would like you to tell me about Mrs Eccles.'

'What do you want to know?'

'Was she, in your opinion, a good and caring daughter, who would have done everything in her power to make her father's last few days on earth as comfortable as they could possibly be?'

'You're suggesting that Fred Howerd didn't die from lung cancer at all, aren't you?' Paniatowski asked.

'I'm not suggesting anything,' Shastri countered. 'I'm merely asking you if Mrs Eccles was a good daughter.'

'Aren't you?' Paniatowski persisted.

'Yes,' Shastri admitted.

'So what *did* kill him?'

'The autopsy revealed that he died as the result of being injected with a massive dose of morphine,' Shastri said.

'*The sergeant, hearing the disturbance, goes upstairs to see what's happened,*' said the tinny voice from the small tape recorder on the chief constable's desk. '*Then, when he realizes that what his boss is doing is throwing up, he thinks he might just have a look in the girl's bedroom himself. That's when he sees the pencils – and what particularly attracts him to them is that they have the girl's teeth marks on them. "Hello, that might come in useful," he tells himself. He pockets the pencil, and goes back downstairs before his boss has finished his business in the lavvy. Then later, when they're in – for example, and still hypothetically speaking – a pigeon loft, he takes the opportunity to drop the pencil the floor.*'

Paniatowski reached across the desk and switched the recorder off. 'I could have played you this before, but there didn't seem much point,' she said.

'And there's still not much point now,' George Baxter said. 'I can think of at least four good reasons why it was a waste of time my even listening to it.' He began to count them off on his fingers. 'One: you didn't have official authorization to make the recording. Two: there are no witnesses to confirm that it was, in fact, you who made it. Three: Hall says nothing that he can't explain away as being no more than a joke in bad taste. And four: you can't prove that the whole tape isn't a complete fake.' He laid his hand back on the desk. 'In other words, as a piece of evidence, it has absolutely no value at all.'

'I know that,' Paniatowski said. 'But you believe it shows Charlie Woodend's innocence, don't you?'

'Oh yes, *I* believe it – as a man,' Baxter said. 'As a man, I'm more than willing to accept that Charlie Woodend is as pure as the driven snow and that Bannerman is a real snake in the grass. But, don't you see, that doesn't make any difference – because, as a *chief constable*, I still know Fred Howerd was wrongly imprisoned for a crime he didn't commit, and that *has to be* investigated. And if the evidence points to Charlie Woodend fitting him up – and apart from this tape, which is *no evidence at all*, it does – then Charlie will just have to take the fall.'

'I think I may have found a way for you to be able to forget all about the pencil and still be able to sleep at night,' Paniatowski said.

Baxter shook his head slowly from side to side. 'You're wrong about that,' he said. 'I know you're so desperate to save Charlie Woodend that you'll believe almost *anything* yourself, Monika, but there's no way in hell that I could ever even contemplate overlooking that pencil.'

'The pencil doesn't matter,' Paniatowski said. 'The pencil doesn't *change* anything.'

Baxter looked at her pityingly. 'A lot of this is my fault,' he said. 'It was a big mistake to put you in charge of this investigation. It's all been far too much of a strain on you – I can see that now – and that's why, effective from this moment, I'm sending you on sick leave.'

'The pencil doesn't change anything,' Paniatowski repeated firmly. 'And once I've explained to you what really happened back in 1951 – and what really happened only last week – you'll see that for yourself.'

Baxter sighed. 'I'll give you five minutes for this explanation of yours, but you'll have to promise to do something in return.'

'What?'

'When the five minutes are up, you'll hand me your warrant card . . .'

'My warrant card!'

'. . . and I will keep it here – in my desk drawer – until I decide you're fit enough to return to your normal duties.'

'That's not fair!' Paniatowski protested.

'Those are my terms,' Baxter told her. 'Take them or leave them.'

'I'll take them,' Paniatowski said resignedly. 'What choice do I have?'

* * *

Baxter had promised her five minutes, but the conversation which
followed went on for nearly an hour. When Paniatowski had
finally finished explaining, Baxter said, 'It's just a theory. You
do know that, don't you?'

'It all hangs together, though, doesn't it?' Paniatowski
asked.

'There is a certain logic to it,' Baxter agreed, reluctantly, 'but
there's also very little you can actually *prove*. Most of the
evidence is circumstantial, at best.'

But he was weakening, Paniatowski thought – he was definitely weakening, and the time had come to go for all or nothing.

She took her warrant card out of her pocket, and placed it on
the desk, as she'd promised she would.

'Tell me honestly, sir, do *you* think I've got it right?' she
asked.

He could have swept up the warrant card in his big hands and
placed it in his desk drawer. But he didn't.

Instead, sounding as if the words were being dragged from
him, he said, 'Yes, Chief Inspector, I *do* think you've got it
right.'

The warrant card – the magic key to the life she loved – was
still sitting there on the desk, but she did not trust herself to look
at it.

'So, in the light of that, might I ask what action you are
proposing to take, sir?' she said.

'The only way you're ever going to make your case is by
getting a confession,' Baxter said.

'The only way *I'm* ever going to make my case is by getting
a confession,' Paniatowski said. 'Does that mean I'm still *on* the
case?'

Baxter shrugged awkwardly. 'You've put so much work into
it that it would be both wrong and unprofessional of me to take
it off you now.'

She could have kissed him. She *wanted* to kiss him.

But she didn't.

She simply said, 'Do I have your permission to pick up my
warrant card again, sir?'

'Yes,' Baxter told her. 'You have my permission.'

She forced herself not to grab at the card, but to reach for it
slowly and calmly. Then, when it was safely back in her pocket,
she said, 'There is the other thing, sir.'

'What other thing?' Baxter asked.

'Assuming *I* am right about what happened, and I *do* manage to get the confession that's needed . . .'

'Yes?'

'. . . then can I also assume that you'll forget all about the coloured pencil which was planted in Fred Howerd's pigeon loft?'

'Yes,' Baxter said heavily. 'You can also assume that.'

TWENTY-SIX

The sun was just setting as Paniatowski and Beresford pulled into the driveway of Robert Howerd's large detached house on the edge of Whitebridge.

It would soon be setting in Spain, too, Paniatowski thought – and perhaps, if she didn't get the next half hour totally right, it would never *really* rise for Charlie Woodend again.

The chief constable's words kept bouncing around in her head.

'The only way you're ever going to make your case is by getting a confession . . . the only way you're ever going to make your case is by getting a confession . . . the only way you're ever going to make your case is by getting a confession . . .'

They were met at the door by a uniformed maid.

'Mrs Eccles is expecting you,' the woman said.

'And Mr Howerd?' Paniatowski asked.

'Mr Howerd is there, too,' the other woman replied, in a voice which suggested that she thought that really wasn't important.

The maid led them down a polished teak-wood corridor to a large parlour at the back of the house.

Robert Howerd and Elizabeth Eccles were sitting together, on a large leather sofa which must have cost almost as much as the terraced cottage in which Elizabeth had spent the last twenty-two years.

Howerd's appearance came as a shock to Paniatowski. The last time she had seen him, it had been on the television screen, and he had been full of fire – an angry man who knew his own influence and was determined to wield it to maximum effect. But now the fire had gone out, and only the smouldering embers remained. His eyes were dull, a muscle in his left cheek twitched erratically, and even the smart three-piece suit he was wearing hung on him like sacking.

Elizabeth, on the other hand, offered no surprises. Her face was a blank, and she was wearing a simple black dress which gave no clue at all as to what she was feeling or thinking.

She'll deny everything, Paniatowski thought miserably.

Elizabeth simply had no choice in the matter, because she was sitting atop a pyramid which had Lilly's and Mottershead's deaths as its base, and her father's death at its pinnacle – and while she didn't give a damn about the former, she had to do her best to protect that base, or the whole structure would come tumbling down.

Two upright chairs had been positioned to face the sofa.

Robert Howerd gestured towards them and said, 'Please take a seat.' Then, as if he realized he'd made a mistake, he turned to his niece. 'I'm so sorry, Elizabeth, I should have asked if that was all right with you.'

'It's all right with me,' Elizabeth Eccles said, through tight lips.

Paniatowski and Beresford sat down.

'I assume that the reason you've come is to report on your findings to me,' Howerd said.

'If that *is* what you assume, then you're very much mistaken,' Paniatowski told him. 'The only person we *report* to is the chief constable. We're here because we've *decided*, purely as a matter of *courtesy*, to inform you of the latest developments in the investigation.'

The *old* Robert Howerd might have leapt to his feet at this point, demanded an apology and then told them to leave.

But the *new* Robert Howerd was a spent force – as even his maid had realized – and all he said was, 'Well, I suppose it doesn't really matter how you phrase it, as long as justice is done.'

'Oh, justice will be done,' Paniatowski said. She paused for a second. 'Your brother was a very bad man, Mr Howerd, but that should come as no surprise to you, because – deep down – you always knew it.'

As she was speaking, she risked a glance at Elizabeth. The other woman's face was impassive – as fixed and rigid as if it were made out of wax.

She knows most of what's coming, and she's prepared to bluff it out, Paniatowski thought worriedly.

'My brother was sometimes a weak man, and sometimes a

foolish man, but he was *never* a bad man,' Robert Howerd said.

'Is that right?' Paniatowski asked. 'So how would you describe the numerous visits he made to under-aged prostitutes? Was *that* weak – or was it merely *foolish*?'

'My brother never patronized prostitutes,' Robert Howerd protested. 'If he had done, I would have known about it.'

'Perhaps you would, if it had been one of his long-term habits, like getting drunk or stealing cars,' Paniatowski conceded. 'But it wasn't – it only really started when Elizabeth reached the age at which she stopped being attractive to him.'

'My father never touched me,' Elizabeth said flatly. 'He never laid a hand on me.'

Despite herself, Paniatowski found her heart going out to Elizabeth Eccles.

'I was an abused child myself, Elizabeth, so I understand,' she said – knowing it was a mistake, knowing it undermined everything she was there to achieve, yet unable to stop herself. 'I've had the same feelings of shame and self-loathing that you must have had. I've felt the same urge to kill myself, just so it would all finally be over. But denying it ever happened won't help – you'll never heal as long as you're in denial.'

A smirk flickered briefly across Elizabeth Eccles's tight lips. 'You're pathetic!' she said. 'You're an emotional cripple yourself, so you think I must be, too. But I'm not – because *nothing* happened!'

She'd blown it, Paniatowski thought, close to despair. She'd had her chance – and she'd blown it.

A silence followed – a terrible crushing silence.

Then Beresford said, 'Why don't you tell us about your daughter, Mrs Eccles?'

'My daughter?'

'That's right. We'd be most interested to learn who her father is.'

'Her father's Mike Eccles – my no-good husband.'

Beresford shook his head. 'No, he isn't. You were already pregnant when you married him.'

'Of course she was pregnant – that was no secret – and Michael Eccles was the father of that unborn child,' said Robert Howerd, drawing on what reserves of strength he still had left, in order to defend his niece.

'Didn't you find it strange at the time, Mr Howerd, that

Elizabeth should even have been going out with someone like him?' Beresford asked.

'None of us can choose who we fall in love with, can we?' Howerd asked, awkwardly.

'I spent some considerable time talking to Mike Eccles this afternoon,' Beresford said. 'He's a wreck. He's dirty, shifty, stupid and idle – and he can't have been *that* different when he married Elizabeth. So I'll ask you again – didn't you find it strange that she should have been going out with him?'

'He . . . err . . . he wouldn't have been my ideal choice for my niece,' Howerd admitted.

'He wouldn't have been *anybody's* ideal choice,' Beresford said.

Thank you, Colin, Paniatowski thought. Thank you for saving me from myself.

'Eccles wasn't exactly Elizabeth's choice, either,' she said aloud. 'But she had to do *something*, didn't she – because she was carrying her father's baby?'

'That's a wicked lie,' Elizabeth said.

'So he was never more than camouflage,' Paniatowski said, ignoring her. 'And what did he expect to get out of it? Well, he expected his share of the family's fortune. But once Fred was convicted of the murder, there *was* no fortune – just a modest monthly allowance.'

'In the past, I treated Elizabeth very badly,' Robert Howerd said, almost in tears. 'I admit that. But I have made up for it now.'

'How?' Paniatowski asked.

'This is no longer my house. It belongs to Elizabeth, as does the family business.'

No wonder he was now no more than a shell, Paniatowski thought. He'd just given away everything he'd ever worked for, everything – outside his religion – which was important to him.

'I can see from your face that you think that I'm no more than an old fool,' Robert Howerd said. 'But you're wrong – I have paid my penance, and now I am at peace with myself.'

Of course he'd tell himself that, Paniatowski thought. He *had* to tell himself that – but he certainly didn't *look* at peace.

'I blame myself, but I also blame the *police* – because none of this would have happened if my brother had not been convicted of a crime he did not commit,' Howerd said, and now there was real anger back in his voice.

'Ah, but you see, he did commit it,' Paniatowski said. 'And not only that, but he killed Bazza Mottershead, as well.'

'Who's Bazza Mottershead?' Howerd asked.

'Why don't *you* tell him, Elizabeth?' Paniatowski suggested.

'I can't. I've never heard of the man,' Elizabeth Eccles said.

No more mercy! Paniatowski cautioned herself. The time for mercy is long past.

'Of course you've heard of him,' she told Elizabeth Eccles. 'Your father brought Mottershead round to your house to "play" with you, didn't he?'

'No!'

'But Mottershead got bored with you at around the same time your father did. That was when they started visiting prostitutes together.'

'You're insane,' Elizabeth Eccles said.

'I think they must have found the whole experience rather disappointing after having you, and they soon decided that what they needed was another *non-professional*. So they started cultivating Lilly Dawson, a sad little girl who missed her father and was delighted to be shown the pigeon loft by a kind man.'

'You can't prove any of this,' Elizabeth said contemptuously.

Too bloody right, I can't, Paniatowski agreed silently.

'Fred's plan, I believe, was to take things slowly,' she pressed on. 'But Bazza was too impatient for that, and one Saturday afternoon – when Fred was out of town, recruiting a new member, by the name of Terry Clegg, to the ring – Bazza persuaded Lilly to go with him to the allotment. He drove her there in his own car – which is why the police could find no trace of her in Fred's van – and once they were there, he raped her.'

'And we know *he* was the one who raped her, because his autopsy report reveals that there were scratch marks on his arm,' Beresford said.

'Then, surely, he was the one who killed her, *too* – and my poor dead brother had nothing to do with it,' Howerd said.

'He couldn't have killed her,' Paniatowski told him. 'Whoever strangled Lilly needed two strong hands, and Mottershead's right hand was crippled with arthritis.' She shook her head. 'No, Fred did it, all right, and he did it for the same reason he married off his daughter – to protect his secret. That's probably why he killed Mottershead, as well.'

'And we know that Fred killed him because of the wound on his arm,' Beresford said. 'Woodend and Bannerman thought it

was self-inflicted – that he'd cut himself to disguise the scratch
marks Lilly had left. But Mottershead was the one with the
scratch marks, and Fred's injury was as a result of the fight to
the death that they'd had.'

'Even so, it's true that it was when Bannerman saw the wound
that Fred decided to confess to Lilly's murder,' Paniatowski
added.

'I . . . I don't understand,' Howerd said, in a gasping voice. 'If
you say that the wound had nothing to do with Lilly's death—'

'It didn't,' Paniatowski interrupted. 'But it had a lot to do with
how Fred saw his own future.'

'His . . . his future?'

'Bannerman had worked Fred up into a state of terror by
telling him just what it would be like to be hanged. And then
the sergeant offered him a way out. If Fred would confess to
Lilly's murder, he'd be spared the rope. And what Fred was
afraid of, once they'd seen his wound, was that if he *didn't*
confess, they'd take a closer look at it, hoping to prove that Lilly
had scratched him. They wouldn't be able to prove that, of course
– because she hadn't – but there was a risk they might suddenly
connect the wound to Mottershead's murder. And if they did
that, he was doomed – because he might escape hanging for *one*
murder, but he certainly wasn't going to escape it for *two*.'

'I don't believe any of this,' Howerd said shakily. 'With
almost his dying breath, and in the presence of a priest, my
brother protested his innocence.'

'Yes, he did do that, didn't he?' Paniatowski agreed. 'But then
he had to – because that was part of the deal he struck with
Elizabeth.'

'What deal?'

'Fred didn't want to die in prison, so he asked her if she'd
take him into her home. And Elizabeth, who had been living
under a cloud of shame and humiliation – and *near-poverty* –
for nearly a quarter of a century, saw a way to turn it to her
advantage. If Fred would only act out the little play-let that she
would write for him, in front of a priest, she told herself, it would
be as if everything she had suffered had never happened at all.
Her father would never have been a killer. The people who
shunned her would accept her again – more than *accept* her,
they'd be all over her, because they'd feel so guilty.'

Elizabeth Eccles was still sitting perfectly still, her hands
lightly clasped on her lap and her face giving away nothing.

She should be starting to crack by now, Paniatowski thought, but there was no sign that she was even close to it.

It wasn't going to work, she told herself. It wasn't going to bloody work!

'Yes, everyone would feel guilty, but her uncle would feel guiltiest of all,' she continued, going through the motions because that was all that she had left. 'Her uncle would have to give her what was rightfully hers. Tell me, Mr Howerd, was it you who *offered* to pay the penance, or Elizabeth who *demanded* it?'

'It was her right to ask, and my obligation to give her what she wished for,' Howerd said mournfully.

'We'll see if you still think so when you've heard the rest,' Paniatowski told him. 'Elizabeth knew that by making her father lie during his confession, she'd done a wicked thing. And since she was a good Catholic, she went to church and took confession herself.' She turned to Elizabeth Eccles. 'But instead of going to *another* priest, you went to the one who had heard your father's confession – and that was a big mistake.'

'I really don't know what you're talking about,' Elizabeth Eccles said.

'You unburdened yourself, and he forgave you – because that's what priests do. But you left him with a burden of his own, because now he knew that the witch-hunt he'd instigated against Charlie Woodend was based on a lie, and, try as he might, he couldn't forgive *himself* for that – which is why he started calling me, and dropping hints that things weren't what they seemed.'

'Father O'Brien always was a weak-willed fool,' Elizabeth said. 'That was why I—'

She stopped herself before she could say any more.

But she had *almost* made a slip, Paniatowski thought, so perhaps there was still hope.

'"That was why I . . .",' Paniatowski mused. 'Why you *what*? Chose him to hear your father's confession?'

'No.'

'Then what *were* you about to say?'

'Nothing.'

'But you weren't just relying on a weak-willed priest to make sure the confession went well, were you? Your real secret weapon was the fact that you controlled the supply of morphine.'

'You're surely not suggesting that Elizabeth withheld my brother's morphine, are you?' Howerd gasped.

'She had to,' Paniatowski said, matter-of-factly. 'She couldn't trust Fred to do as he'd promised, otherwise.'

'I would never have done such a terrible thing,' Elizabeth said, in the same flat voice she'd been using all along.

'Morphine's not handed out to all and sundry, as if it were sweeties, you know,' Paniatowski said. 'It's carefully measured and carefully regulated. Fred was due to have his prescription renewed just before he died.'

'Well, there you are then – he must have been getting his regular shots, mustn't he?' Robert Howerd said, with some relief.

'It was the final shot which actually killed him,' Paniatowski said. 'It was a massive dose. And how did Elizabeth get her hands on enough morphine to give him a *massive* dose? Simple! She'd done it by saving it up – by watching her father suffer, and giving him nothing to relieve the pain.'

'It . . . it can't be true,' Robert Howerd moaned.

'It *is* true,' Paniatowski insisted. 'Naturally, she gave him the morphine once he'd done what she wanted him to. She had no further use for him at that point. And, anyway, it was too risky to let him live, because there was always the chance that the priest would visit him again, and this time Fred might tell him the truth. So, all in all, it was much better to kill him right away.'

This was the point at which Elizabeth should finally break down and confirm that everything was true – but looking at her impassive face and her calm demeanour, it was clear that it was not going to happen.

She knew that if she kept quiet, she just might get away with it all, Paniatowski thought miserably.

If she kept quiet, Fred remained – at least in most people's eyes – innocent of the murder for which he'd been convicted and the murder for which he hadn't.

If she kept quiet, she might be able to persuade a jury that though she'd killed her father, she'd never meant to.

And worst of all – from Charlie Woodend's point of view – if she kept quiet, it still *mattered* that someone had planted the coloured pencil in the pigeon loft.

She had one last card to play, Paniatowski told herself – one last trick to pull. And if that didn't work, it was all over.

She took her handkerchief out of her pocket, and blew noisily into it.

'I'm sorry, Elizabeth,' she said, when she looked up. 'I'm so terribly, terribly sorry. I got it all wrong, didn't I?'

A fresh look of malicious triumph flashed briefly across Elizabeth's face, and then was gone again.

'Yes,' she said. 'You certainly did get it all wrong.'

'You were quite right when you said earlier that you're not like me,' Paniatowski told her. 'I can see that now. I hated the man who abused me. I knew that it wasn't *all* his fault, and that I should forgive him, yet I just couldn't bring myself to do it. But you're a much better woman – a much more worthwhile *person* – than I could ever be.'

'What are you talking about?' Elizabeth asked, mystified.

'I understand now,' Paniatowski said softly. 'Really I do. I can finally see that when you killed your father, it was an act of love. You simply couldn't stand to see him suffering any more, could you?'

It was as if a switch had suddenly clicked in Elizabeth's head. Her body stiffened, her eyes blazed with something akin to madness.

'An act of love?' she screamed. 'Couldn't stand to see him suffering? Yes, he *was* suffering – suffering so much that I almost decided to let him live a little longer, just so he could suffer some more!'

'Elizabeth!' Robert Howerd said.

'He forced himself on me when I was just a little girl. I didn't want him to, but there was nothing I could do about it. And, God, it hurt, it always hurt. He liked to see me suffer. And then, when I started to grow up, he decided that he didn't want me any more – and that hurt, too.'

'You knew he'd killed Lilly Dawson, didn't you?' asked Paniatowski, dropping all pretence – because pretence was no longer necessary.

'Yes, I knew. From the moment I heard she was dead, I knew that he was responsible. But I didn't have the details at the time. They came later, when he'd been released from prison, and I had him in my power. Then, I made him tell me everything – made him describe exactly how he'd killed Lilly Dawson and exactly how he'd killed Mottershead.'

'Why would you do that, Elizabeth?' Robert Howerd asked, in anguish. 'For God's sake, why?'

'I wanted to know how Mottershead had died because, after what he'd done to me, I had to be sure he'd suffered.'

'And what about Lilly?' Paniatowski asked softly.

'I had to be sure she'd suffered too. She deserved to – because she'd taken him away from me.'

'None of this is your fault, Elizabeth,' Robert Howerd said soothingly. 'You're a very sick woman.'

But it was doubtful if, by that stage, Elizabeth was hearing any voice but her own and the ones in her head.

'My father was never a particularly good Catholic,' she said pensively, 'but I think that he held on to his faith right up to the end.' She smiled, and in some ways it was a beautiful smile, though it also a mad one. 'I certainly *hope* he held on to it,' she continued, and now her face transformed itself into a mask of rage and hatred, 'because Hell has a special place for Catholics like him!'

EPILOGUE

Alicante and London – three days later

Woodend didn't like the big airports you found in places like London and Manchester, but he was really quite fond of the one in Alicante.

It was small enough for you to feel involved, he thought. You could see the planes landing close to the terminal, and when you'd been there a few times – as he had – you started to recognize the waiters in the bars, and be recognized in return. In a way, he supposed, it was a bit like the town bus station of his youth, except that these 'buses' were bound for far more exotic destinations than Wigan and Chorley.

He looked across at the barrier, and saw Joan walking towards him.

She'd been a big girl when he'd married her, and she was even bigger now, but given the choice of spending his nights with his wife or with a film star with an hourglass figure, he'd plump for his missus every time.

'It's good to see you, lass,' he said, kissing her and then hugging her to him. 'An' how's our Annie?'

'She's champion,' Joan said.

Woodend grinned. There was no middle ground for folk from Lancashire, he thought, they were either 'champion' or they were 'poorly'.

'She sends her love,' Joan told him.

'Well, I should hope she would,' Woodend replied.

He picked up his wife's bag, and led her out of the chilled terminal and into the warm air of a Spanish afternoon.

'An' how you've been, Charlie?' Joan asked, as they walked towards the car. 'What have you been gettin' up to while I've been away?'

'Nothin' much,' Woodend told her. 'Paco came round once or twice . . .'

'Now that *does* surprise me!'

'. . . an' we usually ended up wanderin' down to the bar for a few games of dominoes.'

'I worry about you sometimes, Charlie,' Joan confessed.

'Worry about me? Why?'

'Well, all them years that you were out solvin' murders, you were usin' your brain, weren't you?'

'Well, it certainly helped to,' Woodend admitted as he opened the boot of the car.

'An' now that you hardly seem to be usin' it at all, I'm concerned that it might just waste away.'

Woodend thought back to the time – only four days earlier – when he had been sitting on his terrace – the large sheet of paper spread out in front of him – trying desperately to work out who Monika's anonymous caller could possibly be, and why he kept insisting that he *couldn't* tell her what she wanted to know.

'You've gone all quiet all of a sudden, Charlie,' Joan said.

Woodend slammed the boot of the car closed.

'I was just thinkin',' he told her. 'Maybe you're right about using my brain again – perhaps I should take up crossword puzzles.'

'Then, when he realizes that what his boss is doing is throwing up, he thinks he might just have a look in the girl's bedroom himself. That's when he sees the pencils – and what particularly attracts him to them is that they have the girl's teeth marks on them. "Hello, that might come in useful," he tells himself.'

The Commissioner of the Metropolitan Police switched off the tape recorder. 'Well?' he said.

The man sitting opposite him – who was in his late forties and was on the edge of looking distinguished – thought for a moment, then said, 'Where did you get that from, sir?'

'It was sent, anonymously, through the post, Mr Bannerman, but I don't think there's any doubt about who sent it, is there?'

'No,' Bannerman agreed. 'I don't think there is.'

'And that is DCI Hall's voice on the tape, isn't it?'

'It would never stand up in court,' Bannerman said.

'No, it wouldn't,' the Commissioner replied. 'It wouldn't even stand up before a disciplinary board, where the burden of proof is much less stringent.'

'So we can forget it, can we?' Bannerman asked hopefully.

'To all intents and purposes, yes, we can most certainly forget it,' the Commissioner agreed.

Bannerman breathed a silent sigh of relief. 'Thank you, sir,'
he said.

'But it does lead us on to another somewhat related matter,'
the Commissioner continued.

'And what might that be, sir?'

'I assume that in the career path you have mapped out for
yourself, you're planning – at some time in the near future – to
apply for the position of chief constable somewhere in the shires,
and that after that you'll have your eye on my job when I step
down.'

'Yes, that is roughly the plan,' Bannerman agreed.

'Well, I'm afraid I must tell you that I don't feel I'm in a
position in which I can support any such application for promotion. And I should further add that, while you will remain an
assistant commissioner here in the Met, you will certainly go no
higher, and it might be an idea to look for alternative employ-
ment in private industry.'

'I see,' Bannerman said. 'Might I ask what's caused you to
reach this decision, sir?'

'I'm afraid I no longer have the confidence in your judgement that I once had, Ralph.'

'Because of what happened twenty-two years ago, when I was
a young sergeant?' Bannerman demanded. 'Look, sir, whatever
I did back then affected nothing – Howerd was guilty of the
crime for which he was imprisoned.'

'That's true,' the Commissioner agreed. 'And I'm sure there's
not a high-ranking officer at the Yard who didn't make some
kind of mistake on his way up the ladder. I certainly know there
are a few skeletons in my closet. But it's not what you did
twenty-two years ago that we're talking about now.'

'Then what *are* we talking about?'

'You had carte blanche to send whoever you wanted up to
Lancashire to bury your mistakes. And you chose an officer who
blabbed the whole thing out to a turnip-top chief inspector in a
provincial railway station.'

'Hall had been a very good man up to that point,' Bannerman
protested. 'I can't imagine what made him—'

The Commissioner raised a hand to silence him. 'It doesn't
matter that he was a good man up to that point,' he said. 'It
doesn't matter that no serious damage was done. What *does*
matter is that you made a serious error of judgement in selecting
him, and that means, in turn, that I can never again have the

confidence to entrust you with the more "delicate" aspects of policing which pass through this office.'

'But, sir . . .'

'Thank you, Mr Bannerman, that will be all,' the Commissioner said coldly.

Bannerman rose heavily to his feet. 'Thank you, sir,' he replied, trying – with no success – to mask his misery.